Her Sweetest
REVENGE

Also by Saundra

Her Sweetest Revenge

Her Sweetest Revenge 2

Her Sweetest Revenge 3

If It Ain't About the Money

Anthologies

Schemes and *Dirty Tricks* (with Kiki Swinson)

Published by Kensington Publishing Corp.

Her Sweetest
REVENGE

SAUNDRA

Kensington Publishing Corp.
www.kensingtonbooks.com

DAFINA BOOKS are published by

Kensington Publishing Corp.
119 West 40th Street
New York, NY 10018

All Kensington titles, imprints, and distributed lines are available at special quantity discounts for bulk purchases for sales promotion, premiums, fund-raising, and educational or institutional use.

Special book excerpts or customized printings can also be created to fit specific needs. For details, write or phone the office of the Kensington Sales Manager: Kensington Publishing Corp., 119 West 40th Street, New York, NY 10018. Attn. Sales Department. Phone: 1-800-221-2647.

Dafina and the Dafina logo Reg. U.S. Pat. & TM Off.

Published by arrangement with Delphine Publications.
Previously published as *Her Sweetest Revenge*.
First trade paperback edition: June 2012

ISBN-13: 978-1-61773-979-8
ISBN-10: 1-61773-979-0
First Kensington Trade Paperback Printing: July 2015
First Kensington Mass Market Printing: January 2018

eISBN-13: 978-1-61773-978-1
eISBN-10: 1-61773-978-2
First Kensington Electronic Edition: July 2015

10 9 8 7 6 5 4 3 2. 1

Printed in the United States of America

I would like to dedicate this book to the state of Mississippi.
Mississippi has been the foundation of many talents that
always go unrecognized. Mississippi: Stand up and take a
bow. This one is for you.

Acknowledgments

First I would like to give honor to God. I want to thank Him for blessing me with the strength and ability to create.

To my grandmother Inez Addison, who left this earth way too soon. I regret being too young when you died to remember you. But you will forever remain in my heart. I love you.

To my mom: I want to thank you for being there for me and supporting me all my life. I still remember the times you made a dollar out of fifteen cents. You're the best.

Onester aka Jay (LOL): I feed off of your strength and independence; it inspires me. Thanks for being my husband. I love you.

Angie, thank you so much for reading all my rough draft manuscripts even though sometimes you were extremely tired from working seven days straight. Love you, Sis. Shout-out to my brother Cordell—keep making those beats and writing those lyrics because dreams do come true.

Jeanette, I want to thank you for encouraging me daily to continue with my writing; it was a big inspiration to me. Latunya Jones, what's up, sister-in-law? You know I got to give you a shout-out for supporting me from day one.

To my dad, Roy McClure: Thank you for always being proud of me no matter what.

To my editor, Selena James: Thank you for reading my manuscript and giving me the opportunity to reach readers across the world. I am proud to be a part of Kensington/Dafina. To both of my beautiful daughters, Dj and Cj: You both inspire me to work hard. I love you.

Tamika Newhouse, thanks for believing in me. Now I want to send shout-outs to my family and friends: Zaleika, Corlunda, Corlexus, Mya, Lil Travis, Aunt Debra, Lil Carl, Mary, Stacy, Rolunda, Veronica, Sharon, Karon, Quatesha, Tiana, and Denise. Also shout-outs to my stepmother, Mary, and my baby sister, Saidah.

To my best friend, Shanta Brown, your independence rocks. Keep setting that example for single mothers. I'm so proud of you. Ms. McKinney, you thought I forgot about you, huh. To my brother-in-law Mario who's always asking me if I'm still writing, "here it go." Eleasha, where you at? (LOL). I hope I didn't miss anyone. To all my fans, I would like to thank you for your support. May every page keep you entertained and intrigued.

Saundra Jones
1 keystroke at a time

Chapter 1

Sometimes I wonder how my life would've turned out if my parents had been involved in different things, like if they had regular jobs. My mother would be a social worker, and my father a lawyer or something. You know, jobs they call respectable and shit.

Supposedly these people's lives are peaches and cream. But when I think about that shit I laugh, because my life is way different. My father was a dope pusher who served the whole area of Detroit. And when I say the whole area, I mean just that. My dad served some of the wealthiest politicians all the way down to the poorest people in the hood who would do anything for a fix. Needless to say, if you were on cocaine before my father went to prison, I'm sure he served you; he was heavy in the street. Lester Bedford was his birth name, and that's what he went by in the streets of Detroit. And there was no one who would fuck with him. Everybody was in check.

All the dudes on the block were jealous of him because his pockets were laced. He had the looks, money, nice cars, and the baddest chick on the block, Marisa Haywood. All the dudes wanted Marisa because she was a redbone with coal-black hair flowing down her back and a banging-ass body, but she was only interested in my dad. They had met one night at a friend's dice party and had been inseparable since then.

Life was good for them for a long time. Dad was able to make a lot of money with no hassle from the feds, and Mom was able to stay home with their three kids. Three beautiful kids, if I may say so. First, she had me, Mya, then my brother, Bobby, who we all call Li'l Bo, and last was my baby sister, Monica.

We were all happy kids about four years ago; we didn't need or want for nothing. My daddy made sure of that. The only thing my father wanted to give us next was a house with a backyard. Even though he was stacking good dough, we still lived in the Brewster-Douglass Projects.

All those years he'd been trying to live by the hood code. However, times were changing. The new and upcoming ballers were getting their dough and moving out of the hood. Around this time my dad decided to take us outta there too.

Before he could make a move, our good luck suddenly changed for the worse. Our apartment was raided by the feds. After sitting in jail for six months, his case finally went to court, where he received a life sentence with no possibility of parole.

My mother never told us what happened, but sometimes I would eavesdrop on her conversations when she would be crying on a friend's shoulder. That's how I overheard her saying that they had my father connected to six drug-related murders and indicted on cocaine charges. I couldn't believe my ears. My father wouldn't kill anybody. He was too nice for that. I was completely pissed off; I refused to hear any of that. It was a lie. As far as I was concerned, my father was no murderer and all that shit he was accused of was somebody's sick fantasy. He was innocent. They were just jealous of him because he was young, black, and borderline rich. True, it was drug money, but in the hood, who gave a fuck. But all that was in the past; now, my dad was on skid row. Lockdown. Three hots and a cot. And our home life reflected just that.

All of a sudden my mother started hanging out all night. She would come home just in time for us to go to school. For a while that was okay, but then her behavior also started to change. I mean, my mother looked totally different. Her once-healthy skin started to look pale and dry. She started to lose weight, and her hair was never combed. She tried to comb it, but this was a woman who was used to going to the beauty shop every week. Now her hair looked like that of a stray cat.

I noticed things missing out of the house, too, like our Alpine digital stereo. I came home from school one day and it was gone. I asked my mother about it, and she said she sold it for food. But that had to be a lie because we were on the county. Mom didn't work, so we received food stamps and cash assistance. We also received government assistance that paid the rent, but Mom was responsible for the utilities, which started to get shut off.

Before long, we looked like the streets. After my father had been locked up for two years, we had nothing. We started to outgrow our clothes because Mom couldn't afford to buy us any, so whatever secondhand clothes we could get, we wore. I'm talking about some real stinking-looking gear. Li'l Bo got suspended from school for kicking some boy's ass about teasing him about a shirt he wore to school with someone else's name on it. We had been too wrapped up in our new home life to realize it. When the lady from the Salvation Army came over with the clothes for Li'l Bo, he just ironed the shirt and put it on. He never realized the spray paint on the back of the shirt said *Alvin*. That is, until this asshole at school decided to point it out to him.

Everything of value in our house was gone. Word on the streets was my mother was a crackhead and prostitute. I tried to deny it at first, but before long, it became obvious.

Now it's been four years of this mess, and I just can't take it anymore. I don't know what to do. I'm only seventeen years old. I'm sitting here on this couch hungry with nothing to eat and my mom is lying up in her room with some nigga for a lousy few bucks. And when she's done, she's going to leave here and cop some more dope. I'm just sick of this.

"Li'l Bo, Monica," I shouted so they could hear me clearly. "Come on, let's go to the store so we can get something to eat."

"I don't want to go to the store, Mya. It's cold out there," Monica said, pouting as she came out of the room we shared.

"Look, put your shoes on. I'm not leaving you here without me or Li'l Bo. Besides, ain't nothing in that kitchen to eat so if we don't go to the store, we starve tonight."

"Well, let's go. I ain't got all night." Li'l Bo tried to rush us, shifting side to side where he stood. The only thing he cares about is that video game that he has to hide to keep Mom from selling.

On our way to the store we passed all the local wannabe dope boys on our block. As usual, they couldn't resist hitting on me. But I never pay them losers any mind because I will never mess around with any of them. Most of the grimy niggas been sleeping with my mom anyway. Especially Squeeze, with his bald-headed ass. Nasty bastard. If I had a gun I would probably shoot all them niggas.

"Hey, Mya. Girl, you know you growing up. Why don't you let me take you up to Roosters and buy you a burger or something?" Squeeze asked while rubbing his bald head and licking his nasty, hungry lips at me. "With a fat ass like that, girl, I will let you order whatever you want off the menu."

"Nigga, I don't need you to buy me jack. I'm good." I rolled my eyes and kept stepping.

"Whatever, bitch, wit' yo' high and mighty ass. You know you hungry."

Li'l Bo stopped dead in his tracks. "What you call my sister?" He turned around and mugged Squeeze. "Can you hear, nigga? I said, what did you call my sister?" Li'l Bo spat the words at Squeeze.

I grabbed Li'l Bo by the arm. "Come on, don't

listen to him. He's just talkin'. Forget him anyway."
I dismissed Squeeze with a wave of my hand.

"Yeah, little man, I'm only playing." Squeeze
had an ugly scowl on his face.

Before I walked away I turned around and
threw up my middle finger to Squeeze because
that nigga's time is coming. He's got plenty of ene-
mies out here on the streets while he's wasting
time fooling with me.

When we made it to the store I told Li'l Bo and
Monica to watch my back while I got some food. I
picked up some sandwich meat, cheese, bacon,
and hot dogs. I went to the counter and paid for a
loaf of bread to make it look legit, and then we left
the store. Once outside, we hit the store right next
door. I grabbed some canned goods, a pack of
Oreo cookies for dessert, and two packs of chicken
wings. When we got outside, we unloaded all the
food into the shopping bags we brought from
home. That would get us through until next week.
This is how we eat because Mom sells all the food
stamps every damn month. The thought of it
made me kick a single rock that was in my path
while walking back to the Brewster.

When we got back to the house, Mom was in
the kitchen rambling like she's looking for something. So she must be finished doing her dirty
business. I walked right past her like she ain't even
standing there.

"Where the hell y'all been? Don't be leavin' this
house at night without telling me," she screamed,
then flicked some cigarette butts into the kitchen
sink.

"We went to the store to get food. There is nothin' to eat in this damn house." I rolled my eyes, giving her much attitude.

"Mya, who the hell do you think you talking to? I don't care where you went. Tell me before you leave this house," she said, while sucking her teeth.

"Yeah, whatever! If you cared so much, we would have food." I got smart again. "Monica, grab the skillet so I can fry some of this chicken," I ordered her, then slammed the freezer door shut.

Mom paused for a minute. She was staring at me so hard I thought she was about to slap me for real. But she just turned around and went to her room. Then she came right back out of her room and went into the bathroom with clothes in hand.

I knew she was going to leave when she got that money from her little trick. Normally, I want her to stay in the house. That way I know she's safe. But tonight, I'm ready for her to leave because I'm pissed at her right now. I still love her, but I don't understand what happened to her so fast. Things have been hard on all of us. Why does she get to take the easy way out by doing crack? I just wish Dad was here, but he's not, so I got to do something to take care of my brother and sister and get us out of this rathole.

Chapter 2

Lying in bed too lazy to get up, I kicked the covers off me. This always helps wake me up because if I keep lying here I will never get up. Waking up early in the morning is always tough on me, but I have to wake Li'l Bo and Monica up so they can go to school.

I couldn't tolerate school anymore so I dropped out about a month ago. I got tired of going to school, being the butt of people's jokes because my clothes looked like I stepped right out of the Salvation Army. Last month alone I had to beat the shit out of two bitches for just lookin' like they were talkin' about me.

My best friend Rochelle would try to get me to wear some of her gear, but she knows that isn't my style. If it doesn't belong to me I don't wear it. The one thing I don't engage in is stuntin'. But that's not the only reason I quit school. I have other stuff on my mind, like how I'm going to feed and clothe my brother and sister.

I don't want to get caught up stealing food and end up in juvenile detention. Then who will Monica and Li'l Bo have? I need to come up with something else legit and quick.

I used to do hair at home, but our house started to look like the city dump since Mom sold our furniture. The county brought over some couches, but they looked like they came out of the Dumpster. So I just gave up doing hair at the house.

Now I go over and do a little hair at Rochelle's house during the day while her mom is at work. But I still don't make that much money because all my clients are at school. Basically, a bitch still needs another plan.

I opened the door to my mom's room to see if she came home last night, but the bed's empty so that's my answer. I don't know why she does this; it worries the shit out of me when she doesn't come home.

I went into Li'l Bo's room and started shaking him so he would wake up. This boy is so hard to wake up. Sometimes I have to stand him up on his feet to wake him up.

"Come on, Li'l Bo. Wake up. You gon' be late for school." I continued to shake him.

"Man, I don't care. I don't want to go anyway." He pulled the cover over his head and rolled back over to go to sleep.

"Boy, you better get up before I set it off up in here. GET UP!" I screamed.

"Damn, you getting on my nerves, girl." Li'l Bo sat up in the bed and threw the covers on the floor.

That's his favorite thing to say, but he loves his big sis. Li'l Bo is my protector; if any nigga gets in my face, he be ready to kill them. I'm trying to keep him on the straight and narrow, but even I know that's hard to do in this damaged neighborhood. Plus, he's growing up. Fifteen in this neighborhood is grown. Each day I can keep him off the block, I'm doing good.

Next I woke up Monica. We share the same room, but I always go wake up Li'l Bo first since he's the hardest to wake. I know Monica heard me get out of the bed to go wake Li'l Bo, but she's going to stay asleep as long as she can. Monica is the quiet one in the family. She doesn't talk too much, but she pays close attention. She turned fourteen a few months back, and lately, she seems to be opening up more, saying exactly what's on her mind. I think the crazy life we have is waking her up to reality. Our dad is gone to prison, and he ain't coming back, at least not while we're young enough to enjoy him.

"Monica, get up and get dressed." I pulled the covers off her.

"Did Mom come home last night?" are the first words out of her mouth. Monica is worried the most about our mom. I guess it's because she's the baby, and when Mom doesn't come home, Monica hates to go to school.

"No. But she's okay. So just get dressed for school."

"No, Mya, I'm staying here until she gets here. How will I know she's okay?" Monica looked like she was about to cry.

"Look, she's okay. She just fell asleep somewhere else. Now get dressed, Monica. I have stuff to do today, and you're not staying here alone."

Reluctantly she started to straighten her hair scarf but kept her eyes on me. It makes me feel so bad, but what else can I do? She needs to go to school, and I need to go do this head so I can make a few bucks. I ain't about to miss no money sitting here waiting on my crackhead momma. God! She is ruining our lives! My eyes started to swell with tears, so I looked away from Monica because I have to be strong in front of them. I don't have time to cry.

"I'll go to school, Mya." Monica threw the covers back and got out of the bed. "But you have to promise that if she ain't home when I get out of school, you'll take me to look for her," she bargained with me.

"I promise. Now get dressed." I pointed to the clothes she had laid out on the edge of her bed.

Chapter 3

After walking Monica and Li'l Bo to school, I headed straight over to Rochelle's house to do Charlene's hair. Charlene is skipping her first- and second-period class, so I know she's going to be on time.

Rochelle is my best friend. She dropped out of school about a year ago to have her baby, who we call Tiny. Rochelle had planned to go back to school, but she got her GED instead. Now she's on the county until Tiny gets a little older.

Rochelle is cool people; we've been best friends since we were about six. Whenever I need someone to talk to, she is right there. Thick and thin is how we roll.

By the time I got back to the projects I saw Luscious pull up in his all-white Escalade truck sitting on twenty-two-inch chrome rims. His truck came to a stop as he dropped off one of Brewster's known tramps. Luscious is one of the dope boys that run with this crew called the Boone Squad.

It's the same squad that Squeeze runs with. Squeeze is actually the leader. Luscious is like his right-hand man. Neither one of them lives around here, but they're in the hood all day trappin'. As Luscious passed me, he looked me up and down, then winked at me. He wishes I was like the ho he just dropped off, fucking for an outfit, but that will never be me. I'd rather look broke-down the way I do. Forget them niggas and their money. I rolled my eyes at him and headed into Rochelle's apartment, where the smell of bacon hit me from the door since Rochelle had it cracked open.

"I saw you coming up the walkway. That's why I cracked the door open. That nigga Luscious was checkin' you out. That whole squad is checkin' for you. I have told them niggas to get over it." Rochelle started mouthing off as soon as I entered the apartment.

"That's what they better do. Only thing any of them niggas can get from me is a stray bullet. I can't stand they ass." The frown on my face looked like I just ate something sour.

"I told 'em," Rochelle said, laughing. "You hungry? I got some bacon and eggs. I woke up hungry this morning."

"You know I want to eat. Charlene ain't showed up yet?" I bounced down on the living-room couch so I could watch cable television. We ain't had cable in so long it's a treat when I get to watch it.

"Nah. Ain't nobody been here. Mike finally done got locked up, and he's calling here all day, bugging me. I told him last night don't be calling me from no jail. Those damn calls are expensive. Nigga gon' have Wynita going upside my head about them long-distance charges shit," Rochelle complained. Wynita is her momma, and Ms. Wynita don't play.

"What he locked up for?" I asked out of curiosity.

"He all the way down in Flint selling dem bricks. I told him if he wanted to talk to me he shoulda stayed out of jail." Rochelle rolled her neck. "But nooo . . . This nigga thinks he the next kingpin of Detroit."

"You so crazy, Rochelle." I laughed at her. "But he is paid, girl," I reminded her.

"I know, right? But he needs to get his priorities together. Besides, we ain't got nothin' to talk about except Tiny. I ain't messin' wit' him no more. Nigga think he my daddy. And you know the one thing I won't put up with is somebody tryin' to control me. Scratch all that."

Someone knocked on the door. Rochelle got up to unlock it. Charlene entered.

"Hey, what's up, y'all?" Charlene said, stepping in the door with a smile on her face and rocking a pink and blue Rocawear short sweat suit with some white Force. Charlene never leaves home looking like a bum.

"I'm ready, Mya. You know I need to make my third-period class on time," she said while she checked out her freshly manicured nails.

"Well, let's go in the kitchen. I already got everything set up," Rochelle said. "Because I already knew Mya was gon' sit on that couch as soon as she got here."

"Shut up, Rochelle," I said while getting off the couch.

"So, y'all going to that party that the Height Squad's giving at the Ripple Turn this weekend? It's about to be off the chain." Charlene grinned.

"Hell, no," I said. "You ain't either because you have to be twenty-one to get in that club. And they be cardin' people at the door, hard," I informed Charlene.

"Never mind all that." Charlene gave me a re-assuring glance. "All I need is a fake ID or this big booty. Trust me, I will be there with all those ballers come Saturday night. Besides, I was invited by Pig." She beamed.

"Pig? You like that nigga?" Rochelle had a dis-gusted look on her face.

"I didn't say all that, but that nigga got mad paper. He's gettin' money like a motherfucker, and I like that, so it's all good. If the two of you want to go, I can get you in." Charlene put a stick of gum in her mouth.

"Count me out. I got other stuff to think about instead of some party," I replied.

"You can count me in if I can get Wynita to babysit Tiny. Oh, what am I saying, girl? You know Wynita gon' watch Tiny. Count me in," Rochelle replied while snacking on bacon.

"Saturday I'm going down to visit my dad. I haven't seen him in a minute, and that trip takes me a whole day on the bus," I replied smugly.

"Yeah, I feel that," Rochelle said, still snacking on the bacon. "How is he?"

"He wrote about a month ago saying every-thing was cool. But I just need to see him. I need to talk to him about some real issues."

"Look, forget about the party. Charlene, you

can count me out. I'm rolling with my girl to go see her dad. She needs me." Rochelle gave me a concerned look.

"No, Rochelle, go ahead to the party. I need to do this alone. This visit needs to be between me and my dad, but thanks. I always know you got my back," I assured her.

Rochelle was always so emotional, so she stood up and gave me a hug. Charlene looked at us like we're trippin'.

"So what y'all tryin' to say? I ain't down because you been my girl forever, Mya. So don't even play." Charlene rolled her neck and popped her lips. Not to mention she's chewing on that gum so hard I think she might break one of her teeth.

Rochelle and I both looked at her.

"Girl, shut up and come fix yourself a plate right quick. You trippin'," Rochelle replied with a smile.

"And fix me one too 'cause I'm hungry." I started rubbing my growling stomach.

Chapter 4

I open my eyes. The sun was shining through the window. I hastily grabbed the clothes I laid out last night and put them on. "Shit!" I said out loud, realizing that I overslept, and if I didn't hurry, I was going to miss the early-morning bus to the prison. Visitation is over at four p.m., and the next bus doesn't leave until ten a.m. The bus ride takes five hours to get there; I would really be pushing it.

I had to let Li'l Bo know I was leaving. I knocked on his bedroom door before going in. "Li'l Bo, wake up. I need you to watch Monica. I'm catching the eight a.m. bus to the prison to see Dad. I won't be back until tonight. So just watch her for me."

"Why I gotta watch her? She's fourteen. And when can I go see Dad? I miss him too. You get to see him all the time." Li'l Bo sat up, rubbing the sleep out of his eyes.

"Look, I know what you feeling, but I don't have extra bus money. If I did I would take Monica, too. Besides, this isn't a social visit with Dad today. I need to talk business."

"I need to talk business too. Dad is the only one who can tell me how to get money off these streets. I need to be takin' care of you and Monica. Not going to some sucka-ass school every day."

Before I knew it, I grabbed him out of the bed by his shirt. "What are you saying, Li'l Bo? You ready to get out here in these streets and start hustlin'? You ready to die? Because that's what's gon' happen. That's all that happens in these streets; they grimy."

"I got to learn how to be a man, Mya," he said, looking me straight in the eyes. "That's what Dad would expect me to do. I can't keep sittin' back watching us suffer. There's money in the streets, and I can get it." He had tears in his eyes.

I released my grip on him. "What I need to know is that you and Monica are safe. I'm going to take care of us. Don't worry. I will get us out of here. I'm the oldest, and it's my responsibility. But I can't do that if I'm worried about you out here hustlin'. Just go to school and help me with Monica. Promise me, Li'l Bo."

He hesitated. "A'ight, I promise. But I still want to see Dad. I only seen him twice since he been locked up."

"Give me some time and I will take you and Monica down to see him. But I got to get going before I miss that bus." I double-backed to my room to grab my key before I left.

Before I shut the door, Li'l Bo yelled at me. "Yo, this some bullshit. I got to be a man in this neighborhood, Mya. FUCK!" he screamed.

Chapter 5

While sitting in the phone-booth stall waiting for my dad to be brought out, I felt a little nervous. My hands started to sweat, and I wished they would hurry up and bring him out. I have a lot on my mind, and sitting here was wracking my nerves. Nobody in their right mind would like sitting between two walls. It felt like this stall was closing in on me. For a moment I felt my chest was getting tight, like I'm about to lose my breath. I squeezed both of my hands into fists to help with the anxiety.

I finally saw him being escorted my way by one of the guards on duty. He reached out and touched the window with both hands. Since he was convicted of several murders, he was in a maximum-security prison. That means no physical contact with the inmate. So we only get to see each other through this fucking glass.

"Baby girl, I been missing you!" He smiled at me. The window was soundproof so I could only read his lips. I stood up and put both of my hands on the window to match his. For a moment we just gaped at each other before we picked up the phones. I could feel my heart breaking all over again. I think it even skipped a beat.

"Hey, Daddy," I all but whispered into the phone receiver. I tried to control my tears, but they just started rolling down my face.

"Come on, baby girl. You can do this. Tell me what's up."

"I just don't know what to do anymore. Everything is harder than ever, and I'm trying to be strong, Daddy, but I'm only seventeen, and a girl at that." I wiped the tears off my face with the back of my hand.

"Mya, look at me. I'm sorry the way I left things, but I couldn't control that," he pleaded.

That statement is complete bull to me. And even more it just made me angry. "You could have controlled it. Everyone has a choice of how they live their life. I'm only seventeen, and even I know that. For all the dope you served on the streets, we don't have shit now. You left us flat broke. No house, no cars, not even an ounce of coke to sell. So what was it all for? We have nothing to show except a father in prison and a mother on crack. Maybe instead of selling crack, you and your beautiful wife should've had a legit job. At least we would have our parents." I felt a lump growing in my throat, and I could barely breathe so I laid down the phone.

He pointed at the phone for me to pick it back up. I stalled for a few seconds before I picked it up.

"You have every right to be angry at me. I

know that. I beat myself up every day knowing how y'all out there suffering. But the feds took everything." His voice started to get choked up so he stalled. Then he cleared his throat and continued.

"I had money set up in a bank account for us to move and get that new house out in the Auburn Hills suburbs. I knew that would at least get us out of the heart of the projects. And being stupid, I had money in safes around the house. They found all that money. I fucked up; I was just used to things being the way it had always been. Used to livin' the good life. I was just too caught up into gettin' money. The whole time I was out there in the streets I never made one good decision and, baby girl, I had been in the streets a long time. I had been dealing for almost twenty years. I thought I was on top. But it wasn't until I noticed all the young cats coming into the game around me, making moves and getting up out of the projects that I knew I needed to make a move. That's when I decided to get y'all up outta there, but by then, I was just getting rusty. I'm sorry, baby girl."

"I know you didn't want any of this stuff to happen. It's just so fucked up, Dad."

He tried to change the subject. "How is everybody? I bet Monica and Li'l Bo getting tall like me, huh?" Dad smiled, thinking about them.

"Yep, they want to come see you too, but I don't have the money. Li'l Bo talkin' about hustlin.' Dad, if he gets out there in the streets, he gon' end up dead or in here with you. He listens to me now, but I don't know how much longer he will. I got to do something."

"He said something to you about hustlin'?" Dad asked me.

"This morning was the first time. He said wants to come see you so you can teach him the game."

"Shit!" Dad hit the window with his fist. Two guards rushed over to contain him, but he explained and they let him go. "I don't want to see him in here or dead, but I can't do jack for him in here." He paused for a minute; his breathing was rushed. "I just ruined it for everybody. DAMN!" His voice boomed across the room again.

"It's okay, Daddy. I will do what I can for now to keep him off the block, but you and I both know it's just a matter of time. Those niggas from the Boone Squad be after little niggas every day," I reminded him.

"I know." He had a distant look in his eyes. "You try to bring him up on the next visit. I'll talk to him." He paused again. "Your momma . . . How is she doing?"

I looked down to keep from looking him straight in the eyes. I just hated to put all this on him while he's in here. "She's worse. Losing weight, skin color fading, just not the same anymore. That's why I need to step up, Dad. Monica and Li'l Bo only have me, and if I keep stealing from the food market, I'ma end up in Juvenile. I can't leave them; I need to know what to do." I looked him straight in the eyes. "You can't show me, but you can tell me how to survive." I beseeched him for help.

Again he hesitated. "Baby girl, you got to get what you can outta the streets. Not by being weak like your momma. I spoiled her. Kept her looking good, but I didn't teach her nothing. That was my first mistake. The only thing she knew how to do was look good and be my woman. That's my fault. But you, baby girl, you can get it. The streets got something that you can get and on your terms. You don't need anybody to get it, especially no nigga. Fuck that! You fatten your own pockets. Now, if you happen to find a sucka on the way, that's different. And another thing I want you to get is your GED. You need that; it completes you."

"But, Dad, what are you saying? In what way does that get me up out of the projects?" I asked, totally confused by everything that he just said. It sounded like random chatter.

"Baby girl, the streets don't want nothin' from you. But you want from the streets because it's your survival. The streets ain't gon' give you nothing free. Whatever you want out of the streets, baby girl, you gon' have to take it. On your own terms; it's as simple as that."

I started smiling. "Dad, the only thing you said that I understand is GED. And I plan on gettin' that when I get straight. But for now, we gotta eat and get out of the projects."

"Baby girl, once you sit down and think about what I said, it'll come to you. The picture will be clear, but look at me when I say this. Don't you ever become a trophy for any nigga, because ain't shit he can give you that you can't get for yoself. You remember that."

Chapter 6

After the visit with my dad I headed straight back to the Brewster feeling a little relieved and trying to figure out what he was talking about. As I approached my building I could see Li'l Bo standing in the hallway. Before I got to him, I could tell that he was upset.

"What's up, Li'l Bo? Why are you standing out here?" I questioned him as I felt myself getting nervous.

"Momma!" Li'l Bo eyes were filled with tears. "One of these sucka niggas beat her. And she won't say who," Li'l Bo said in short, hurried breaths.

"What!" I screamed. I pushed past him and rushed up the ten flights of stairs to get to our floor since the elevator was broken again. Shit is always broke in these damn projects. I'm so tired by the time I run up all those stairs I can barely breathe. The door was wide open to our apartment, and the living room looked like it'd been tossed.

"Ma!" I shouted out, heading straight to her room. "Oh, GOD!" I screamed but I didn't even hear the words as they left my mouth. One look at her face sent rage through me. Her naturally redbone face was black and blue, her right eye was swollen shut, and her bottom lip was covered in crusty dried-up blood. "Come on, Momma, we gotta get you to a hospital." I reached down and tried to lift her off the bed.

"No, Mya. I'll be okay." One single tear rolled down her already soaked face.

"I've been trying to get her to go to the hospital, Mya, but she won't listen." Monica tried to speak through her choked-up voice. Her face was also swollen from crying.

"You need to go to the hospital, Momma. Something could be broken, and why are you holding your arm like that? Can you move it? Do you think it's broken?" I reached over to help her lift the arm up, but she quickly pushed me off.

"Ugh, ugh, Mya, don't touch it." She tried to lift it herself. "AGGHH!" she screamed in agonizing pain. "I don't think it's broken, but it hurts like hell." She bent over in pain.

"Fuck all this, I'm calling the cops." I rushed over to grab the phone off the dresser, but the cord got caught under my shoe and it fell to the floor.

"No, no, Mya!" she shouted. "Don't do that. You'll only make it worse. I'll be okay," she begged me.

"Well, tell me who did this. Who did this to you?" I shouted again.

"That doesn't matter. I'm okay," she said, trying to convince me.

"Monica, leave the room." I pointed toward the door.

"But—" Monica tried to protest.

"Monica, leave the room. *Now!*" I screamed.

Monica got off the bed slowly and walked out. I slammed the door behind her. In a quiet voice I demanded answers from Momma.

"I want to know who did this to you and why. I won't leave this room until I know."

"Why does it matter, Mya? I ain't shit but a prostitute and crack ho," she said calmly while looking off into space. "This type of thing is bound to happen to me . . . or worse. I'm lucky every day if somebody don't rape me and leave me for dead in an alley."

Trying not to hear a word she was saying, I broke her trance when I got directly in her face and started screaming at her. "Do you think it's okay for someone to do this to you? And then you try to protect him? Tell me now, goddammit!" I screamed again. "Who did this to you?" The look in my eyes had to be raging because my insides felt like they were on fire.

I think I surprised her with my rage because she had shock in her eyes. "Mya, I'm still your mother regardless of my fucked life," she said, her voice still calm.

"Right now you are acting like a teenager, Ma, but you don't have to tell me who did this to you. I already know. This got Squeeze's name all over it." I turned to leave the room, but before I did, she started talking.

"He came over while y'all was gone, okay? Is that what you wanna hear, Mya?" With agonizing pain written across her face, she repositioned herself on the bed. "We had sex. When we were finished he went to the bathroom to take a shower. He came outta the bathroom and started getting dressed, and then he went into his pants pocket and started counting his stack. All of a sudden he starts accusing me of stealing from him. I told him I didn't touch his stuff. And, Mya, I swear I didn't." She looked me straight in eye convincingly.

"I didn't move out of this bed when he went into that bathroom. I would never steal from a crazy-ass nigga, but he wouldn't listen to me, Mya." She started to cry. Seeing my momma cry sent me into more tears. "The next thing I know he was punching me. I must've passed out sometime during the beating. I don't know what happened after that. When I woke up, Monica was standing over me screaming."

"I *knew* he did this." I broke down on the floor. "I hate living here. I hate our life." At that moment everything my dad said to me suddenly seemed clear. These streets were grimy, and the only thing that was free in the street was hurt and pain. I stood up, wiped my face, and walked toward my mother's bedroom door.

Mom jumped off the bed and grabbed me with her good hand. Unable to see straight because of that swollen eye and the pain, she stumbled. "Mya, don't tell Li'l Bo. I'm afraid for him, and if knows he might try to kill Squeeze. I don't want to see him locked up or shot up by the Boone Squad. I just couldn't take it." She reached out and wrapped her good arm around me. For the first time in four years I felt like I had my momma back.

I quickly released myself from her embrace. "Even though Squeeze deserves exactly what he'll get one day, I won't tell Li'l Bo. But only because I love my brother. I don't give a fuck about Squeeze or what may happen to him."

I opened the door and left her room with a calm feeling that for some reason sent chills down my spine.

Chapter 7

Waking up early this morning, the first and only thing on my mind was getting on my grind. I had shit that I needed to put into place, and I mean ASAP. A nigga like Squeeze wants to screw with my family? Then it's on. Like my dad said, the streets ain't gon' give you nothing for free, so it's up to you to take from the streets. And I meant to do just that by taking from grimy niggas like Squeeze who don't mean these streets any good. From this day forward, Squeeze and his whole squad are targets for me. The money they work hard at getting by selling crack over in these projects is going to be my proceeds really soon. Because when I put the steel to their heads, they better drop it off. If they don't, they better be ready to die. I have never killed anyone before, but this was personal.

"Yo, Mya, get the phone," Li'l Bo yelled from outside my door.

"Who is this?" I said into the phone with a hint of attitude.

"What you mean who is this?" Rochelle questioned on the other end of the phone. "Why didn't you call me when you got back from the prison? How was the trip? I know how you hate those long rides."

"You know I do, but it was cool. My dad is doing really good, but he wanted to see Li'l Bo and Monica. I'ma take them down soon, though. Other than that, the trip was cool. We got to talk about a lot of important stuff, you know."

"That's what's up. I'm glad you got to see him. Girl, let me tell you about the party last night." From the sound of her voice I could practically see the excitement on Rochelle's face over the phone.

"I'm all ears," I said. I took a seat on one of our brutally battered living-room couches.

"Mya, everybody was there. It was wall-to-wall packed. The DJ was on fire. I don't think I sat down the whole night. Girl, we were in VIP with the Height Squad. They got mad money, Mya. They were poppin' bottles all night long. I'm talkin' about that expensive shit."

"Were you drinking?" I rudely cut in.

"Hell, yeah. I was fucked up. Matter of fact, I'm still buzzed." Rochelle started laughing.

"All right, you remember the last time Wynita kicked your butt for drinking and throwing up all over her carpet?" I reminded her.

"I know. That's why I stayed out until some of my buzz wore off. She didn't notice a thing when she brought Tiny in my room this morning."

"Well, did you meet any of those low-life niggas?" I asked sarcastically.

"Girl, please, I was havin' too much fun to be

thinkin' about a nigga. I was not tryin' to be no-body's wifey. Those niggas ain't ready for no ready-made family, so I was just enjoying the free liquor and music. But you already know niggas was tryin' to holla," Rochelle confirmed. "Especially this nigga called Li'l Lo. But, of course, I was giving that nigga a hard time. All niggas wanna do is one thing, and right now, I'm like, forget that. Oh snap, and wait a minute before I forget. Let me tell you about Charlene. This bitch pulls up in Pig's black Beamer with tint so dark that you couldn't see through it if helicopter lights beamed on it." Rochelle was talk-ing so fast she didn't even take a breath.

"For real?" I asked in shock.

"I'm not bullshittin'. Then they get to the club all in VIP slobbering each other down. They were actin' like Mr. and Mrs. in that motherfucker for real. If Nina didn't go, I would've been on my own. Not that I would complain or anything, 'cause I was gettin' krunk all night long. But I just had to tell you about that hot mess, 'cause I knew you would trip." Rochelle continued to laugh.

"That's some hot topic right there. I can't be-lieve she let that ugly nigga put a hand on her." I laughed and twitched in disgust at the thought of Pig. This nigga is major ugly. Pig is as black as that burnt soot around your stove. He got a big head, with eyes that look like they are about to pop out of his head, and pink lips. The only reason he looks decent is because he can dress. The only rea-son he can dress is because of all at the dope he pushin' in the hood. Charlene, on the other hand, looks like Trina. You know, *Da Baddest Bitch*. But I guess in some people's case money does really talk. Not in mine, though, because a ho or gold digger I will never be.

"I was thinkin' the same thing, Mya. When I saw them kissing I thought I would throw up all my liquor. It was on some beauty and the beast–type stuff for real. They looked cool together, though. I really think he likes her too. So what's up with you today? You got some heads to do or something? I told you Wynita was going to church all day today," Rochelle reminded me.

"Nah, I ain't got no heads today. But I'm going to come over later. We got some business we need to discuss. And I would rather not talk over the phone."

"Aye, that's cool. I'll be here all day. I ain't got shit to do today, so I'll see you when you get here."

"A'ight, see you in about an hour." I hung up the phone, got out of bed, and started to get dressed. The first thing I needed to do was go and meet up with Rochelle. My plan was to inform her from now on we hittin' the club hard because that's where I need to be to get the drop on the Boone Squad. Them niggas can't help but try to get with a bad bitch, and they're always after me, so this should be easy. I might be one of the youngest chicks in the club, but I'll be one of the baddest. With a look just like my mother's, I stood five feet six inches tall, with almond-shaped eyes; thick, black, long eyelashes; and long, coal-black hair down the middle of my back. Guys are always after me like hound dogs. Especially the Boone Squad with their nasty ass, but the mind game is on. I would use my looks to pick them niggas to get the information I need to rob them of their own dough. I needed Rochelle to provide me with the gear I'd need to hit the club looking flawless until I fatten my pockets, which should be very soon. I'd have to be very careful because, although Rochelle is my best friend, she can't ever know what I'm doing. Nobody can know. It's like they say, the only way you can keep a secret is if you are the only one who knows it. That's how I intend to keep it. Don't get me wrong, Rochelle is down with me and whatever I do, but this situation was about to get ugly, and I don't want her or anybody else involved. This situation is on my hands. This shit is personal.

Later that day, I finally made my way over to Rochelle's house. I had to beat the door down for about five minutes before it finally swung open. "Yo! What took you so long to answer? I been banging on this raggedy door for about twenty minutes," I exaggerated and pushed my way past Rochelle into the apartment.

"My bad. I decided to go ahead and take my shower while Tiny was still asleep. I didn't hear your knock until I turned off the shower. I'm surprised you didn't wake Tiny with all that damn banging you were doing. Anyway, what's up?" Rochelle sat down and grabbed a pack of Newports off the coffee table. It's a habit I've been trying to encourage her to break, because the smell stinks so bad. Her habit only got worse the more I complained, so I decided to leave well enough alone.

"What do you mean what's up?" I asked, stalling for no apparent reason.

"Look, Mya, stop bullshittin'. We've been best

friends since forever. I know when something is bothering you. So spit it out already."

All of sudden tears just started rolling down my face. The thought of my mother being beaten by a trifling low-life like Squeeze was just more than I could stomach. The thought of it made me want to get a gat and put a bullet in his head, but I know something that will hurt that nigga more than that. That so-called empire he's running means more to him than his life. Yeah, his money being taken, *that* will hit that nigga where he lives.

Wiping the tears away from my face, I told Rochelle about my mom's beating without giving her the details of who was to blame. "You know yesterday I went down to visit my dad. When I got back to the house my mom had been beaten. I'm talkin' about she is *fucked up*, Rochelle."

"What? What the hell happened? Who did it?" Rochelle screamed as she put her cigarette out in a green astray shaped like a frog, all while firing questions at me.

"I don't know." I lied, but for a good reason. "And according to her, she don't know who did it either. She said she was jumped from the back. She wasn't raped or anything. They just beat her up and took the money that she was holdin'; that's about all I know. But, Rochelle, she looks bad. One of her eyes is swollen shut, her face black and blue." Without warning, the tears start progressing down my face again. Rochelle's face was also wet.

"I can't believe this happened to her. Probably some thirsty dope fiend. That is so messed up. How is Monica? I know she a mess right now," Rochelle said as she got up off the couch and grabbed some Kleenex off the coffee table.

"She cool now, right at home up under Mom. At least until Mom gets up and gets back into those streets again. I am just so sick of this shit, but I don't want to talk about this no more. It's just bringing down my good news," I said, then put on a fake smile, because at this point, I was about to tell my best friend a lie. As much as I hated doing this, it was for her own good that she not know my true intentions.

"Good news? What good news?" Rochelle asked, looking directly at me.

"Well, I didn't tell you everything over the phone that my dad and I discussed at our meeting." I took a deep breath because this would be the first serious lie I ever told my best friend. This would be the first lie of many I would have to tell to keep her in the dark and to keep the first lie in place. "Remember when you used to ask me did my dad leave us any money if something like him getting killed or going to prison ever happened? Well, the answer to that question has always been no, but yesterday, I found out different." I braced myself because this lying just doesn't seem to be coming easy for me. My mouth seemed to get drier with every word that came out of it.

"Apparently my dad had this friend named Big John. Big John had been locked up since recently, and he owed my dad some money for a big delivery job they did together. He promised my dad that when he got out he would pay him. Except now my dad is locked down. So, of course, my

dad never expected to hear anything from him."
Rochelle was staring at me so hard it was making
me nervous. I almost feel like she can sense I'm
lying, but I continued on because it was too late to
turn back.

"Well, about a week ago, my dad said he received a visit from Big John. Dad said he thought
he was coming to tell him why he couldn't pay him
his money, but the visit turned out to be the exact
opposite. Big John said he would have his money
in like three weeks and wanted to know what he
wanted him to do with it. He knew Dad had been
married, but, of course, he didn't know Ma was a
crackhead now." I stopped talking and kind of
laughed a little under my breath. It seemed fucked
up to be calling my own mother a crackhead. It is
what it is, so I brushed past that and kept the lie
moving.

"Dad said he told him he knew exactly what he
wanted to do with it. And that was to give the
money to me. He told him he would get word to
him on how to get the money to me. Long story
short, I showed up Saturday out of the blue to see
him. So I guess it was fate or some shit," I said, glad
to have it out just like I practiced at home in my
bedroom mirror. Of course, Rochelle had to start
asking questions.

"Oh my God!" She was excited. "So how much
is it?"

"How much is what?" I asked, caught off
guard.

"The money, how much is it?" Rochelle quickly
repeated.

"It's a lot, enough for me to get an apartment and live for a while, a few years maybe."

"Dang, that has to be a lot of money then. I am so happy for you, Mya."

"Dad wants me to get a safe deposit box at the bank because he don't want anyone asking where that money came from. Big John should be contacting me this week. Dad is going to be contacting him Monday to make sure everything is straight. So now all I have to do is wait," I lied.

"What about your mom? If she knows you got that money, Mya, she gon' be tryin' to get some. She gon' be pissed when she finds out he givin' it to you instead of her." Rochelle looked concerned.

"Who cares about her being pissed? She knows he ain't gon' give no money to her to smoke up. What does she think, he's crazy or something? That money is for me to take care of Monica and Li'l Bo," I confirmed. "Dad made that shit clear. Until Mom gets clean, she can't even stay with me when I get a crib."

"Oh hell, yeah." Rochelle had a big smile on her face. The thought of me getting my own crib put her on the edge of her seat. "Where you plan to get a place? I know you not moving into these damn projects." Rochelle put a disgusted scowl on her face.

"Ugh, no. I'm getting up outta here, but I can't do anything until I turn eighteen. Ain't nobody gon' rent to me if I'm under age. So in a few weeks I'll hit the rent ads. Another thing, from now on we are going to be hittin' the club. It's

time I start to have a good time. All this stress with
my mom is turning me into a seventeen-year-'old'-
ass woman." I stressed the last part.

"Wait a minute. You want to go out to the club?"
Rochelle asked. She put a stunned look on her face.
"Because I just want to make sure I heard you
right."

"That's what I said." I smiled for the first time
since I started talking. "As a matter of fact, let's celebrate my good news this weekend coming up."

"*That's* what up. Now *that's* the Mya I been
looking for," Rochelle replied.

"Oh, just one thing. I need something to wear.
You know normally I would not wear your clothes,
but this one time I will make an exception. Because when I do hit the club I want to be laced."

"Dang, you must be desperate, because you
know how you trip about wearing other people's
clothes. But don't worry, I got you." Rochelle
jumped off the couch and grabbed me by the
hand. We headed to her room to raid her closet
for name-brand clothes. Her daddy was a well-
known dope pusher who was gunned down like six
years prior. Although her mother, Ms. Wynita, was a
new self-proclaimed Christian who wouldn't spend
any of the money he left, she did give Rochelle an
allowance out of it every so often. Most of the
money was for Rochelle to go to college, but she
still hadn't gone yet so Rochelle was just getting
geared.

Chapter 8

Saturday, the night we were going to the club, came so fast. At first I was a bit nervous. All day I was jumpy and kind of agitated. It was obvious that something was wrong because Monica asked me, "What's wrong with you?" while she was standing at the mirror in our bedroom taking the braids out of her head that I had put in about two months ago.

"Ain't nothing wrong with me," I replied quickly. The last thing I needed was for her to know that I was going to the club, because if Li'l Bo knew that shit, he would be tripping. The first person Monica would tell if she knew would be Li'l Bo. The boy thinks he's my dad sometimes instead of my baby brother. I have to keep him in check, and in this case, hide the fact that I am about to hit the club hard tonight.

So instead of getting dressed at home, I told Li'l Bo and Monica that I was going over to Rochelle's house to watch videos. I also told them not to wait up for me because I may not come home until late since I had a couple heads to style.

I added the hair bit to keep Monica home. She hates to sit around and wait on me when I do hair. Plus, the girl is an early bird. Monica's in the bed every night no later than nine. So now that was it. My plan was in motion.

Charlene had heard through Rochelle that I was interested in hittin' the club this weekend, so she immediately offered to pick us up. Since she was now officially dating Pig, word on the streets was that he had picked her up a new candy-apple-red Mercedes-Benz CLK 550 convertible sittin' on twenty-two-inch chrome rims. That chick was riding hard, and we all know what came with that: "the haters." Her being Pig's girl, I knew she wouldn't have any problems.

Later at Rochelle's crib we started getting dressed about ten thirty. My chosen outfit was a white Coogi button-up dress lined in gold that stopped above my knees and fit every curve just right, with a pair of white, gold-lined Coogi stilettos. I had on big gold hoop earrings with a string of gold bracelets for my wrist. Of course, all this came à la Rochelle, who was beaming when I stepped out of the bath-room. I had done my hair in an updo, which com-plemented my outfit and high cheekbones. Rochelle had done my makeup, and I looked flawless.

I must admit, stepping out of that bathroom I felt like a new person. I couldn't remember the last time I made myself up. Since my dad had been locked up, I never had any new or nice clothes. Plus, now, I also had added stress, so this just wasn't reality to me. Right now, I felt really good about looking good. I felt like a seventeen-year-old girl with no worries. Stepping out of my normal shell, I modeled the outfit around the room for Rochelle.

"You like?" I turned around and made one final strut. "Do I look like new money or what?"

"Mya, girl, you gon' be fuckin' 'em all up tonight." Rochelle grinned from ear to ear. "And keep that smile on your face too. You always look so damn serious these days. But I knew you was gon' be bad in that outfit. You go, girl!" Then Rochelle stood up to show off her outfit.

"Girl, we gon' both be turnin' heads tonight." Rochelle looked down to check out her outfit. She had on a strapless blue Prada dress with a pink belt wrapped around the waist and Prada heels to match. Earlier today I had cut her hair in that new Rihanna short cut and added a light-colored rinse that she had been bugging me about. My girl looked runway ready. She was right; we were going to be turnin' heads, which made me kind of nervous. Unknown to Rochelle, I was more interested in meeting my targets than turnin' heads.

My thoughts must have shown on my face because Rochelle asked, "Mya, what's on your mind, girl? A few minutes ago you were glowing, and now you look like you want to snatch off the Coogi and run home."

"Really?" I asked, surprised at how well Rochelle had read my facial expression. "I didn't know that." I immediately jumped back into party mode. The last thing I wanted Rochelle to think was that I had changed my mind about the club. Oh hell, no, because the club was on. I had shit I had to do. And I planned to do just that. "What time Charlene gon' be gettin' here? I'm ready to party." I smiled.

"Good, because I'm ready to drink," Rochelle informed me. "Charlene should be pulling up soon; let's head to the living room. Come on, my baby." Rochelle reached down and picked up Tiny, who had crawled over to her and started grabbing at her legs to be picked up. Tiny is so adorable. She is fudge-chocolate brown with thick black curls in her head. Rochelle kissed her on her big chocolate cheeks, which made her smile. "Let's take you to Granny."

Just then, Rochelle's mother, Ms. Wynita, yelled, "Rochelle, Mya, get in here. Charlene outside blowing."

"A'ight. We comin'." Rochelle doubled back and picked up the pink and blue Prada bag that matched her dress, and we headed out the door. The only thing I thought before I climbed into the backseat of Charlene's candy-apple-red Benz is, *It's on.*

Chapter 9

Getting inside the club was easier than I thought it would be. They didn't even ask me for an ID, which, if they would've, Charlene said Pig was already in the club waitin' on her and he would get us in. Rochelle had gotten me a fake ID just in case, though. Still feeling a little nervous inside, I made sure not to show it on the outside. If my face didn't show my confidence, the swirl I put in my hips did, because I sashayed up in that club like it was something I did every Saturday night. Rochelle and Charlene headed straight to the dance floor. Nina, one of Charlene's friends, had come along. We both paused for a split second and took in the whole scenery.

The DJ was blasting "Rockin' That Thang" by The-Dream. Something about that song gave my strut an even bigger ego than I was capable of having on my own. Feeling like all eyes were on me, I kept my cool and headed straight to the bar. Nina followed me like this was her first time coming to this club instead of it being my first time. To be honest, I wasn't even sure why I was headed to the bar. My feet went so I followed. When I reached the bar, there was some dude standing there. He was rockin' one of those 'fits from T.I.'s new clothing line.

While staring at me, he said something to the bartender and wandered off. Nina, who had been looking off in the other direction, turned to the bartender and ordered something to drink. I didn't even hear what she said until she asked me again.

"Mya, what are you drinking?" The question was totally foreign to me because I didn't drink, but instead of saying that, I replied to the bartender. "Give me what she's having." And without giving it any thought, my mind drifted back to that guy who had just wandered off into the crowd.

I wasn't sure what it was about him besides the fact that he was so damn handsome that it made me think twice about him. I had seen some of the finest guys that Detroit had to offer, and I never gave them a second thought, but not this guy. Something about him made the pit of my stomach tingle. Without any notice, Charlene and Rochelle broke my trance as the bartender passed me my drink.

"Why are you guys sittin' at this bar?" Charlene asked, out of breath from dancing.

"Forget the bar. Mya, why do you have a drink in your hand? I *know* you not about to drink that," Rochelle asked with sarcasm in her voice.

With a smile on my face I took a drink from my glass and, to my surprise, it was good as hell. Two more gulps and the glass was empty. Then I asked the bartender to hit me with another one.

"Now *that's* what I'm talking about. It must be a new day. Mya is here at the club with us, and she just took a drink. Charlene, pinch me so I can know I ain't dreamin'.'"

"No, trust me, you ain't dreamin'. Her ass is gettin' bent right here with us," Charlene threw in.

We all started laughing. "Charlene, I thought you said your man was here waitin' on you," I said curiously.

"Oh yeah, he's with his crew up in the VIP section. I'm 'bout to go up there now. Y'all gon' roll? When you get up there, you ain't got to buy no drinks or shit," she bragged.

Just as Charlene started talking about her man, I saw my targets hit the club, the fucking Boone Squad. Who do I see leading the pack? Squeeze with his nasty self. Then his crew followed. My two targets were with him: Luscious and Phil. Just who I needed to throw a wrench in their operation. Elated, I zoned back into Charlene still running her mouth.

But what I didn't notice was she was asking me a question. "So you gon' roll or not, Mya?" Charlene asked me directly.

"Damn, Mya, are you daydreaming again?" Rochelle asked, then took a step closer to me.

"No, I'm cool. But I'm gon' hang right here for minute and finish my drink. Y'all go ahead. I'll be up there to VIP soon."

"You sure?" Rochelle asked. "Because I'ma about to go up there and get lit. I don't want you hangin' by yourself. We came together; we gon' stick together. You never know if these niggas wanna get crazy."

"I'll be up there soon. Don't worry; go start having fun." I smiled and took a sip of my drink to reassure Rochelle, who seemed dead-set against leaving me alone.

"Okay, suit yourself," Charlene said. "But hurry up. I want to introduce you to my man's crew, 'cause them niggas is fine. Tell her, Rochelle."

"Hell, yeah, those niggas look good. Too bad my family already made."

We all started laughing at Rochelle's lame comment. "Bitch, your family ain't already made. You just got a baby. Those niggas don't even know much about you. You were too busy partying last time you were here," Charlene said with a grin on her face.

"I was gettin' wasted the last time I was here," Rochelle bragged. Then she looked at me with a serious look on her face. "A'ight, we goin' roll up to VIP. You be careful and hurry up."

"I would stay with you, Mya, but I got to get krunk for free, if you know what I mean," Nina said before trailing off behind Charlene and Rochelle, tugging at her thigh-high skirt that wouldn't stop mounting up her ass. She knew that shit was too little when she left home.

My only thought about Nina leaving me behind was deuces. Because with them gone, I could get down to business.

Chapter 10

Taking slow sips from my drink, I watched Squeeze and his crew like a hawk. Still standing next to the bar, I swayed my hips to the music to make myself look extra sexy. Even though I had practiced this at home in the mirror many times during the week, I was still a bit nervous, but the more sips I took from my drink, the closer I got to comfort. Before long, I saw Luscious headed toward the bar with two dudes in tow. I noticed one of my targets who goes by the name Phil. Phil is one of the dumb flunkies of the crew, and he was just who I had in mind to pull this shit off.

Pretending not to see them coming toward the bar, I took another slow sip from my glass and continued to act indulged in the music the DJ was mixing. Just as I predicted, Luscious noticed me first and couldn't resist flirting.

"Aye, what up, Mya? That is yo' name, right? Because I would know you anywhere." He looked me up and down.

"Yeah, it's Mya. And yours is Luscious, right?" I pretended to care.

"That's right. You musta been checkin' up on a nigga." He smiled.

With a fake smile plastered on my face I replied, "No, but when you hang out in the Brewster-Douglass Projects it's hard for people not to know your name."

"She right, dawg," Phil butted in. "What's up, Mya?" he asked in a casual tone of voice.

"Nothing, just listening to the DJ." I took another sip from my glass, which was threatening to be empty. "I see you dropped outta school." I started up a conversation with Phil, hoping to get rid of Luscious.

"Yeah, I had to let that shit go. It wasn't bringin' in no dough. Gotta eat. You know how it go." Phil polished off his drink and ordered another round. "You should be about to graduate though, right?"

"No." I paused for a minute. "I had to drop out too."

Luscious, who was still standing next me, looked at me and Phil like we was wasting his time so he decided to butt back in the conversation. "Shit, you don't need school anyway. I mean, what's a beautiful girl like you need to spend half your day in a classroom for? You already equipped with wealth."

Without responding to him I gave him a shut-the-fuck-up look with an insinuation of a smile on my face. "You know, I do hair over in the Brewster for a lot of our classmates. It used to be a hobby, but now it brings in cash." I turned my attention back to Phil.

"Aye, that's what's up. Gotta do what you gotta do." Phil downed his shot.

Luscious, realizing that he was being ignored by me, grabbed his drink and gave me a once-over glance and walked away. His swagger let me know that he was pissed, but I couldn't care less because he was slowing up my process.

Phil looked at me and smiled. "Don't mind my nigga. He's just feelin' you. That's why he trippin'. Shit, you can't blame him for tryin' to holla."

"Whatever. His ass is rude. The nigga just stood here and told me to give up my education and sell some pussy," I spat out bluntly.

"He didn't mean that, Mya. I mean, but look at you." For the first time since he approached the bar, Phil let his eyes slowly roam my curvaceous frame. "You fine as hell, fully stacked. Girl, you changed just this year alone," Phil complimented me.

Tired of Phil's ranting I gave him a way out. "A'ight. Okay. I get it. I'ma fucking sex symbol. Please just let it go." I pretended to be upset. Obviously it worked.

"Damn, I'm sorry. I guess I didn't help the situation with my compliment," he tried to apologize. "Look, let me buy you a drink. You still my classmate, even though we both dropouts."

He and I both started laughing at that comment.

"Come on, let me buy you drink," he continued to beg.

"Only one." I pretended to be giving in.

"Aye, give her whatever she wants," Phil yelled at the bartender.

"Just refill my drink I had earlier."

"So this is my first time seeing you in the club.

I've seen your girl Rochelle in here before, and she likes to shake her ass," Phil joked.

"She does like to get krunk." I grinned. "But your observation about me is right, though. This is my first night out. I like to keep a low profile."

"Well, let me show you how to have a good time. First, ain't no standing at the bar all night. You have to hit the dance floor."

Just as he said that, Hurricane Chris's song "Halle Berry" started blaring out of the speakers. I grabbed him by the hand and strutted my way to the dance floor. With a stunned look on his face, Phil stood back and watched me do my thang.

———⊕———

Three drinks and five dances later, Phil and I sat down at a table near the bar.

"I guess you like to dance too, huh?" he asked me in a seemingly slurred voice. I had been drinking light so I was only feeling a little tipsy. Phil, on the other hand, had been taking vodka shots straight, and from the looks of it, that vodka was taking effect.

"Yeah, my sister and I dance all the time at home," I lied.

Sweat was starting to pour down Phil's forehead, and I realized that he was drunk. Now his words were obviously slurred, and he was getting way too relaxed. I decided this was the perfect time to get him to talk about his crew.

"You sure your crew don't mind you kicking it over here with me all night? You did come out with them tonight," I quickly threw that out to change the direction of the conversation.

"Aw, shit, they don't give a fuck," Phil's words slurred. "As long as the hoes surround them until they leave, they cool. All they gon' do is pop bottles and smoke it up in here. I am missing out on the smoking, though," he grinned.

"Well, I had fun dancing with you. And thanks for all the drinks, but you can go back with your crew. I don't want you to miss blazing up on my account."

Realizing he was being dismissed, Phil started to protest. "Oh, but I'm cool. I can get you another drink. I can blaze anytime. Shit, I got pounds of that smoke, and then some." He bragged like an idiot.

"Look, I don't want to come between you and your crew tonight. You guys might have a meeting or something. And the last thing you want to do is miss a meeting with your crew because you were hanging out with me." I screwed with his head.

"I told you, them niggas ain't thinkin' about my black ass. Besides, our meetings are on Tuesdays, Fridays, and Saturdays. I just sat in a two-hour meeting before I even got here, and I'm glad that shit is over. So unless someone gets shot or busted tonight, I don't want to hear the word *meeting* until Tuesday."

"Wow, you guys have two-hour meetings? Sounds like a real business or something. I always thought crews were just a bunch of dope boys running together to make money and scare off other crews."

"That is what we do, but it's also about business. Do you have any idea how much money passes through these crews in a week?"

Playing stupid, I gave a weak number. "About ten thousand? It can't be much more than that. I mean, after all, these crack fiends live in the projects."

"That may be true, but we work all over the city and out of the city. Shit, crews can bring in anywhere from one hundred to two hundred thousand a week."

"Damn, Phil, that's dangerous work. Nobody makes that kind of money without a price." Then I decided to take the conversation to common ground to ask specific questions to get specific answers.

"Do you ever have to be responsible or do you have like leaders and shit?" Without hesitation, Phil started singing like a bird. Not sure anymore if it was the liquor or just a case of the big mouth, I gave him my undivided attention without being obvious, because I didn't need to miss a word of his tell-all.

"Squeeze and Luscious them niggas run this shit. They got this operation on lock. They're some smart-ass niggas; they keep everything running smoothly. The rest of us niggas is the block. We push the dope and report to them. Luscious collects the ducats from the crew and delivers it to Squeeze."

"What if someone is short in dope or money when Luscious come out to collect? 'Cause he look like he don't play. I wonder all the time if he the reason for them dead bodies in the Brewster." I gave a fake laugh suggesting that I'm joking and took a sip from my drink.

"That shit don't happen, Ma. Luscious meets with Squeeze every Wednesday. This happens to be the same day he collects from the crew. So if someone don't have they money or dope, that nigga dead before Luscious even gets to Squeeze. If Luscious is short when he gets to Squeeze, he got some explaining to do. You feel me? Dead." Phil's eyes hardened on that last part, but they immediately softened, and without warning, he reached out and grabbed my right hand. "Mya, you got a beautiful smile." He immediately realized that I wasn't comfortable so he let go of my hand. "I'm sorry; I didn't mean to grab your hand," he apologized.

"It's cool. Thanks for the compliment," I said while fighting the urge to get up, spit in his face, then slam his head on the table up and down until I see red. But out of nowhere he is saved by the fucking bell. I heard a voice that I recognized as Rochelle calling my name.

"Mya!" Rochelle yelled again, this time catching my full attention.

"What?" I turned around facing her. "Why are you yellin'?" I pretended like I'm annoyed.

"What the hell is taking you so long? You said you would meet me in VIP in a minute, but according to my time, it's been about an hour." Rochelle continued to fuss a mile a minute before she noticed Phil sitting with me. She then shut up and stared at Phil like he just committed a criminal offense. Then she gave me a puzzled look before turning her attention back to Phil. "Hey, Phil."

"Yo, what's up, Rochelle?" Phil replied while looking at me with a smirk on his face.

"Well, um. I hate to interrupt, but, Mya, you have some people waiting to meet you in VIP."

"Oh yeah, I was about to come up," I said, feeling relief. I had planned how I would pry info from

Phil, but I didn't plan how I would get away once I had enough info. Rochelle had saved me. I had to thank her later. I couldn't help but think that Phil was a sucka-ass nigga.

"Phil, it was nice talking to you, but I have to go party with my girls. You know how it is."

"No doubt. I guess I can go blaze with my crew. See you around." Phil grabbed his drink and bounced.

As soon as he walked away Rochelle started with the million questions. "Mya, what are you doing sitting here with Phil? Was he trying to hook up with you? I know you ain't feelin' him, 'cause you know he a part of the Boone Squad. And you hate them, remember?" Rochelle reminded me.

"Rochelle, calm down. I was only talking to him about school. Plus, he was buying me free drinks. Now let's go to VIP and drink some more for free. The night is still young, and this DJ off the chain. I see what you were talking about. I already been shaking my butt on the dance floor," I said as I followed her to VIP.

When we entered the VIP section I was blinded by bling. When the bling finally cleared, I saw faces that I knew from this crew called the Height Squad. They were this other rival crew that sold dope in the Brewster and all over the Michigan area. This was the same crew that Charlene's new man Pig ran with. As Rochelle started to introduce me to everyone, I realized that I knew most of them. There was Li'l Lo, Pablo, Rob, and, of course, Pig. Then she introduced me to the one way in the back that I couldn't see from the door where I was standing. Hood. Hood happened to be the guy that was staring at me earlier while he was at the bar. When Rochelle introduced Hood, he never looked up. He was texting on his phone. The sight of him made me feel a little nervous and speechless. I was never speechless, especially over some guy, some thug. That simply wasn't my style. So at that moment I chilled. Hood spoke up first.

"Mya, that's it, right?" he asked without looking up at me.

"You got it," I replied, trying to sound cool while feeling like all eyes in the room were on me.

"We have an open bar in here so help yourself. If you don't see anything you want in here, the waitress will be back in a minute. You can order whatever you want."

"Thanks," I said as I followed Rochelle over to the bar.

"Girl, did you see the way Hood looked at you when you entered the room? He likes you, Mya," Rochelle babbled.

"No, he don't. He was not lookin' at me. He don't even know me. He was only trying to show off, and you know that don't impress me," I reminded her and rolled my eyes.

"Mya, you can say what you want. Hood wants you. These hoes have been breaking this door down trying to get to Hood since we got here. They did the same thing last week, and when they do get in here, he don't give them the time of day. But when you first stepped in here, he couldn't take his eyes off you. Trust me, he wants you." Rochelle beamed.

"First off, when we first stepped in, the nigga was texting."

"Girl, that was a front because while I was introducing you to everyone, he was checking you out. I'm telling you, he wants you."

"Well, I don't want him or any of these other niggas up in here. I got better shit to do with my time." Rochelle handed me the drink she was mixing for me. Pretending not to give what she said another thought, I took a sip of my drink, threw my head back, and started relaxing to the beat.

Chapter 11

My plan for this morning seemed like it was already off track. I was supposed to get up and catch the bus to go meet my dad's friend Big Nick at the crack of dawn. I would have reached out to Big a long time ago to help us with money for food, but Mom had been against that. She knew the word was out on the streets about her doing drugs. And she felt like reaching out to Big Nick would bring him too close to our business. But now I had to do what I had to do, and he was the only person I could trust with this. So I called him last week to see if he could get me some clean guns, and he said he would take care of it. He told me when, where, and what time to show up, which happened to be first thing this morning, but this morning I woke up late and with a little unwanted anxiety. Not that I was chickening out or anything, but just the reality of this robbery actually taking place slowed my pace a little bit, I think.

But squash all that. I got up and got moving. I

had missed the bus that I planned on catching, which meant I had to pay a cab about fifty bucks to take me across town. I didn't want to pay that money, but forget it. Yesterday I did six heads so I'm straight. Plus, I hit the supermarket on Friday, so we are good on food, but still, I could've used that money on something else, but I couldn't be late to meet Big Nick. If I'm late, he ain't gon' even deal with me. My dad used to always say, "Big Nick is a timey nigga." That means be on time or forget it.

When the cab finally pulled up to the penthouse that Big Nick lived in, I couldn't do anything but stare up at the huge building for a minute. It was really nice. This is definitely some shit I haven't seen in a long time. Before my dad went into prison, we would ride out of the hood all the time to go shopping and to eat at expensive restaurants, but that's been a whole lifetime ago, so standing in front of the Pavilion Penthouse, a huge high-rise building on the north side of Detroit, left me impressed. This building looked like something only well-off people lived in for sure. It had those huge Italian windows and a doorman in uniform standing outside waiting to let me in.

After gathering my composure, I spoke to the doorman who greeted me. He then directed me to the front desk where they would let Big Nick know I was in the lobby. There was security, so unless you were a resident, there was no way you were just going to get on the elevator to go up, and from what Big Nick told me, he lived on the twelfth floor, so the elevator was a must. When I got to the front desk, Big Nick had already given them preapproval of my arrival. I handed the password that he gave me to the front-desk attendant, and she quickly alerted him that I had arrived.

At that moment another attendant came over and directed me to the elevator, where he took me up to the twelfth floor. When we reached it, he walked me all the way to Big Nick's apartment and rang the doorbell. Finally the door swung open, and I was standing face-to-face with Big Nick. I hadn't seen him since my dad went up to prison, but he still looked the same. Big Nick was about six feet seven, weighed at least 250 pounds, and had a look on his face that said, "Don't fuck with me." Somewhere along that line he acquired the name Big Nick.

"Baby girl," he said, as soon as the door swung open. "Come on in here and give me a hug."

Hugging Big Nick made me feel like I had my daddy back, because my dad and Big Nick were the same height. They probably weighed about the same except my dad was light-skinned and Big Nick had a milk chocolate skin tone. Needless to say, they both were very handsome men.

"Hi, Nick," I said in a casual tone.

"It's been way too long. I really miss you kids."

"Likewise." I tried to sound really grown up. "I was glad to find out that your number was still the same," I said to keep the conversation going.

"Well, I'm just glad you called. Ain't nothing been right since your dad went to jail. I just want you to know I never forgot about your mom, Monica, Li'l Bo, or you. The police was trying to hassle everyone who associated with your dad. I mean, your dad's occupation and mine was totally different, but the feds didn't give a fuck. They just wanted to get everybody who was associated with him in any way. So I just stayed away. I go up all the time to see him, though. He told me about your mom. That situation is killing him while he's inside. Anyway, I was glad when you called, but I was a little concerned about you needing guns. You okay?" His forehead had a slight frown.

"Yeah . . . Yeah," I said, having to clear my voice. Big Nick talking about my family was making me get emotional. "Just need some protection. You know how it is over in the Brewster. That neighborhood ain't changing, and I want to feel protected. Tha . . . That's all." I had to clear my throat again.

Big Nick gave me a long look like he was trying to see inside me for a minute. "Follow me," he finally instructed me. I followed him as he led me to the back of his luxurious penthouse. He led me to this room complete with a fully stocked bar and a pool table. It also had two big-screen TVs on opposite walls. On the pool table lay two guns that shined so brightly I could literally see them sparkle.

As he picked up the gun and ran his hand across the rim, I saw a light inside Big Nick that only a killer gets when he puts a gun in his hand.

"This here is a Ruger GP100 complete with a silencer. With you being a young lady, this is all you need for regal protection. You think you can handle this gun?"

I picked up the other Ruger from the table to feel the weight of it. "This is some real heat," I said with an unbelievable look in my eyes. A true feeling of excitement raced straight to my heart while holding the gun in my hand. I was so focused on the gun that I didn't even hear Big Nick when he asked me the question.

"Damn right it's real. Now again, can you handle this gun or do you need something smaller?"

"No. I can handle this," I said matter-of-factly.

"I thought you could, but I had to ask. I'm giving you both of these because you said on the phone you need two. I also got a few boxes of bullets for you. I didn't load them, but I will show you how. All you have to do is pop this up and the chamber will open. You take these bullets and load it." He opened up a box with bullets and inserted them in the chamber of the gun. "Pop this clip and it will close back up. I want you to keep it on safety at all times, loaded or not, okay? Both guns are clean, so if you get caught with them, all you have to say is that you found them. That's it."

"Got ya. You don't even have to worry about that. Lester didn't raise no damn snitches," I reminded him. "Thank you so much, Big Nick. But I have one more favor to ask you."

"What's that, baby girl?" he asked with sincerity in his voice.

"My dad can't know about this. Could you please not tell him?" I begged.

"Mya, I don't know if I should keep this from him. I just gave his baby girl two Rugers. How can I not mention it? He'll be pissed," he tried to explain.

"I know I am asking a lot, but this will only worry him if he knows I have guns. He'll be worried that Li'l Bo is going get them and do some stupid shit. On my last visit I told him about how

Li'l Bo is ready to get in the streets and hustle. So if he knows I have these guns he'll worry about Li'l Bo. Please, Nick, just don't tell him," I continued to beg. I let my thick eyelashes flutter up and down. It used to make my dad give in. Maybe it would have some effect on Big Nick.

"All right, I won't tell him, but if your mom catches you with these guns, you can't tell her you got them from me. Because if you do, the first thing she will do is tell your dad."

"I promise," I said before giving Big Nick a hug. "Thanks, Big Nick. I have to get going before my mom starts worrying. She didn't see me this morning before I left. Lately she turns into a real bitch if I make her mad, so I don't feel like pissing her off today," I said while bending down to put one of the guns in a clip on my right ankle. I put the other gun in my waistband. My dad kept clips around the house for when he strapped up, and he'd stayed strapped. So I figured it would be a good idea to bring a few along with me to hide the heat.

"Wow," Big Nick said with a shocked look on his face as he watched me suit up with my Rugers. "You came prepared, huh? I was going to give you this gun case." He pointed to a black case on the pool table next to where the guns had been resting.

"I can't take that on the bus. It would bring too much attention, especially to those who can't wait to rob and take advantage of a young girl alone on a bus."

"You're a thinker just like your dad." Big Nick

smiled. "Go on and get back before your mom misses you. Call me if you need me. "

"I will," I lied. Calling him would be my last resort. This was on me. "Oh, and thanks for supplying the bullets."

"No doubt." He smiled.

I headed out the door back toward the elevator, where the attendant was waiting to take me down to the main floor. I couldn't help but think, *Damn, it must be nice to live like this.*

Chapter 12

"Hertz Rent-a-Car," the lady at the sales counter answered the phone with a snide attitude. "Hold for just for a moment. I'll transfer you to my supervisor."

"May I help you?" she said, giving me a look like I was wasting her time as she hung up the phone.

"Yes." I stepped up to the counter. "I'm here to rent a car."

"Do you have a reservation?"

"No."

"Without a reservation, I have to check to see if we have anything available." She started typing on the computer in front of her. "Yes, looks like we have a Ford Taurus available. How long will you need the vehicle?"

"Just till tomorrow," I replied quickly.

"Okay. Well, I will need your driver's license and a credit card to set this rental up." She kind of stared me up and down like she was trying to figure me out.

Credit card. I started to get nervous. I had a fake driver's license that Rochelle had made for me to get in the club, but a credit card I didn't have nor could I get legally. Thankfully I had called first to find out what all I needed so I gave her this information because this ghetto tramp had a look on her face like she was losing patience.

"Uh, I called before I came over, and I was told that at this location I could use a money order for the payment."

"Well, do you have a money order?" she asked with attitude.

Now I was about to lose my patience 'cause if this bitch caught one more attitude with me, I was gon' snatch her from behind that counter. Of course I had the money. I had borrowed it from Charlene. Did this dumb bitch think I would show up without the money? Ugh. With all the strength I could gather without cursing her out, I gently laid the money order and my ID on the counter. While investigating my ID she started smacking on some gum she clearly had hidden in her mouth.

"This you?" she asked me while giving me a once-over glance. "Because this ID says you twenty-five, but you look like you sixteen."

"Look, do they pay you for thinkin' or rentin' cars? If the ID says I'm twenty-five, then, bitch, I am twenty-five." I went Brewster projects on her before I could control myself. "Now, are you going to rent me a car or what? Because I don't have all day for this." I was starting to get pissed.

"Rude too, huh? Well, whatever. Anyway, I was just asking." Without another word she finished up the paperwork and handed me the keys. I gave her a snide grin as I snatched the keys from her hands.

I hate putting up with people like her, but finally I had the car. That bitch and her jacked-up weave hates her life so she wants to take it out on the customer. Scratch her. I headed out to the parking lot to find the car. Talk about a piece of junk, Taurus is one of the ugliest cars ever made. But whatever. As long as it gets the job done. I hopped inside, turned the volume up, and hit the interstate to clear my mind before getting on the job because this shit goes down tonight.

Chapter 13

After grabbing something to eat I went back to one of the main exits out of the Brewster to get ready to follow Luscious. Brewster is his first pickup from the young dope boys in the projects. He should pick up sixty thousand easy out of Brewster alone. The hard part was sitting here waiting for him to come out. I was already in place when he arrived about an hour before. He jumped up out of his ride, giving strict instructions for the future wannabe kids to guard his wheels. I just wished he would hurry his ass up. He should be about to come out. I just gotta chill until he does.

While I sat and waited, I went over the plan in my head and all the information that I'd collected to get to this point. Shit has been hard and easy. The first bit of information I got that I planned on using in this whole setup is a piece that I got from Squeeze himself a long time ago. Well, he didn't give it to me personally; I was kind of eavesdropping.

One day I had come home from school early, and I was in my room when my mom brought him home for another one of their sex romps. Squeeze was high, and, of course, my mom was too, except she was high on crack. He was in the living room on the phone talking to someone about going to Luscious's house to pick up a last-minute package. Squeeze thought this conversation would be okay to have because my mom was asleep; he had no idea that I was home. Whoever was on the other end of the phone was worried about running into someone at the pickup house besides Luscious. According to Squeeze, no one was ever allowed at that house but Luscious, so he would definitely be alone.

So I got all that information as a freebie. I never knew I would need it because I would have never thought I would be robbing Luscious or anyone else from the Boone Squad. I need to thank Squeeze. Because of his big-ass mouth, that bit of information will be useful. Another bit of information that Squeeze gave during that phone call that I could use is the name of the pickup house. The pickup house was on the north side of Detroit, Seville Point Apartments. Earlier today I was able to ride by the spot and familiarize myself with the area so when I made my getaway it would be clean. I just wished he would hurry up so we can get this on the road.

"Shit, there he is," I said out loud to myself. I ducked my head to be sure he didn't get a glance at me. I let two cars go by before falling in two places behind Luscious. I quickly gathered my thoughts and put the car into slow motion to get behind him. My heart was beating so fast I thought it might bust right through my chest. My hands were sweating so much they were sliding off the steering wheel. It was dark out so it would be hard for him to notice he was being followed unless he had a reason to be suspicious, which, at this point, he shouldn't. Today he was riding in a different car. He has quite a few cars he shows up in when he's on the block, but normally, he drives his Escalade. Tonight he's riding in a rusty orange 2009 or '10 Ford Mustang with dark tinted windows, and, of course, he's sittin' on twenty-four-inch rims.

We rode for another three hours, making frequent stops where Luscious would get out of the car, go in and come out, seemingly empty-handed, but the money was strapped to him. Once he gets inside the car he unloads it into this black bag. I got this bit of information from Phil's drunk ass on the dance floor. Damn, what a nigga won't say when he's loaded and thinking he's scoring some points with a bitch. Finally, we pulled into the Seville Apartments. I parked in a dark spot where there was no streetlight.

Luscious got out of the car and looked around for a minute. Then he walked to his trunk and opened it. Not getting anything out of the trunk, he closed it and again took a look around to make sure everything was clear. Feeling secure, he reached back into the front seat, grabbed the bag, and headed for his building. I noticed he was keeping his left hand close to his left side near his hip. That must be where he's holding his heat.

I got out of the car slowly with both my Rugers locked and loaded. Then I quickly sped up my pace to get up to the door behind him. Luscious took a quick glance around, took his hand off his left hip, put it in his pocket, and grabbed his key. Taking one final look around, he put the key in the lock. That's when I made my move.

My right hand went up with the Ruger to the back of his head. My left hand with the other Ruger centered on his spine. He froze, shocked. There was silence for a brief moment.

"What the fuck is goin' on?" Luscious finally muttered.

"Don't say shit," I said in the best man's voice I could muster. If nothing else, I had to hide the fact I was a girl. I had on all black with a black ski mask and black gloves. I had practiced a low, deep drawl with my voice, and so far I was doing good. I thought I sounded just like a real dude.

"Take your left hand, open up the door, and keep your right hand on the bag. Any sudden move and you a dead motherfucker," I said, meaning every word, knowing that if he saw me I wouldn't have any choice but kill him or be killed. Being killed wasn't an option for me.

Once inside, I ordered him on the floor, face-down. "Lay on your face right here."

"Look, man, you making a big fucking mistake. You're dead tomorrow," Luscious attempted to threaten me.

"No, man, you're dead if you don't shut the fuck up right now," I warned him as I lifted the safety on both Rugers. Luscious flinched when he heard that click from the safety.

I stood over him and put both Rugers to the back of his head, showing him I meant business.

"Now, reach on your left hip and throw your gun to the side. Then spread both of your hands out in front of you." He quickly but carefully followed my rules.

"Please don't kill me, man. Not over money. Just take the fucking bag. It got about three hundred thousand in it."

"Stop beggin' for your life like a bitch, dude. Have some heart."

I reached over with my right hand and opened the bag. Like I thought, the bag was full of stacked bills, fives and tens, bound by rubber bands. With my heart racing I finished the job. With the Ruger in my right hand, I struck Luscious on the back of the head. To make sure he was out cold, I repeated the blow. This blow turned red. I grabbed the bag and made a dash for the front door, hoping for Luscious's sake he woke up or somebody found him before he bled to death.

———◈———

I was so nervous that I felt sick to my stomach. I found the closest hotel possible to gather my thoughts. Inside the hotel room, I headed straight to the bathroom, where I washed my face in cold water. I then threw my exhausted body across the bed with a million thoughts racing through my mind. My exhaustion turned to panic. What if Luscious wasn't unconscious and followed me? He could be outside with his crew waiting to blast me. So I got up and started looking out the window.

Finally I realized my paranoia for what it was. I was having a panic attack, and I just needed to calm down. First, I needed to get out of the clothes I had on. I had already taken off the mask and gloves. I had on regular clothes under the baggy ones, so I just stripped down.

Sitting across the room from me was the black bag full of money that I had taken from Luscious. Once I calmed down, I grabbed the bag and took the money out and started counting. Four unbelievable hours later, I had counted three hundred thousand, eight hundred sixty dollars of cold, hard cash. I couldn't believe I had pulled this off all by myself. Me, Mya—a seventeen-year-old 115-pound girl. It must be true what they say: niggas without they heat is soft.

But it wasn't over. I had to make this money not noticeable. Of course, I told Rochelle that I would be coming into some money from my dad. That was easy; she is my best friend. I could tell her just about anything, and she would believe it. Telling others would be a whole other story. No one else would believe some guy owed my dad some money and paid it to me while Dad was locked up because shit doesn't normally happen in the hood like that. I would just let the money surface slowly by telling Li'l Bo and Monica bits of what I told Rochelle. They are my family, and like Rochelle, they are bound to believe me. As for my mother, I would tell her what I felt like telling her, which was nothing. You can never tell a dope fiend the truth about sudden riches or money—period.

First thing tomorrow I'll open up a safe deposit box at the bank where I'll put in all this money except for a few hundred. Then I'll return that rental car. From there, I'll lay low and keep my ear to the streets and keep doing heads. That is what I do, right?

Chapter 14

The last two weeks were like murder on me. Keeping my ear to the streets, lying low, and trying to keep my same routine is how I had been maintaining. I didn't want to do anything out of the ordinary to bring any unwanted attention. Today was a little different, though. I decided to spend a little change to buy a weave to braid Monica's hair. Monica had been bugging me for the past couple of days to braid her hair. So I decided to get up this morning and surprise her.

So for the last eight hours I'd been going hard on braiding Monica up and it was coming out pretty. The only downside is my damn fingers were in pain like usual when I braid.

"Mya, are you almost finished? My butt's starting to hurt, and these shabby pillows with no cushion aren't helping," she complained and twisted in a circular motion like she's trying to get comfortable.

"Girl, I know you ain't complaining the way

you been bitchin' every day to get these braids. Besides, *I'm* the one with the cramps in my fingers."

"Oh, poor Mya's fingers all cramped up like a cripple." Monica made fun of me.

"Shut up." I laughed at her. "I just want to see you half decent is all."

"Yeah, half decent. You remember when we was little, you would practice braiding my hair and you always ended up giving me pigtails instead? Dad would say, 'Mya, take them snakes out of that girl's head. She look just like Beetlejuice.' " Monica tried to mimic my dad's voice.

"I remember that." I thought back while laughing.

"I miss those days. I miss Dad. I miss our old family, period. But even still, I feel lucky to have you and Li'l Bo. Now we just got to work on getting our momma back." Monica started to get emotional.

I stopped braiding her hair for a minute. "Look at me," I said. "Even though times have been rough, we gon' make it. As for Momma, we just got to give her time, but everything is going to work out. I just need you to trust me."

"Mya, how did you get to be so strong?" Monica started wiping her running tears with the back of her hand.

"I kinda had a little training from my dad, Lester. You do know him, right?" I joked. I reached out and hugged Monica. "Now, turn around. I'm almost finished with yo' big watermelon-shaped head." We both started laughing.

KNOCK, KNOCK, KNOCK.

"Get the door, Monica." I stopped braiding her hair again.

Monica rushed to open the door. "Oh, it ain't nobody but Rochelle." Monica tried to be sarcastic. "Girl, why you knocking like you the police? We busy; we ain't got time to be answering doors." Monica gave Rochelle her latest unfriendly attitude, but we know it's all love.

"Hi to you too, li'l mama. I see you woke up on the floor this morning instead of the bed." Rochelle stepped in the apartment past Monica as Monica closed the door.

"What's up, girl?" I greeted Rochelle.

"Nothin'. Just thought I would get outta the house for a minute today. I think I'm starting to miss Mike. I need to find me a man," Rochelle informed me as she bounced down on our already brutally battered couch.

"Girl, I know you trippin'. Have a seat!" I laughed. "I'm almost finished braiding Monica's hair."

"That's right, so don't be talkin' to her too much. I don't need her messing up my head. And where is Tiny? How you goin' come over and don't bring her?" Monica asked.

"She's with Wynita. They out shopping," Rochelle confirmed.

"Umm," was Monica's reply. Everyone knows how much Monica loves Tiny. Every time Rochelle brings her over she takes her over without Rochelle even asking.

One hour later I was finished braiding Monica's hair. Monica had started to nod off as we both sat there listening to Rochelle babble on and on about how she misses Mike. I chalked that whole conversation up to the fact that she's just lonely.

The Rochelle I know can't stand Mike, and if he wasn't locked up, they still wouldn't be together. They would be broke up from a previous fight. So all that this Rochelle on my couch needs is some fun. One thing I know for sure, she doesn't miss Mike.

Yawning, Monica rose up off the pillow she had been sitting on. "I think I'm going to take a nap. I'm getting sleepy." She stretched all the way to her room.

"Mya, I thought Monica would never leave." Rochelle sighed with relief. "The streets have been crazy since Luscious got robbed a couple of weeks ago. People have been gettin' shot. The streets just ain't been safe. That's why I been telling you just go where you have to. Last night someone in my building got blasted in the face. Supposedly about that Luscious incident. I'm telling you, it's a war zone out there."

"Word? I had heard about some of that on the late-night news, but they don't even mention the robbery. Maybe they don't think the two are connected." I tried to sound casual.

"I don't know, but you already know they ain't gon' talk about that until they have some proof. And you know ain't nobody from the hood gon' give them that. Luscious didn't even report that shit, I'm sure. But the streets is talkin', and the word is somebody gon' pay for that. So you know what that means."

"Have you heard anything about any suspects on who did the robbery?" I asked casually.

"Nope. At this point, everybody's a suspect. That's why niggas been getting blasted." Rochelle pulled out some Certs and popped some in her mouth.

"That's crazy." I shook my head in fake disbelief.

"Mya!" Momma came out of her room yelling.

"What?" I said, irritated, without turning around to face her.

"Hey, Mrs. Marisa," Rochelle said.

"Hey, Rochelle. Mya, you got any money? I need to get me some Newports."

"Nope."

"Ain't you been doing hair? Don't lie to me, girl. All I need is some Newports."

"Look, I told you I don't have any money. And if I did, I wouldn't give it to you." I caught an attitude.

"You wouldn't give it to me? What the hell does that mean? I been taking care of you since you was shittin' up diapers. And you wouldn't give me four stankin' dollars? Well, ain't that a bitch." She really got upset.

"All right," I said impatiently. "I will get you some Newports. But I ain't giving you no money. I'll go out and get some. Come on, Rochelle, let's walk over to the store." I bent down and laced up my shoes.

"And make sure you pick up that mess before you leave," Mama said, pointing to the leftover hair I used to do Monica's hair.

I rolled my eyes and started gathering up the hair with Rochelle's help.

On the way to the store, everything looked peaceful, which kind of relaxed my nerves. Everybody was hanging on the block, even my brother

Li'l Bo. I started to scream at him, but I decided to chill since I had shit on my mind.

"So what's up with the money, Mya? A week has passed since you were supposed to pick it up. And you ain't said nothing, plus you been acting funny."

I stopped dead in my tracks. I knew she would ask at some point. I just didn't know when. But I guess now was as good a time as any to continue with my lie.

"I got it."

"You got it? Well, when did you get it, and how much?" Rochelle fired questions at me. "And why you ain't happy?"

"Calm down, Rochelle. It seems to me you're happy enough for both of us." I grinned. "I am happy and nervous. I don't know what to do with all that money. I haven't even told Li'l Bo and Monica about it," I confessed.

"You haven't? When are you going to tell them? And you still haven't told me how much money you got. I thought you were my best friend, but you're holding out on me. What's up with that, Mya?" Rochelle played at being mad.

"I'm not holding out. I just haven't told you. I was afraid you might lose it. You know how excited you get about anything that glitters." I stopped for a few seconds. "But the amount was about a hundred thousand," I lied calmly. Rochelle stopped, almost in slow motion. She looked at me in disbelief and screamed.

"Oh my Goddd!! Mya, you rich, girl!" Rochelle jumped up and down and grabbed me in a big hug.

"Shhh, girl!" I looked around and put my hand over her mouth. "Girl, you gone tell the whole projects and get me robbed. Calm down; it's only money. Besides, I wouldn't want Li'l Bo or Monica to find out from anyone but me."

"Why haven't you told them? You can't keep this a secret from them."

"I know. I just gotta get used to the fact that I even have all that money first. I already safely put it away. But having that much still makes me nervous."

"Nervous? It should make you happy as hell. I know it makes me happy. I know Li'l Bo and Monica will be too." Rochelle had a grin on her face so wide it looked like her face was going to pop. "I know your dad is happy Big John showed up with that money."

"Yeah, he is," I lied with a grim smile on my face.

"Okay, look. You have to tell Monica and Li'l Bo soon. Maybe you should take them out to eat or something and do it," Rochelle suggested.

That sounded like a good suggestion, I thought as I stopped walking to face Rochelle. "Yeah, I think that's what I'll do. I'll take them out later today and tell them. That way, if they get too excited, my momma won't hear. Rochelle, thanks." I gave her a fake push while we continued to walk.

"Now what are you going to do for your eighteenth birthday?"

"Oh snap, Rochelle. Girl, I forgot all about my birthday, I've been so busy."

"Mya, how you gon' forget your own birthday?

I didn't forget. It's next Saturday, and we gon' party." Rochelle threw her hands up in the air.

"No, doubt." I smiled. "I *know* we gon' party." I got hyped.

"Damn right. And you're gon' spend some of that money to go shopping too. I don't wanna hear shit, and do your hair. You'll be the main bitch that night. You only turn eighteen once, so it's on." Rochelle gave me a serious look to make her point.

She's right, I only turn eighteen once, and with all the drama I've been going through the last four years, I deserve to celebrate my eighteenth birthday. And that's just what I plan to do. As for shopping, I haven't done that in a while so it should be interesting. Not only am I going to go shopping for myself, I'm going to take Li'l Bo and Monica on a shopping spree. Spending money ain't something we've been accustomed to in the last couple of years, but I'm pretty sure we won't screw it up.

Chapter 15

"Give me that bread back, Li'l Bo. I had it first. You know I had it first," I heard Monica scream at Li'l Bo when I entered the front door.

"I don't know shit. If you had it first, why didn't you eat it?" he asked calmly.

"Because I went to the bathroom. Now give it here." Monica snatched the bread out of his hand. The bread crumbled when she snatched it. "You see what you've done? Now the bread is torn up. How am I supposed to eat it?" Monica continued to yell at him.

"Why don't you ask yourself that, since you the one snatched it?" Li'l Bo started laughing.

I stood back in silence and watched them argue. They have been arguing like that since I became too old to argue with Li'l Bo myself. So now I get to sit back and referee their petty bullshit arguments. Monica always wins because Li'l Bo always lets both of us get our way in the end. Just when the argument was over, Momma came out of her room.

"What is going on in here? Why all the hollering?" She headed in the kitchen.

"It's *him*." Monica pointed her finger at Li'l Bo.

I started laughing out loud, and Momma turned around. "What's so funny? Don't you hear them in here about to kill each other?" she asked.

"Yeah, and can you believe over some bread?" I answered, still laughing.

"It ain't funny, Mya. He knows I was about to make a sandwich with that bread." Monica pouted.

"Stop whining like a baby. The next time you take the bread out, use it. Females." Li'l Bo breathed out loud.

"Whatever, boy, get yo—"

"Hold it." I cut Monica off before she could say anything else. "Could both of you stop about that damn bread. We can get more bread. As a matter of fact, both of you get dressed. We going to the store," I ordered them.

"Why are we going to the store? I don't feel like it. Besides, I just took my clothes off. If you lookin' for me, I'll be in my room trying to beat the next level on my game." Li'l Bo walked off.

"Li'l Bo," I yelled, "boy, you better get dressed before I act a fool," I warned him.

"I'm already dressed." Monica smiled. "All I have to do is put on my sneakers."

Li'l Bo gave both of us a malevolent look before going to his room to get dressed.

"Speaking of the store, did you get my Newports?" Momma asked. In the mix of everything I had forgotten all about the Newports that Rochelle and I had walked to the store to pick up. I reached inside my pocket and handed them to her.

"Thanks." She smiled as she grabbed the pack out of my hand. "You taking your brother and sister to the store so you must have some money. Why don't give your momma some, because I sure could use it."

"I already told you I don't have any money. Now I got you those Newports just like you asked."

"I know that. I just thought you had some money. If you ain't got no money, why you going to the store? You better not be on no stealing shit, because I ain't coming down to Juvenile to get your asses," she warned.

"Who gon' be stealing?" I fired back at her.

"I'm just telling ya." She frowned at me and lit a Newport. I hardly even recognize this mother in front of me. She has changed so much since my dad left. Feeling sorry for my own mother, I decided not to argue with her today.

"Yeah, I hear ya."

Li'l Bo came out of his room with a look that said, "Let's go now."

"We'll be back later if you still here," I said before we headed out the door.

Chapter 16

Once outside the apartment we started walking like we're going to the store, but I decided to take a detour. I sped up my walking pace and stopped in front of Li'l Bo and Monica.

"Let's stop a cab."

"Stop a cab for *what?*" Li'l Bo looked at me like I have only one eye. "Mya, what's up with you today? You got us out here walking in this damn heat like we going to the store. Now you talkin' about let's stop a cab." He started walking again. Monica looked at me, confused.

"Look, Mya, are we going to the store or not because I'm hungry. I ain't got time for this neither." Monica looked defeated as she ran her hand through her braids to get them out of her face.

I turned around and waved down a cab that happened to be passing by, and it actually stopped. I can't help but think this must be my lucky day because it's rare to get a cab to even slow down in the Brewster. I stepped off the curb up to the cab.

"Where you headed, little lady?" the male cab-driver asked me. I almost threw up before I could answer because his bad breath slapped me in the face.

"Downtown," I was able to answer before having to catch my balance.

"They with you?" He looked past me and pointed at Li'l Bo and Monica.

"Yeah," I answered.

"You got money?"

"Uh-huh," I answered, sick to death of his killer breath.

"Then hop on in."

I opened the back door, and Li'l Bo and Monica hesitated for a minute. "Would y'all get in the cab," I said in a demanding tone.

As soon as we all piled inside the cab, the driver took off. He didn't even give us a chance to put on seat belts. By the time we hit the interstate headed downtown we had all settled comfortably in our seats. I, for one, was just hoping the driver kept his damn mouth shut since I had come up close and personal with his foul breath. To be honest, the whole cab smelled just like his stank-ass breath. So him not talking only eased the funk just a little bit, but just my luck, he didn't stay quiet for long.

"Where ya headed downtown, little lady?" he asked while looking through his rearview mirror, which had me worried, since he was driving like a bat out of hell.

"Not sure yet; just keep driving." I looked over at Li'l Bo and Monica, who were quiet as hell.

"Where would y'all like to get something to eat

from downtown? Like what restaurant?" I asked them, hoping to get a response.

"You got some money?" Li'l Bo asked, giving me a suspicious look.

"I asked what did you want to eat, didn't I?"

"I want a greasy burger with mustard and pickles," Monica said, without a doubt.

"Yeah, that does sound good." Li'l Bo cosigned with a slight nod.

"A'ight, bet. You know there's only one place to get that downtown. Aye, driver, you know where Motown Café & Grill Burgers is?" I asked.

"Absolutely. I'll have you there in five."

We pulled up in front of Motown Café, and I paid the cabdriver and we got out.

"Thank God! I thought we'd never get outta that stanky-ass cab," Monica revealed, taking a deep breath. Li'l Bo and I started laughing.

We stared at Motown Café for a while before going in. This place brings back memories for us because my dad used to take us here all the time for burgers. A waitress seated us and took our orders. After she left the table, Li'l Bo started with the questions.

"Okay, Mya, what's up? How you gon' pay for all this? And after all that food I just ordered I don't plan on running up outta here. Not today. So you better have a better plan or some money," he informed me.

"Don't worry about that. I got money, so you can eat your food in peace. Monica, you can order dessert if you want."

"Now *that's* what I'm talkin' about," Monica

said without questioning anything. But I decided to go ahead and fill them in on our new financial gain before the food arrived.

"Look, I brought both of you out to eat for a reason. I need to talk to you about something important. What we discuss is not to leave this table for no reason. Understand?" I gave them both a serious look.

"Spit it out—" Li'l Bo stopped because the waitress approached the table with our drinks.

"A'ight, I'll get to the point," I said, knowing what Li'l Bo was about to say before the waitress walked up to our table. "Remember when I went to visit Dad the last time?" I paused, and they both gave me a nod.

"Well, Dad told me he had a friend that owed him some money. Just so happens that friend had come by to visit him to let him know he was ready to pay up. Well, to make this story short, Dad told him to give me the money for us. I met with the guy about two weeks ago, and he gave it to me."

"How much money?" Monica asked.

"Two hundred thousand," I lied, not giving them the exact amount. I couldn't disclose the actual amount. I didn't want my money to add up to the robbery.

"Stop bullshittin', Mya," Li'l Bo stated, giving me a sideways glance.

"I'm not." I gave him a smile. "I promise."

The waitress came back to our table with the food. "Let me know if you need anything else," she said before walking away.

"This looks good," Monica said, staring at her plate.

"Yeah, it does," I replied before biting my burger.

"So what did you do with it?" Li'l Bo said with a mouth full of burger and a few fries also stuffed inside.

"What did I do with what?" I played dumb.

"The money," Monica jumped in the conversation and inserted a fry in her mouth.

"I put it up and don't ask me where." I looked at Li'l Bo, knowing that was his next question. "Look, we have to be really careful. No one can know about this, especially Ma. If she knows about that money she will lose it. Dad said not to give her none because she will only smoke it. If she needs something like clothes or Newports we can buy it for her. As for other people they aren't to know either. We don't want to get robbed, so we need to continue on like we were doing. Except I'm taking you two shopping," I informed them, and they both started smiling.

"When are you taking us shopping, because I need some of everything?" Monica said, giving me an assuring look.

"No doubt." Li'l Bo started on his second hamburger, since he ordered two.

"Eat up and we can head to the mall," I said, feeling like a weight had been lifted off my shoulders by telling them about the money. Now that I had got that out, we could move forward. My eighteenth birthday was just around the corner. I didn't want to feel no burden riding my back. This shopping trip for me was going to be a huge stress reliever.

Chapter 17

When we got back from shopping last night Momma was out so we didn't have to worry about hiding all the bags that Li'l Bo and Monica had. They were really happy. They both got a lot of what they wanted. By the time we got through shopping they had spent two thousand dollars so I knew it was really time to get up out of the store. We took a cab back home because I didn't want to ride the bus back with all those bags. In our hood, we would've been asking to be robbed. Speaking of being robbed, I knew Momma would notice Li'l Bo and Monica had new clothes. I wasn't worried about her asking where they came from as much as I worried about her trying to sell them for money. While we were out shopping I picked up locks for our bedroom doors. That would keep her out of our rooms when we were not home.

This morning when I got out of bed I decided to get dressed and head over to Rochelle's house. I figured we could do some shopping so I could pick me up some new 'fits. Yesterday I didn't really do any shopping for myself; I just let Li'l Bo and Monica shop. Today was my day, and I was going to let my girl Rochelle shop as well since she's been the best friend a girl could have.

When I knocked on the door I could hear Rochelle's mom, Ms. Wynita, fussing about something. When the door swung open, it was none other than Ms. Wynita, and I knew from the look on her face I had come over at the wrong time. It was Sunday, and Ms. Wynita got this "church/she-will-cuss-your-ass-out" thing going on. She had on her Sunday best and her Bible in one hand which means she was ready for war.

"And why ain't you dressed for church?" she asked me right off the bat.

"Uhhhh, I told you before, Ms. Wynita, I wasn't brought up in the church," I answered, knowing it was the wrong answer. But the words escaped my mouth before could I catch them.

"You wasn't brought up in the church? Chile, that ain't no excuse." She gave me a hard stare like she's considering what I just said. "Well, what's Rochelle's problem? I took her to church every Sunday. Now she done turned into a regular Satan. Going to the club is the only thing she thinks about."

"Ma," Rochelle screamed from the other room, "would you stop terrorizing my company?"

"Shut up and bring me my baby. You gon' me make me late for the sermon. And if I'm late, I'm gon' kick your ass," Ms. Wynita threatened.

"Here she is." Rochelle brought Tiny out and handed her over to Ms. Wynita.

"There's Grandma's baby. She ain't gon' turn out like you. Humph," Ms. Wynita said before storming out the door.

"Damn, girl, she woke up trippin' and shit." Rochelle looked at me and pulled a cigarette out of her pocket.

I immediately started laughing. "Ms. Wynita don't play. She be hoeing you." I pointed at Rochelle while laughing so hard I had to catch my breath.

"Shut up." Rochelle smiled as she lit her cigarette. "Why you out so early?" she asked before taking a deep intake on her cigarette.

"I came by to scoop you up. Let's hit the mall. I need to pick me up some 'fits for my birthday bash. I took Li'l Bo and Monica out yesterday, but I didn't get anything for myself. So how about you roll with me?" I smiled.

"Hell, yeah. I got to make sure you pick the fly 'fits," Rochelle complimented as she got off the couch. "Let me get dressed. I can't go to the mall lookin' like no wack ho. You know the whole Detroit be at the mall on Sunday. And you know I'm looking for Tiny's new dad," Rochelle joked.

"Girl, please." I laughed. "Hurry up."

Twenty minutes later Rochelle stepped out of her room looking like she just stepped out of a fashion magazine. "Ya like?" she modeled around in circles.

"Yeah, I like." I smiled. "But I don't know about them heels. We ain't just going to one store. We about to shop for real." I dropped a hint to let her know that I'm taking her shopping as well.

"We about to shop," Rochelle repeated back to me like I didn't just hear what I said. "You takin' *me* shopping?" She got excited and screamed. "Girl, these heels are fine. Can't you see they are for shopping only? Let's go." Rochelle, overly excited, grabbed my hand and dragged me out the door.

Three buses later we were at the mall, and it was jam-packed. Rochelle and I didn't waste any time hittin' up the stores. Our first stop was Charlotte Russe. They didn't carry any name brands, but their clothes were stylish. Rochelle and I hung around at Charlotte Russe about an hour before we decided we didn't want anything outta there.

"Okay, Rochelle, there's a lot of cute things in here, but I don't see anything I want. Nothing says 'Mya' all over it. And that's what I need. How about we head over to Macy's?" I finally suggested. And just like that, we were off to Macy's fighting our way through the hundreds of people walking through the mall. Like us, they were either looking to spend money or window-shop.

Macy's was like a dream come true for shopping. Everything you could name in fashion they had it. All the Coogi, Gucci, Prada, you name it, they had it. Rochelle went crazy. She must have put her hands on about everything in the store.

"Look, I like these jeans. I'm going to try them on," Rochelle said about some blue Baby Phat jeans with a purple Baby Phat logo on the back pocket.

"Yeah, those are hot." I turned around and glanced at the jeans. I picked up a pair of Guess skinny jeans with no pockets on the back. Then I picked up the shirt that went with it. It was a navy blue and white tee shirt with no sleeves on one side. The shirt was really trendy. All I needed was the right heels to match. This outfit turned out to be one of many I picked up at Macy's, but I still hadn't found the outfit I wanted to wear for my eighteenth birthday celebration. I stumbled upon this Dereon V-neck shirtdress. It was exactly what I was looking for; the color was peacoat navy blue with a belt around the waist. I immediately picked up my size and scattered to the dressing room. Once I tried it on, I knew I had to have it.

Rochelle and I wrapped up our shopping at Macy's once we had spent a whopping thirty-two hundred dollars. The saleslady handed us our bags.

"Shit," Rochelle murmured, as she tried to balance her bags in her hands. "Clearly we can't do any more shopping."

"No way. What are we going to do about shoes? We got to have the right shit," I replied with a smile. "Flawless, remember?"

"I remember." Rochelle almost tripped while still struggling to balance her bags.

"Tell you what," I said, as I dropped one of my bags and the saleslady rushed over to help me. I finally gathered all my bags in my hands. "How about we take these home and come back later for shoes?" I suggested.

"Cool. Hit the exit," Rochelle ordered as she led the way.

We were almost out of Macy's when we ran into Charlene, who apparently had been yelling our name from behind us.

"Hey," Charlene said, out of breath after she caught up with us. "What y'all doing up in here?" she asked casually.

"Just shopping, picking up some much-needed gear," Rochelle replied as this other chick approached Charlene, looking like she had been running a marathon, breathing all hard.

"Damn. Charlene, why are you running? You know a bitch can't keep up. I'm not young like you," the girl with Charlene squabbled while fixing her eyes on Rochelle and me.

"Sorry, I had to catch up to my girls." Charlene waved her hand toward us. "Sorry for her rudeness," Charlene apologized to us. "This is my cousin Bambi. Bambi, these are my girls, Mya and Rochelle."

One good look at Bambi and I immediately knew who she was. Bambi was the same female from Hertz Rental with the stank attitude. I damn near dropped all the bags out of my hand trying to contain my composure. The last thing I needed was for this chick to recognize me. I tried to remain casual.

Bambi seemed like she was trying to size us up before she finally spoke. "What's up?"

"Hey," Rochelle and I replied at the same time.

There was this odd silence, but Charlene instantly put a stop to that. "So, what y'all out here picking up? I see Macy's had to kick you out with all those bags," Charlene said as she eyed all the bags in our hands.

"Yeah, we picked a few 'fits," Rochelle bragged. "I see you been hittin' up the stores your damn self."

"You know it. That's why I got Pig. If nigga can't keep my pockets laced and me looking fly, then what's the point, right?" she babbled with a little laugh.

"I know, right?" Bambi cosigned with a smile. Clearly she didn't have a baller because her cheap weave still looked jacked up.

"You bitches musta hit the lotto, though, 'cause ain't neither one of you got no man," Charlene seemingly joked.

"You got jokes, right?" I said to downplay her comment to keep from bringing attention to myself. "But we straight. Too bad we can't all have a baller, though."

"Yeah, you know how it is," Charlene bragged. "But anyway, Mya, we kickin' it for your birthday or what?" Charlene got hyped. " 'Cause I'm ready to party and get krunk."

"Why you think we in here shopping? It's on just liked we talked about," Rochelle replied, just as krunk as Charlene.

"Oh, so y'all been planning my birthday behind my back," I shot off with a fake angry smirk on my face.

"Hell, yeah. You only turn eighteen once." Rochelle beamed. "And I can't wait."

"I know, right?" Charlene cosigned.

"Well, we about to jet up outta here. We've been in here for a while, but I will call you later and we can polish off the details," Rochelle informed Charlene.

"Cool, me and Bambi gon' get outta here too."

"Hell, yeah. I'm tired, besides my feet are killin' me," Bambi responded with her mouth twisted in a circular position. "It was nice meeting both of you."

"Later," Charlene said as she and Bambi turned to walk away.

Rochelle and I started to follow suit when Bambi turned around.

"Mya, I knew you looked familiar. I rented you a car about two weeks ago. Hertz. I'm the lady with all the questions."

"Yeah, I remember," I said. Clearly my cover was blown.

"So you just turnin' eighteen? I knew you weren't twenty-five. That ID was fake, huh?" She laughed.

"Guess so." I shrugged my shoulders, not at all amused by her little comment.

"Wait a minute. You two know each other?" Charlene finally butted in the conversation.

"Well, not know each other, but I rented her a car." Bambi nodded in my direction.

"Dang, Mya, girl, I didn't even know you could drive," Charlene responded.

"You didn't know that? She's been driving for a long time. Her dad used to let us both drive before he went up, but how you gon' rent a car and not tell me?" Rochelle turned her attention to me.

"It was only for a day. I had some business I needed to tend to." I gave her a shut-the-fuck-up look. The last thing I wanted was a big discussion about that rental car.

"Umm, you renting cars and going on shopping sprees. Both you bitches holding out on me," Charlene said in an unusual tone that caught Rochelle's and my attention.

I'm not sure, but I could have sworn it was a hint of jealousy, but maybe I heard it the wrong way because jealousy would not be normal from Charlene.

"Well, we gon' get up with you later," Rochelle responded. "These bags are heavy."

"A'ight," Charlene replied. "I will see you bitches at the celebration."

"Again it was nice meeting you too, and if you ever need to rent another car come see me, Mya. No need to bring ID," Bambi added.

"I'll remember that," I quickly replied.

Rochelle turned and headed toward the exit in a hurried walk. "I still can't believe you rented a car and didn't tell me," she complained.

"Look, Rochelle, I needed the car for business. There was no joyriding involved," I replied, hoping to end this conversation.

"You still could have told me. We are best friends, Mya. And since when do we not tell each other everything? Especially when one of us rents a car."

"Oh, for crying out loud, Rochelle." I stopped dead in my tracks. "I rented the car to go pick up the money from my dad's friend. I didn't want to ride the bus with that type of package on me. I didn't tell you because I had so much other shit on my mind. So would you please drop it?" I screamed.

Shocked by my reaction, Rochelle looked around to make sure no one was looking in our direction. "Okay. I'm sorry. Let's just go home." She looked defeated.

Chapter 18

"**H**appy birthday to you, Happy birthday to you . . ."

I heard people singing "Happy Birthday" and I thought I was dreaming until I opened my eyes and found Li'l Bo and Monica standing over me. "What is going on?" were the first words out of my mouth as I rubbed sleep from my eyes.

"It is your birthday, isn't it, or are we in the wrong apartment?" Monica inquired, holding a tray that was filled with breakfast. Pancakes, eggs, sausage, bacon, and grits.

My stomach immediately started to growl. "Is all that for me?" I asked, my mouth watering.

"Yes, and it's all made by me and your dear brother." Monica handed me the tray when I sat up in the bed.

"Yeah, and whatever you don't eat, I will," Li'l Bo informed me. "Happy birthday, sis." He bent down and gave me a hug, then Monica followed suit by giving me a huge hug.

"Thank you so much. I wasn't expecting this." I forked some pancakes into my mouth. "So where did you guys get all this?" I asked curiously with a mouth full of food jammed inside.

"Me and Li'l Bo went shopping," Monica proudly answered.

"Just like you taught us," Li'l Bo proudly added.

I immediately stopped eating. "Wait a minute. You guys went shoplifting?" I asked.

"Hell, yeah. You know we didn't pay for it," Li'l Bo answered with a serious look plastered on his face.

I paused for a minute with my eyes closed and took a deep breath. "Look, I know both of you meant well, but you cannot be stealing for any reason. I don't want you getting into trouble for doing something stupid. I know in the past that is how we got by, but not anymore. Now we have money, so whatever we need, we will pay for it."

"That sounds cool. But we"—Li'l Bo pointed between himself and Monica—"don't have any money. You took us shopping, but you never gave us any cash. So *we* broke."

"A'ight, I'll take care of that. I will make sure you have money but no more stealing. Agreed?"

"Agreed," Monica replied without hesitation.

"Li'l Bo?" I nudged his leg with my fist knuckles.

"A'ight. I won't shoplift," he said, sounding annoyed.

"Cool, now leave so I can eat in peace." I smiled.

"Uhh, this is my room, too," Monica reminded me.

"Oh, sorry, you can stay. Li'l Bo, get out."

"I'll go but call me if you get full," he reminded me.

Li'l Bo left the room, and Monica started to straighten the covers on her bed. With all my excitement I still noticed one important person was missing.

"Monica, where is Mom?" I asked before stuffing my mouth with more pancakes and taking a sausage and dipping it in the maple syrup.

"She ain't here; didn't come home last night. Mya, I just knew she would be here this morning for your birthday." Monica looked sad.

"Yeah, at least." I continued to eat, trying to sound unconcerned. "I can't believe you not freaking out about her not being home. I know you worried."

"Not today. My only concern was wishing you a happy birthday. Like you always tell me, I'm sure she's fine, right?" Monica tried to sound convinced.

"Right," I said, pissed at the fact she ain't home to wish me a happy birthday but also determined not to let her mess up my day. So I announced my plan for this morning. "Guess what?" I took a bit of my bacon and smiled. "I'm going to get my hair done after I eat this breakfast. A new look is what I plan to get."

"Wow! What look do you have in mind?" she asked with excitement.

"I haven't made up my mind yet. But I was thinking that short haircut like Kandi has on *The Real Housewives of Atlanta* but a little shorter. That's hot!" I got excited thinking about that hairdo on me. "How about you go with me? It'll be fun."

Monica gave me a big smile, and I know she was down. Excited about my day, I started to devour all my food fast so we could get an early start to a salon. Although I wasn't sure which salon I would use, I had one in mind. I have always kept up with all the hair salons in the Detroit area. I keep up with what type of hairstyles they specialize in. I guess this sort of thing comes with the passion I have for doing hair. There was this new salon in the Detroit area called 4EverStylz. Recently I read some good reviews about them in a Detroit local magazine. Maybe I'd stop by to see if they take walk-ins.

"Welcome to 4EverStylz," the redheaded girl behind the receptionist desk greeted us when we entered the hair salon.

The place was elegant and beautiful. When we walked in I was speechless. I lost my voice so Monica spoke up.

"Hello," Monica replied and gave me nudge on the arm.

"Um, um. Hi," I stammered over my words. Embarrassed at my behavior, I apologized. "Sorry. It's just this place doesn't look like a hair salon." I felt like the receptionist and the women standing behind her were looking at me like I was crazy. So I tried to explain. "It's just really nice, very unique."

"Thanks," the woman behind the receptionist replied with a smile.

"How can I help you?" the receptionist asked.

"Well, I was hop . . . I mean, wondering, if you guys take walk-ins."

"Actually, we don't," the receptionist informed me. "But I can set you up an appointment with one of our stylists."

"I kinda figured that. Never mind." I turned to leave.

"You know what? I'll do it," I heard the voice of the other lady who was standing behind the receptionist speak up.

I turned around slowly to see her step from behind the desk. She extended her hand to me. "Hi, I'm Pepper. I'm the owner here at 4EverStylz. I am also one of the top stylists here, and your name is?" she asked.

"Mya." I extended my hand. "And this is my sister, Monica."

"Well, it's nice to meet both of you. Monica, we have a seating area in the back that's complete with a television and all the snacks and drinks you can eat. Normally, I would offer you wine, but neither of you seem old enough." She smiled and led the way.

After we dropped Monica off at the waiting area, Pepper led me to the styling area, and that shit was banging so hard it also left me speechless. There was a fully stocked bar area with big-screen TVs before entering single booths where the screens could be seen from all directions. I would love to work at one just like this someday.

"So how would you like your hair?" Pepper's question pulled me back from my thoughts.

"Do you watch *The Real Housewives of Atlanta?*" I asked.

"Absolutely. In my opinion it's the hottest black show on television."

"So you should be very familiar with that hairstyle Kandi rocks on there. I want my hair cut and styled just like that," I said, proud of my choice.

Pepper ran her hand through my hair but didn't respond for a minute. "That's really short. With this long, shiny hair you could cut it off and sell it. Are you sure you want to cut all your hair off? I can always do a quick weave of the same style," Pepper tried to suggest.

"Look, it's only hair. Besides, I thought about it long and hard. It's what I want," I replied matter-of-factly.

"Okay," was her last response before the scissors made a beeline through my hair, chopping it down row by row like high weeds.

Three hours later I was leaving 4EverStylz looking good. I loved it. My hair was the damn bomb. I couldn't thank Pepper enough. After paying a hundred and fifty dollars for my hairdo, I left Pepper a fifty-dollar tip. It was well worth it. This hairstyle brought out my look. My high cheekbones and brown almond-shaped eyes complemented this hairstyle. Pepper also gave me her number to call her for my next hair appointment. So everything was all good and tonight was the night. I was going to be a bad bitch.

Chapter 19

While getting ready for the party I was feeling pumped. My hair looked good, and the outfit I had picked was banging. I was ready to hit the club. Rochelle was supposed to be picking me up in Charlene's car. Charlene had plans earlier with Pig so she told Rochelle just to keep her whip and pick me up for the party. It was cool, but I hadn't seen Rochelle since the incident at the mall a few days ago. She hadn't even called about shopping for the shoes. So I didn't know if she was over it or not, but looking myself over in the mirror I wasn't worried about that tonight. Tonight was my night. All I wanted to do was have fun and forget about the bullshit.

I heard a knock at the door. Rochelle arrived.

"Mya, Rochelle is here," Monica screamed.

One more glance in the mirror and I grabbed my handbag. When I turned around Rochelle was already in my room followed by Monica.

"Girl, you rockin' that hairdo," Rochelle complimented me. "Mya, that looks so good on you. Who did that?"

"This chick named Pepper over at that new salon called 4EverStylz."

"She hooked you up. Girl, you gon' have niggas droppin' like flies tonight," she complimented again.

"Shit, you don't look bad yourself," I complimented her.

"I know, right?" Rochelle bragged while looking herself over in the mirror. "Let's ride."

I felt good walking inside the club. It was jam-packed from wall to wall. Rochelle led me straight to a private reserved VIP room. The room was set up for my party as well as full of people ready to celebrate with me. "Happy birthday!" they all yelled when I walked in.

Looking around the room I noticed Charlene, Nina, and a few females from the Brewster who had either graduated or dropped out for some reason. There was Mikki, Janice, and Felicia. They were all cool but not who I would invite to my party, but I already knew without a doubt who did invite them. Charlene. Charlene had sort of a reputation for running with gold diggers and hoes. Mikki, Janice, and Felicia happened to be just that. Of course, the members of the Height Squad were present. I'm sure it was Pig's dollar that paid for all this because they had it set up really nice. There were food trays filled with every type of party food you could think of and a well-stocked bar. Charlene and Nina made their way over to give me a hug.

"Happy birthday," they both repeated in a joyful tone.

"Thank you. This is so nice." I smiled while looking around the room. "I can't believe you guys did all this for me."

"Girl, you turned eighteen today. Why not?" Charlene responded with a smile. "And the new look looks good on you," she said, looking me up and down. "I mean, a total change."

"Yes, I like." Nina smiled, admiring my hair.

With a smile on my face I thanked them as Rochelle grabbed me by the hand and pulled me over to the bar.

"Now you get to have your first drink of the night. Just tell the bartender what you want. Matter of fact, scratch all that. Bartender, give me one of them bottles of Patrón," Rochelle told the bartender that was reserved just to serve us in VIP all night.

"Rochelle, I was thinkin' a margarita," I replied with uncertainty.

"Mya, that's all you were gon' have? Girl, we want you to get krunk tonight." Rochelle was hyped.

"I know. Trust me, I plan on gettin' there. Baby steps." I gave her a cute smile.

"A'ight. Bartender, pass me some glasses so we can bottoms-up this Patrón." Rochelle beamed.

One chase of my drink and the DJ started blastin' Trey Songz's, "Bottoms Up." Without a moment's thought, I started swaying my hips to the music. Before the song was over, Rochelle poured me another shot. Tonight it was going down. I was going to party until I exited. Feeling even better with my second drink in my hand, I watched as Hood stepped in the room. When I first entered the VIP room I noticed he was missing, but I just figured an eighteen-year-old's birthday party wasn't on his list of things to do. Now that he had entered the VIP room I had a totally different feeling. Again, he was dressed in the T.I. clothing line, Akoo, and I immediately got the feeling that was one of his favorites. He had on a pair of dark blue Akoo jeans, a V-necked Akoo sweater with the shirt under it, and a pair of Timberland boots. I must say he was rockin' that whole outfit. After hittin' his whole squad with the rock handshake, he headed straight in my direction. Talk about nervous. I was shakin', but I didn't know why. This never happens to me. I never get excited about a dude. I had bigger fish to fry. When he stopped in front of me I was speechless.

"Happy birthday, Mya," he said in the sweetest tone I ever heard from a dude.

"Thanks," I replied casually.

"You look nice. How old are you again?" he asked.

"Again? I never said," I responded.

"Yeah, right. You didn't." He grinned. "Would you like to dance?"

"Umm. No. Maybe later. I think I'ma stand here and talk to my girl for a while," I said, hoping to get rid of him. His straightforward approach happened to be too much for me.

"A'ight, maybe later." He nodded at Rochelle, who was standing close by. He then turned and walked away.

Rochelle, who had been listening close the whole time, moved in on me. "Did you just tell him no? Are you crazy or blind? *Look* at him. He fine as hell. Every bitch in this club wants him, and you turn him down for a dance." Rochelle shook her head back and forth.

"So?" was my only response to her.

Rochelle stared at me for a bit. "You crazy." She smiled.

"I know. My dad's name is Lester. Let's grab something to eat 'cause I ain't ate shit since this morning." I headed toward the food table.

After Rochelle and I got over to the food table and nibbled for a bit, we headed to the dance floor. An hour and a couple of drinks later we had mellowed out. Rochelle hit the dance floor again with Charlene and her girls. I went to have a seat on one of the couches in VIP. It didn't take long before Hood came over.

"I see you like to dance."

"Not really," I admitted. "But we are celebrating my birthday, right?" I reminded him. "So how old are you, Hood?" I asked.

He started laughing.

"Did I say something funny?"

"Naw. I like your style." He continued to smile. "I'm twenty-one."

"Umm, that old, huh? Well, I guess you are of legal drinking age." I smiled.

"Mya, Mya," Rochelle started yelling my name. "Come on, blow out the candles on your cake." Rochelle waved me over.

"Cake?" I sounded shocked. I got off the couch, and Hood followed me. Everyone sang "Happy Birthday" to me again. I blew out the candles and cut the cake so everyone could eat. After almost puking from watching Charlene feed Pig cake, I turned my attention back to Hood, who had already fixed his attention on me.

"You think I could have that dance now?" he asked again.

I almost turned him down until I heard Trey Songz's "Invented Sex" blast out of the speakers.

"Yeah, let's dance. Right here." I stepped up to him and started doing my shit and leaving him very impressed. After that song I danced with Hood on like three more songs. Then we headed back to our seat on the couch to relax.

"So are you going to tell me how old you are?" he asked again.

I had just ordered a margarita, and Hood was drinking a Hpnotiq. I took a sip of my drink before giving him an answer. "I'm eighteen today," I said in slow motion.

"Wow. Really?" He looked shocked.

"Why the shocked look?" I asked.

"My bad. I just thought you were a little older." For a moment there was silence.

"You live in Brewster?" he pried.

"Yep."

"Where do you live?" I asked.

"Out in the suburbs. Chilling with the white folks and shit." He paused. "Maybe I could come by and take you out sometime."

"Well, I don't know. I stay pretty busy," I quickly lied as Rochelle approached us with this guy from the Height Squad nicknamed Li'l Lo.

"Mya, it's time to go. Charlene is going to drop us off, and she's about to leave. Li'l Lo is going to walk me out."

"Okay. I'm right behind you," I replied. I looked over at Hood. "Well, I gotta go. It was nice dancing with you." I stood up.

"Let me take you home," he offered.

"Take me home? Hood, I don't even know you. All I really know about you is your name and your age."

"I won't bite. I promise," he begged.

"Maybe some other time." I didn't give in.

"A'ight." He smiled. "Can I call you?" He tried another approach.

"How about you give me your number and I will call you?" I suggested.

"A'ight." He grabbed a pen from the bartender and handed me his number with a note that said, "Hit me up."

"Can I at least walk you out?" he asked, not giving up.

I nodded my head in agreement, and he walked me out to the car. I told him good night and hopped in the backseat. Rochelle and Charlene immediately started badgering me for answers.

"Did he ask you out? Did you give him your

number?" Charlene started in without taking a break.

"Yes and no," I casually answered while looking out the window.

"You see, Charlene, she keeps doing this. I don't know what's wrong with the girl. I give up." Rochelle waved her hand, sounding defeated.

"Mya, girl, Hood is not one of them niggas you play hard to get with. That nigga is the leader of the Height Squad. Do you know how much money he has? Pig just works for him and look what *I'm* driving. If you know like I know you better get on board," Charlene replied. "Humph, but if you don't want him, I will take him."

"And how are you going to do that? You already Pig wifey," I reminded her.

"Bitch, and that means what? Where there's a will there's a way," Charlene said with a seriousness that made me wonder if she really meant it. The whole time she was looking at me in the backseat through her rearview mirror.

"Well, I don't need no nigga to get ahead in life. My daddy taught me that," I retorted.

"Umm," Charlene grumbled and sucked her teeth.

The rest of the ride was done in complete silence, but I thought about what Charlene had said. Since she had been fooling with Pig, her ego was growing like a mold. Could she really be capable of messing around with Hood or any other nigga while she's with Pig? This guy had been nothing but good to her. Had money changed

Charlene that much, or was she just running off at the mouth like always?

When we pulled up at Rochelle's house I got out with her since I would be spending the night at her crib. What a night. I was tipsy, and I had a good time. I would sleep well, I was sure of it.

Chapter 20

Since my birthday party this past weekend things had been pretty busy for me. Prom was coming up for the high school kids, so my clientele had increased. I had been over at Rochelle's house daily cutting, rinsing, doing some type of style on somebody's head, but today was the day of the prom and I had decided to relax. No styling today. Maybe now I'd get a chance to sit down and reminisce on what happened at my party. I still can't believe my girls went all out for me. That shit was really nice. That's one party I will remember, but not right now, though, since Monica has decided to interrupt my thoughts. She started mouthing as she pounced down on her unmade bed.

"Mya, you think you can take me to the mall? I want to pick up these purple and white Forces. I saw them at the mall the other day after school. They were fly."

"First off, I had no idea you were at the mall

after school the other day. Who did you go with?" I questioned.

"With Li'l Bo. He was checkin' for some girl so I tagged along since you be trippin' about me walking home alone," she reminded me.

"Oh," I replied.

"Can I get the shoes?"

"Monica, I just bought you three pairs of sneakers just two weeks ago," I reminded her.

"Is that a yes or no?"

Someone knocked on the door so I thought I was saved, but Monica got off the bed and started following me, still expecting an answer. Annoyed, I turned to face her. "Monica, why don't you go make up your bed and finish making mine while I think about it."

Monica turned around and headed back to the room. The knocking on the door started up again. I hurriedly swung open the door to give whoever the impatient person was the business for banging on the door, and it better not be Li'l Bo forgetting his key again.

"Stop bang—" I stopped speechless as I came face-to-face with about three dozen white roses. There were so many roses I couldn't see the face of the person holding them, but then came a voice that I'm sure I recognized.

"Mya home?"

"Who would like to know?" I asked for no reason at all, basically being my usual not-impressed self. I didn't have to wonder for long when the person behind the flowers revealed his identity by showing his face.

"Hood?" I said with a hint of shock in my voice.

"These are for you." He handed the flowers to me.

"Umm, I don't really know what to say. Thanks . . . I think." I shrugged my shoulders.

Hood smiled. "It's cool, baby girl. I just wanted to bring you something. I enjoyed kicking it wit' ya at the party."

"Yeah. The party. I haven't had much time to think about it." I stepped out into hall and closed the door to the apartment behind me. There was no way I was letting him into our county-created apartment. "Well, the flowers are nice."

"I thought you would like them. So would you like to grab some food later?" he casually asked.

"Later? I, umm, well, I have to take my sister out."

"Tell you what. Here's my number. You call me when you're free." He handed me a card that had his number on it. At the same time his cell phone started ringing. Totally ignoring it, he gave me all his attention.

"I'ma let you get back, baby girl. Hit me up." With that he turned and walked away.

Stuck standing in shock, I watched him leave. There wasn't a guy on TV, rapper, or athlete that had shit on him. Damn, as much as I hated to admit it, Hood was all that and then some. Shit, I'm never impressed. What the fuck was happening to me? I looked down at the number and wondered if he realized he had already given me his number, but I threw it away the first chance I got. With all this roaming through my mind, I finally opened the door and went back in the apartment. I headed straight to my room, flowers in tow.

"Who are those for? Who bought them?" Monica started firing at me as soon as I opened the door to our room.

"They're for me," I answered.

"Who would buy you flowers?" Monica sounded stunned.

"What's that's supposed to mean?" I acted offended.

"I'm just saying. You always say fuck dudes. That's all." Monica laughed.

"I do, huh?" I admitted. "Well, I didn't today. Besides, it's just a friend who wanted to wish me a happy birthday. Now stop asking questions and get dressed. We're going over to Rochelle's crib."

"Why? I thought you said you wasn't doing heads today," she reminded me.

"I know, but I left some things over there," I lied. "Now just get dressed," I ordered her.

Chapter 21

The Brewster was jumping by the time Monica and I made it outside and headed to Rochelle's building. When I stepped off the curb, I felt blinded by chrome. There were so many twenty-two- and twenty-four-inch chrome rims I felt like I was at a car show. Of course you got the neighborhood hoes showcasing their asses. The only thing I didn't see on them is a sign that says "FOR SALE." Again I saw Li'l Bo hanging out with some li'l niggas. I didn't say anything, though, since they didn't seem to be up to much, but in this neighborhood, they could be up to plenty. I decided to talk to him later about his recent hanging out on the block because he knows how I feel about him doing that. He may be fifteen, but he knows I will bust his ass.

When we made it to Rochelle's building, we saw her outside along with Charlene, Pig, Felicia, and some more people from the block while she was holding Tiny.

"Aye, Mya!" Pig said first since he was the only one who noticed me approach.

"What's up?" I replied. That's when everybody else noticed me.

"Girl, what you doing out?" Charlene asked.

"Yeah, I thought you were chillin' today," Rochelle added.

"I was, but I had some shit I needed to pick up from your crib, Rochelle. Damn. Why you bitches checking me?" I shot back.

"And you got Monica with you. Hey, Monica," Charlene said.

"Hey," Monica replied in an uninterested tone. She headed over to Rochelle and took Tiny from her.

"Charlene, don't you need to be at home getting ready for the prom?" I asked.

"I'm headed that way now. I had to come get this nigga off the block, but I'm leaving now. Come on, Pig," Charlene screamed at him. "You head to your crib now. Shit. You got to get yourself together. Nigga, you ain't gon' have me late."

"A'ight, ma, I got ya. I said I'm leaving, right?" Pig said calmly while Charlene stared at him, smacking her gum and rolling her eyes at him.

"Girl, you see I got to babysit this nigga just so he can get off this block. Ugh," Charlene said as she popped the lock on her car doors. "I'll hit y'all later and tell you how the night went. Yo, Felicia, if you catching a ride, you better hop in." On that note Charlene jumped in her ride and stabbed out.

Pig gave the niggas on the block the Height Squad shake before he jumped in his ride and burned rubber headed to his crib. Surely his crib will be both of theirs as soon as Charlene graduates in a couple of weeks.

"Yo, she be giving his ass the business," Rochelle said, laughing.

"For real," I commented and laughed too.

"Yo, check this out, though. Why does Charlene got Felicia's nasty ass out here for?" I had to ask.

"I don't know. She always ridin' that bitch and her crew around. She better watch them thirsty hoes. Anyway, scratch them. Now, what you really over here for?" Rochelle asked with a smile.

"Why I gotta have a reason to come over here? If that's the case I need blood. Can you help me?" I played around.

"Stop playing, Mya. You so damn crazy." Rochelle laughed. "Come on, let's go sit on the step."

We headed over to the steps where Monica was walking around playing with Tiny.

"Girl, Monica knows she loves kids. She's gon' be a good mother," Rochelle mouthed.

"Bitch, don't play," I quickly snapped. "Monica ain't about to be nobody mother anytime soon."

"Oh my bad." Rochelle grinned.

"Anyway, guess who showed up at my door out of the blue."

"Yo dad?" Rochelle looked taken aback.

"Rochelle, what the hell is wrong with you today? Out of all people, why my dad when you know he locked up for life? Don't get a bitch hopes up."

"Well, I'm lost then." Rochelle gave up with a puzzled look.

"Hood," I hastily replied.

"What the fuck?" Rochelle let fly out of her mouth. "Hood, the leader of the Height Squad, knocked on your door? You, who turned him down a thousand times at your party last weekend?" Rochelle stood up.

"Not only did he knock on my door out of the blue, but he brought so many roses it hid his identity," I said and released, to my own surprise, a smile that spread across my face.

"Oh my God, is that a smile on your face? Wait." Rochelle's smile faded to concern. "Please don't tell me you were rude and kicked him out." Rochelle seemed to hold her breath.

"Wait, whoever said I invited him in? And yes, I had him stand outside our door. There was no way I was inviting him into our tacky apartment. But no, I was not rude. He did ask me to go out, though, and I had to turn him down."

"Why did you turn him down again, Mya?"

"I had to. Monica asked me to take her to the mall."

"Oh no. Don't blame that on me," Monica butted in.

"Stay out of this, Monica." I gave her a fake dirty look, and she smiled.

"Mya, you need to stop making excuses and let Hood's fine ass take you out."

"I can't. I don't have time for dating. That shit is a headache I don't need."

"Scratch the headache. You would have fun. Be a normal eighteen-year-old. Stop actin' like a granny panty. Get up right now." Rochelle started pulling me up on my feet. "Get your butt up and go call Hood. Tell him you would love to go out with him. Beg if you have to. Tell him you'll throw yourself at his mercy for being so ignorant," Rochelle joked.

"Okay, okay. I'll call him." I smiled. "But not today. I have to take Monica to the mall. You and Tiny wanna tag along?" I asked.

"Might as well, as we ain't doing shit else. Let me grab my purse and Tiny's stroller. Be right back."

Chapter 22

I had finally made up my mind to go out on a date with Hood, but I didn't want to make it too formal. So instead of letting him take me out to eat I agreed on bowling. My dad used to take us bowling all the time, and we all loved it. I wasn't that good at it, but it still happened to be one of my favorite games. When I told Hood that I would go out bowling with him he quickly agreed, and to my surprise, he picked AMF Bowling. That was the alley my dad always took us to. So I was excited about being at the alley again. Tonight was the night that he was supposed to pick me up. Since we are only going bowling I didn't have to dress up. I didn't want to look too sexy anyway, but I didn't want to look ghetto either.

After tearing my closet apart with the new clothes I had purchased since I had the money, I decided on these white Blue Label short shorts with an active yellow Blue Label polo long-sleeve shirt and white ribbed high socks with a pair of yellow active Polo Breeana shoes. After modeling in the mirror and in front of Monica it was decided that I looked cute.

"Mya, you look really stylish. Not everyone can pull that outfit off. I mean, how many girls you know from the Brewster would choose that outfit on a first date?" she rambled.

"I know. It's only bowling. I ain't puttin' on no heels for that. I need to be comfortable. Besides, I ain't trying to impress him," I tried to convince myself. I was nervous as hell. What if he thought I looked stupid? Humph, what was I worried about? I looked fly. I took one more turn in the mirror when I heard a knock on the door. I quickly told Monica good night and ran toward the door. There was no way I was letting him into this apartment. Hell no. I had purposely encouraged Li'l Bo to go to his room and play his game so he wouldn't be in the living room when Hood showed up. Mom was out in the streets. So the coast was clear. I could make a clean getaway. Nervous, I paused before I half opened the door just enough to squeeze myself out and step into the hallway.

"Damn, baby girl, are you trying to hide something in there or someone?" Hood asked like he was trying to look past me.

"Yeah, my family." I let out a little laugh. "So you ready?" I asked while giving him a once-over glance. Of course, Hood was dressed in Akoo. This time, he had on some doeskin Akoo Cambridge shorts and a whisper white Akoo Vanni polo shirt with some fresh new Forces. He looked nice. Seeing what he had on kind of relaxed my nerves.

When we got outside, Hood led me to his

black Cadillac Escalade sitting on twenty-four-inch rims. He popped the lock, and we jumped in. When he turned on the ignition I thought T.I. would blast out of the speakers, but instead, he was listening to Rick Ross. Feeling like I was riding on a cloud, I sat back in my seat and relaxed until we reached AMF.

Once inside the alley, Hood ordered our games, then we got our shoes and headed to our assigned alley.

"Do you want to bowl first?" I asked.

"Nah. You can go first," he replied.

"Okay." I tied the last knot on my bowling shoes, then I got up and headed to the lanes. I looked back at Hood to see if he was watching, and just like I thought, his eyes were glued on me. I turned back around and focused before throwing the ball. My ball started off at a good roll, but I side-lined and missed all the racks. I turned around with a smile on my face to find Hood laughing at me.

"You think that's funny, huh? Well, I'm just warming up."

"Do you, baby girl," was his only reply. After I missed several more rounds Hood took the lane by storm, throwing the bowling ball and not missing over and over again.

"Okay. Now I think you trying to show off," I said with a fake frown, throwing my right hand on my hip. "You didn't tell me you were a pro."

"Trust me, I'm not. I just focus."

"Yeah, whatever. You not telling me you were a pro means you cheated," I babbled on as Hood came over and took a seat next to me.

"No, baby girl, I would never do that." He

looked me straight in the eye. "Can I get you something from the snack area?"

"Yeah, I'll take some nachos and a Coke." I had relaxed a lot since the game started and was now enjoying myself.

"A'ight, I'll get that for you." Hood stood up and left.

While he was off getting my food I decided to keep bowling. I thought without him being around I would do better, but my luck was the same. Missing the racks was definitely in my bowling future.

Hood came back with the food so I went over and sat down with him.

"So where did you learn to bowl like that?" I pried.

"Don't know really. Like I said before, I just focus. Can't be that hard." Hood bit into a hot dog he picked up from the snack bar. "Why do you like bowling so much?" he asked me.

Chewing on a nacho, I thought about my dad for a moment. "My dad used to bring us here. We would come here just about every Saturday. Everyone in my family is a pro." I paused for a minute. "That is, except for me. I could never knock down the racks." I smiled.

"Where is your dad now?" he asked, catching me off guard.

"Prison," I said without hesitation.

"Wait, I didn't mean to get personal and shit."

"It's okay. I'm not ashamed or anything. I think it's fucked up seeing how much we need him, but I'm not ashamed. Plus, everyone in the Brewster knows. His name is Lester. He used to be one of the top dealers in the game before he went up. Now he's just an inmate. Yep. Dad's in jail, and my mom is on crack, and I'm left raising my brother and sister. What a life, huh?" I bit off another nacho.

"I would say you holding up good."

"I do okay. So what's yo' line of work?"

"Me." Hood smiled at me again. That's when I realized I was falling in love with his smile. "I'm into profits and brotherhood."

"So is that what the leader of the Height Squad calls himself? Pretty interesting," I responded sarcastically.

"I guess you know all about the crew." He rubbed both his hands together.

"I live in the Brewster, remember?"

"It is what it is, baby girl. You know what I do. I'm building an empire."

"Yeah, I think that's what my dad was building." Again I made another sarcastic comment.

"I got to admit something. I'm not totally in the dark about your dad. I didn't know him personally, but some of the people that I dealt with when I first started in the game had worked with him. They all say he was not to be fucked with, and I think it's fucked up how it went down." Hood sounded sincere.

"What? So you knew? Why did you ask then?"

"I didn't know he was your father, but when you said his name I knew then. Everybody has heard of Lester. He was next in line to be named kingpin of the streets. And I like I said, that situation was fucked up."

"Yep. But time goes on, right?" I stuffed another nacho in my mouth. "You know my dad calls me baby girl," I informed him.

"Oh, my bad again. I just keep steppin' on yo' toes. I don't mean no disrespect, though. You want me to stop calling you that?"

"Nah, you cool. I just thought you should know."

"The first time I talked to you that just came outta my mouth. It just fit you."

"It's cool," I assured him. "So do you have any kids?" I asked, surprising myself.

"Nope. No shorties. Although one day I would like to."

"Do you think it would be a good idea to have kids in your line of work?"

"My shorties would always be straight. No doubt. And I would silence anyone who tried to test that." Hood had a killer look in his eye. "My family has always been small, just me and my moms. Besides that, the only other family I have has been my crew. Pig, that's my nigga for life."

"Charlene says you guys are close," I took a slow sip of my drink. "So where does your mom live?"

"She lives in Phoenix. Been there for about six years."

"Phoenix? That's far. Do you mind her living so far away?"

"It's cool. I fly out all the time. You know, it's better for her out there. Anything for my moms."

I instantly knew he was a momma's boy.

"Sorry about the twenty questions. Just curious."

"You cool, baby girl. Gotta answer questions for the daughter of a kingpin," Hood joked.

"Oh, you got jokes, huh?" I laughed.

"But on the real, you can ask me anything." Hood smiled then took a swig from his cup. "So you spoken for?" he finally asked me.

"You take me out on date and then ask me that? Don't you think you should ask me that first?"

"Really I didn't care because that nigga was gon' have to stand down," Hood said with a seriousness that made me know he wasn't joking. "All bullshitting aside, I wanna be ya man."

"Why? You don't know anything about me. All you know is I'm Charlene's girl."

"There ain't nothing I need to know, period. I wanna take you out. Spoil you."

That statement caught my attention. "Look, I don't need anybody to spoil me. I take care of myself. I ain't nobody's trophy bitch. Got that?" I said with much attitude.

"A'ight, a'ight, baby girl." Hood threw both of his hands up, letting me know he understood. "Can I at least let you beat me in bowling?" he joked again.

"Don't speak too soon. I was practicing when you were gone. I think I'm ready to bring on my A-game." I stood up and grabbed a ball with a huge grin on my face.

We bowled for at least another hour. Of course, Hood won, but he threw some of my balls to get me some extra points. I also caught him watching my ass a couple of times, but it was cool being that he was so damn fine. On our ride home we laughed about Pig and Charlene, how she be bossing him around. It was funny. When we made it back to my crib he walked me to the door. Without a second thought I reached out and planted the biggest kiss on him that I had ever planted on anyone. I had never kissed anyone before, but the way I worked my tongue in and outside of Hood's mouth you would've thought I was a pro. Clearly I was because before I finished Hood let out a moan. Shit, was I that good? For the first time ever my womanhood kicked in. Full speed.

Chapter 23

Almost a week had gone by and I hadn't heard much from Rochelle since she had started messing around with Li'l Lo. I didn't mind much, though, because I had been spending a lot of time on my new cell phone with Hood. I hadn't seen him since our date because he flew up to New York on business. Basically, he had some bricks to pick up, but he only told me in so many words. He would be back on Friday so I decided to get my hair done again so I would be lookin' tight when he returned. We had planned to go on another date, and this time I would impress him.

After eating breakfast with Li'l Bo and Monica, I decided to call Rochelle up to see if she wanted to go with me to 4EverStylz. I had called Pepper earlier in the week and set up an appointment but before I could call Rochelle my cell phone started to ring. I reached for it thinkin' it was Hood.

"Hello." I tried to sound casual even though my heart was pounding from excitement.

"What's up, chick?" Rochelle beamed through the phone.

"Damn, Rochelle. Stop catching me off guard like that," I said, feeling a little disappointed that it wasn't Hood.

"Sorry. I just thought I would call you to see what's up since I had a free moment." I could hear Rochelle smiling through the phone.

"I didn't know you were still alive. I thought maybe you had drowned or something," I joked.

"Girl, you know I been hanging out with my man. Girl, he keeping me busy. You know. he be banging my back out!" Rochelle screamed through the phone.

"Well, I'm happy that your back is being banged, but you shouldn't neglect your best friend." I tried to sound sad.

"Oh, Mya, I am so sorry. You know we're girls. I just thought you had Hood to keep you busy."

"Yeah. He a'ight," I said with a smile in my voice.

"Wait a minute. I heard that. You like him, huh?" Rochelle got excited. "How was the date? Did you kiss him?" she questioned me.

I didn't say anything for a minute. Finally I replied. "Yep, and you would know if you had called all week," I threw in.

"Agggh," Rochelle screamed through the phone. "It's about time!" She was excited. "So are you ready for sex now? You know that comes next."

"Rochelle. Damn. You so nosy." I smiled. "Nasty self."

"Girl, ain't nothin' nasty about that. Mya, you eighteen. You should've been having sex a year ago," Rochelle said matter-of-factly. "You are the only virgin in the Brewster over the age of sixteen." Rochelle laughed. "Did you tell him you were a virgin?"

"Why would I tell him that?" I was horrified by her question. That was my business, not Hood's.

"I will take that as a no, and good; you don't want to scare the dude off."

"Whatever, Rochelle. Your mind stays in the gutter. Anyway, do you want to go to the hair salon with me? I want you to see 4EverStylz."

"I don't know. Wynita ain't here. She's working a double today. And I don't have anyone to watch Tiny."

"I know, but my appointment ain't until four p.m. By then, Monica will be here from school and she can watch her for you."

"Okay," Rochelle quickly agreed.

"Cool. When you get here we can catch a cab."

"No cabs, boo. Not today. I have one of Li'l Lo's whips. I will pick you up," Rochelle bragged.

"A'ight. Later." I hung up happy that we didn't have to catch a damn cab. I hate waving them down in the Brewster. Sometimes that can be like a job but not today. My girl had her man's whip. So I can get dressed and relax.

When Monica made it home I asked her if she would mind watching Tiny, and she gladly agreed, which I knew she would because she loves Tiny. So when Rochelle pulled up in Li'l Lo's all-white 2009 Dodge Challenger with black tint, I was ready to roll. When we pulled up to the salon and went inside, Rochelle was impressed the same way I was when I first saw 4EverStylz hair salon. The receptionist checked me in and took us back to the waiting area. All the ladies were sippin' on wine except me and Rochelle, since we were underage. Finally, Pepper came out to get me. At 4EverStylz, everyone had their own individual salon area so I knew Rochelle would be able to go back with me while I got my hair done.

"Hi, Mya," Pepper greeted me with a hug when she came out.

"What's up, Pepper? Pepper, this is my best friend, Rochelle." I pointed to Rochelle.

"Hi, Rochelle." Pepper extended her hand.

"What's up?" Rochelle gripped Pepper's hand to return the handshake.

"Can she come back with us?"

"Of course, follow me." Pepper led us back to her private area and we took a seat. After about two hours my hair had been washed, set, and was being styled when Pepper asked Rochelle if she was a model.

"Hell, no." Rochelle had a shocked look on her face.

"Well, you should be. You have the height, and your bone structure is astonishing. And your hair is fabulous," Pepper complimented her.

"Thank you, but you should give Mya the shout-out on my head 'cause she did it."

"Mya, you do hair?" Pepper asked me, appearing shocked.

"Yeah, that's right. My girl is fierce with those hands. She does it all freestyle," Rochelle continued to compliment my skills.

"Mya, why you didn't tell me hair was your thing?" Pepper asked.

"Well, when we met I was just trying to get my own hair done. I'm always doing other people's heads. That day I was just worried about my own wig," I added with a smile.

"Do you plan on getting your hair license? Like, are you in school for hair or something?" Pepper inquired.

I stalled for a minute, not knowing if I should reveal I wasn't a high school graduate, but somehow I felt comfortable with Pepper. I had since the first time we met. "I, uhh, I sort of need to graduate high school first, but yes, I have thought about it a lot. Right now, I have real-life issues I need to take care of first," I informed her.

"I understand, but don't let your gift die. You know, before I moved here I had other things going on too, but I had someone who I looked up to that helped me along the way." Pepper talked while continuing to do her magic on my head. "You know what? Would you be interested in working here part-time?" she asked me out of the blue.

"Work here? Doing what?" I asked, shocked at her question.

"Well, you wouldn't be able to do hair because you don't have a license, but you could wash heads and help with other stuff around here. I would like take you under my wing, but the catch is you would have to join this program I just started here called Diploma Cuts."

"Diploma Cuts? What's that?" Rochelle asked before I could.

"Diploma Cuts is a program I started here at the shop where aspiring hairstylists who don't have high school degrees can come and earn their diploma while earning their hair license degree. It's a six-month program. When you're done you will have earned a diploma and your hair license, all at the same time."

"Damn, Mya, that's sounds like a good idea," Rochelle said. "So like, are you a schoolteacher or something?" Rochelle was impressed.

"Actually no. I have an instructor come in that prepares you for your diploma, and another hairstylist instructor and I do the hair portion. So what do you think?" Pepper turned my chair around to face her.

I was so speechless at first. This could be a huge opportunity for me. I could earn my degree like my father wanted, and I could get my hair license, which is part of my dream. All while having a paid part-time job. "When can I start?" I smiled.

"I guess you are interested, then. You can start next week. I'll start you washing my clients' heads next week and class is on Tuesday and Wednesday nights."

I sat there in a daze. With all the crazy things that had been going on in my family, I couldn't believe how my luck was changing for the better. I couldn't wait to get started.

Chapter 24

"So are you enjoying your steak?" Hood asked me.

"It's good, just like I imagined it would be." I smiled. Hood had returned back from his "business trip," so we were out eating at the Outback Steakhouse restaurant. He had picked me up from Rochelle's house. I had been at her house all day styling heads. So I brought my clothes along since I knew that's where I would be all day. Our food had made it to the table, and I was savoring every bit of my juicy steak, and I think Hood was enjoying watching me chew, since he seemed to never take his eyes from me.

"So how was your trip? Did you get to go sightsee in the Big Apple?" I teased.

"Not really. It's business so I didn't leave my hotel much. I made my moves, and I was out, but you know it's a big city. Just like on the TV."

"I know. I wanna go there someday. Actually, I wanna go a lot of places, but New York is definitely one of them," I revealed.

"And maybe you will. What did you do while I was away? Besides let me harass you on the phone." Hood gave me that smile that he only seems to give to me, and it was indeed making my panties wet. I tried to gain control of myself.

Smiling back at him I almost stuttered while shifting in my seat. "I, uh, I . . . you know, hung out with my girl Rochelle and I got my hair done. Oh, I got a part-time job," I revealed, forgetting all about that for a minute.

"A job? Doing what?" He seemed surprised.

"Just washing heads at this salon, but I will be getting my diploma at the same time while earning my hair license."

"Oh well, congrats, baby girl. Maybe one day you can have your own shop," Hood suggested.

"Maybe," I agreed before taking another bite of my steak.

"Yo, do you chop up the fellas?"

I swallowed the steak in my mouth before speaking. "Absolutely, but not that often."

"Maybe I'll let you fade me up sometime, then." Hood smiled while rubbing his flat fade. His haircut was fresh as always.

"Yeah, I'll fade you or bald you up. Whatever you want," I joked.

"Okay, maybe I should rethink that." Hood smiled and behind that beautiful smile were his perfect white teeth. His smile made my heart flutter.

"No, I'm just kidding with you. You know I could hook you up." I gave him a seductive but sweet smile.

"So when do I get to meet your family?" Hood asked.

"Why do you want to meet them? You just met me."

"I just want to meet your family. Let them know who I am."

"Umm, well, how about I will let you know," I quickly replied before I changed the subject. "So when do I get to visit your house?" I boldly asked.

"Whenever you ready. You want to see it tonight?" Hood poured some of the wine he ordered.

Shocked at his question, I thought about it before I answered. "Was that a trick question?" I asked.

"Nope," he replied while taking a drink.

"I just had to ask, and no, I would not like to go tonight."

"Well, it's up to you, girl. Whenever you ready just give me a call." Hood smiled. "You got all my numbers."

After a dessert that we shared, we flirted for a little, and then Hood took me home. On the ride home I actually thought about going to Hood's house, but I decided that I wasn't ready for that. If and when I went to Hood's house I would be ready on every level to go there.

The next morning while brushing my teeth I thought a lot about what Hood had asked me about meeting my family. At first I was trippin' off that shit. I had never thought about letting a dude meet my family, but on the other hand, I had never given any other dude any time of day, mainly because I kept my guard up. My dad had always been the man in my life, and since I was his little girl, he had loved me. So I wasn't craving for a man's love or attention in my life, which meant these lame-ass niggas in the street couldn't get to me easily, their compliments never faze me, but Hood, I'm really feeling him. I haven't quite put my finger on it, but there's something about him. He was cool people. So I thought I would invite him over today before I changed my mind. Plus my momma, who is never home lately, was in her room. So why not?

I decided to knock on Li'l Bo's door first. "Yo, what's up? Let me in," I screamed after I knocked six times and he didn't say a word.

"What?" he asked with a hint of attitude.

"Let me in. That's what." The door finally swung open.

"What are you in here doing?" I stuck my head in and looked around.

"Nothing, chilling. Playing my game." He bounced back down on his unmade bed.

"Well, put it down for a minute. I need to talk to you about something."

"Then spit it out, Mya. You know I don't like being interrupted during my game."

"Look, I have a friend that I want all of you to meet today. He's a guy, so don't be rude."

"Yo, this why you come in here to ruin my game? What you want us to meet him for? Nigga ain't gon' be coming over here anyway," Li'l Bo said as he grabbed his joystick to continue his game.

"Stop being so rude, boy." I pushed his shoulder. "Li'l Bo, you can't tell me who can come over here. I am the oldest. I'm eighteen, so that makes me the next adult up in here." I rolled my eyes.

"Mya, I don't care. It better not be none of these busters from the Brewster."

"Whatever. Look, clean this room and put on some clothes. Don't embarrass me." I walked out of his room and shut the door behind me.

"Yeah, whatever," Li'l Bo said, barely moving his lips.

I knocked on my momma's bedroom door, and she immediately yelled to me to come in. "You must want a visitor because you never say come in that quick."

"Well, I ain't doing anything; might as well have some company," she replied while moving her hand through her still good but brittle hair.

"I have this guy coming over today. I want all of you to meet him."

"What guy?" Ma sat straight up in her bed. "No, Mya. Hell no. Ugh, ugh. Not today. Look at me," she protested.

"Ma, I will help fix you up. I know you only used to the beautician doing your hair, but you can't afford that no more. You ain't been to the salon in years, now. You know I do hair. I can hook you up." I tried to convince her. I had been trying to do her hair for the longest time, but she always turned me down.

"Hell no. You ain't gettin' near my head." She put both of her hands up and covered her hair like she was protecting it from me.

"Ma, I can do your hair. I'm good, and you know it. Stop trippin'."

She sat there looking at me for a minute. "All right. I will let you wash it and moisturize it only." She pointed her finger at me as if to warn me.

"Wash it only. I get it," I lied, because when I got my hands in her head I was going to hook it up. "Go ahead and get up while I go grab my shampoo and stuff."

I made a quick dash to my room before she could change her mind. I had called Hood this morning and told him he could come over around three. It was eleven so I had to step on it.

"Monica, Mom just agreed to let me do her hair. Quick, help me grab the hair supplies," I encouraged her. I had told Monica about Hood coming over as soon as I made the decision, since she already knew about all our dates.

"What did she think about Hood coming over?" Monica asked while moving around helping me grab things.

"She really didn't say, but your brother was trippin' just like I expected. I didn't tell him it was Hood. Let's hurry and grab the stuff for Momma's hair before she changes her damn mind."

By the time we got all the stuff together, my momma was already in the kitchen ready to get her hair washed. After washing her hair and cutting her split ends, I was able to blow-dry it, straighten it out, and put it in a long ponytail with a swoop in the front. That's all she would allow me to do. Her ends were straight, and her hair looked good. She had that long coal-black hair down her back, so it looked like she had on a long weave ponytail. She was rockin' it. Now all we had to do was get her in some nice clothes, which was easy. My mom was still a size six like me with a big butt and a six-pack even though neither of us worked out. So she could fit in all my clothes. By the time Hood knocked on the door everyone was ready. Although I was really nervous, I had managed to give Li'l Bo a dirty threatening look before I opened the door.

"What's up, baby girl?" Hood immediately said when the door opened.

I was so nervous the only thing I could say was, "Come in."

Hood stepped into the apartment past me. Nobody said anything for a brief moment.

"Hood?" Li'l Bo immediately recognized him. "Aye, what's up, nigga?" Li'l Bo got up off the couch and gave Hood a pound.

"What's up, little man?" Hood returned the pound.

"Mya, why you didn't say it was Hood? Shit, you straight then. Hood, man, I thought she was tryin' to bring one of them ol' sucka niggas up in here. But you straight, dawg! Welcome to the family." Li'l Bo grinned, looking in my direction.

"Thanks for your permission, Li'l Bo," I said sarcastically.

"Oh, no doubt, big sis." He had a smirk on his face. "I think I'll go back to my game now. Stay up, Hood." Li'l Bo gave Hood another pound before rushing off to his room.

We all looked at each other and started laughing. "Well, Hood, since my brother introduced you to everyone, I guess I don't have to introduce you to my momma, Marisa."

"Hi, Mrs.—" Hood was cut off by my momma.

"Ugh, ugh, son, ain't no Mrs. here. Just call me Marisa."

"A'ight. Marisa. I'm Hood." Hood reached out and shook her hand.

"And this is my sister, Monica." I pointed toward Monica, who had a big grin on her face.

"What's up, Monica?" Hood walked over to her, and they gave each other a pound.

"Well, this is my family." I shrugged my shoulders.

"Li'l Bo knows you so you must be from around here in the Brewster. You a dope boy?" Momma boldly asked him.

"Ma!" I give her a shocked look. "You can't ask him that."

"It's cool, baby girl." Hood looked at me calmly.

"That's right, this is my house," Momma spoke up in her own defense.

"Marisa, I am a businessman, and no, I am not from the Brewster. I grew up in the Sojourner Projects."

"See, Mya? Ain't no harm done." She gave me a quick glance before turning back to Hood. "I got me one more question." Momma scooted to the edge of the couch. "Do you smoke weed?"

"No doubt." Hood gave her a huge grin.

"Now *that's* what I'm talkin' about. Hood, you come on over here and sit next to Momma Marisa." She moved over so Hood could sit down. Monica started laughing.

We all sat and talked for about an hour. Momma kept begging Hood to roll up some smoke, but he wouldn't until I said it was okay. Finally, I told him to roll her one up and she took it and was off to her room. Monica sat with us a little while but decided to go to her room. Hood sat with me until about ten o'clock laughing and joking. I fixed us a couple of sandwiches while we chilled. His crew kept calling letting him know what was up. So basically, he did his business sittin' right there in our living room but eventually he told me he had to bounce. He said he had rounds to make and to my surprise, I wanted him to stay, but I knew that the streets are thirsty. I remember when my dad would be out in them all night. So after laying a big juicy kiss on him, I released him to the streets, but what I did notice was that I was turning into a woman on the inside and I was falling in love with Hood. My womanhood didn't tell me if this was good or bad. I guess only time would tell.

Chapter 25

Lying in bed trying to get some much-needed rest, I kept hearing doors slam. I know it ain't Li'l Bo and Monica because today was the last day of school for them. And they both woke up and celebrated first thing this morning before they went to school. I stayed in bed this morning because I had classes last night at 4EverStylz. I had been working my ass off part-time at the shop and attending those classes for the past couple of weeks. I liked it and everything, but I had been feeling a little tired. Now I'm lying here trying to get some sleep in peace and quiet, but someone won't stop opening and slamming doors. I know it ain't nobody but my damn momma. She's finally decided to bring her ass home. We haven't seen her in two days, and she was not at home this morning when Li'l Bo and Monica left. Now she's slamming doors like she done lost her mind. I decided to get out of bed since I can't ignore her.

I walked in the living room and stuff was all over the place. It looked like a tornado or some type of storm had blown through it. Shit was literally everywhere. Papers were all over the floor, the pillows from the couch had been tossed up and thrown about the room. With my mouth wide open, I looked in the kitchen, and there was Momma opening and slamming the cabinets again. Next she raided the refrigerator with a dumb look on her face. Finally, she turned around and looked at me like a madwoman.

She looked at me as if she didn't expect to see me standing there. "There you are. I want to know right now. No lies." She pointed her finger at me. "What is going on around here? Where is all this food and shit coming from? HUH?" she yelled at me.

"Are you serious?" I said calmly, then I got pissed. "You are running around here on a rampage because we got food in the house?" I yelled. "We live in this dump that you call an apartment, and you around here rippin' it up because you see some food in it?"

"Damn right. This is my house. I tear it up when I get ready. You don't like it, GET OUT!" She turned around and slammed the refrigerator door. "I want to know where all this stuff came from."

"Why do you care? You ain't buying it. Waitin' on you to feed us we would starve. Monica and Li'l Bo need somebody they can depend on."

"Don't get smart with me, Mya. You must think I'm some kind of fool. You think I don't notice the way y'all been having on new clothes and shoes all the time? You think crack done made me stupid? Then you go put locks on doors, in *my* house, trying to lock *me* out." She started to pace the floor.

"This ain't your house. If Section eight didn't pay for it, we would be out on the streets."

"Well, until they throw you out in the streets, this is *my* house, and I don't get locked out of rooms in my house." She started stabbing herself in the chest with her finger. "You got that?"

"Whatever. I don't have time for this." I turned to go back to my room.

"Is it that boy, Hood? Is that his name? Is he giving you money?" She quickly threw questions at me.

"No, he is not. I told you I got a part-time job, but when you high you can't hear. I don't need a man to give me nothin'. I am not dating Hood for his money," I said with my back still turned to her.

"Then why? Huh?" She paused for a minute, and her breathing was hard, like she was exhausted. "Are you sleeping with him?" She spat those words at me.

Shocked at her question, I stood speechless. I just stood there not saying a thing. I was horrified yet pissed that she would ask me that question.

"You walk around here like you Mya the perfect. Well, let me tell you something. When I look at you, I see me when I was eighteen. All that long, pretty, shiny hair. Your almond-shaped eyes and butter-colored skin. Yeah, that's right. When you look in the mirror you lookin' at me. And even though you went and cut all your hair off, you can't erase that. I used to walk around actin' all perfect with my head in the air and my ass stuck out because

I knew all the dudes wanted me. There wasn't a baller in my neighborhood that didn't want me, and they knew I would eventually give it up 'cause in the end, all a girl wants is nice things. You think I don't know Hood and what he does? You think I ain't ever heard of Hood, the leader of the Height Squad. He's just another Lester, and if you ain't careful, you'll be another me."

I just stood there listening to her while she talked, staring off into space. With tears running down my face I turned around and faced her.

"That dope you smoking really done fried your brain. I will *never* be you like you. You are weak. I may look like you, but that's it. If you slept with my dad for money, then that's yo' problem. I will never sit back and sleep with men for money, have a bunch of kids, and then when it all falls through, turn to crack. No, that will never be me, ever. Unlike you, I have my own mind. I don' need Hood or no other nigga to buy nothing for me. You remember that." I turned around and headed to my room, leaving her speechless.

I slammed my door so hard it vibrated through the apartment. Then, I threw myself across my bed, buried my head in my pillow, and soaked it with tears. I cried these tears for my mother who is so lost without my dad. The tears came because of the way I disrespected my momma with my mouth. I hate talking to her like that. I thought about how happy we used to be when my mother used to caress my head and push me on the swing at the park. Happy times when my mother loved me, loved all of us. She used to put us first. I racked my brain trying to figure out what I must have done to deserve this life, a life without the love and comfort of a mother and father. With no solution coming to mind, I just lay in bed drenched in my own snot and tears.

Chapter 26

After the argument with my mother and all the crying I must have finally dozed off for a minute, then I heard Chris Brown's "Deuces" ringtone start singing on my phone. I wondered who the fuck was calling me. At this point it just seemed useless to try to get some sleep. I reached over and grabbed the phone off the extra pillow I have laying on my bed next to me. It's Rochelle. Normally she texts me so this must be important, so I hit TALK on the screen.

"Yo, what's up?" I said in the sleepiest tone I could muster. I noticed right away that I heard a lot of commotion in the background.

"Mya, girl, this bitch done came over here trippin', and I done had to bust her up."

"Who? What bitch?" I said, trying to sit up while holding my head from the headache that was coming on from the recent argument with my momma, which was only about an hour ago.

"Li'l Lo baby momma. She tried it today. This bitch done came over here trippin'. She busted his windows out of the car that I been driving, cut all the tires, and then acted a fool. She was all outside yelling for us to come out or she gon' burn this apartment down. Yo, Mya, the chick is crazy," Rochelle yelled through the phone. I could hear someone in the background cosigning her every word.

"Wow," I said, shocked.

"So Li'l Lo go out there about to kick her ass for actin' up. He told her he didn't care about the car, just to get on actin' crazy in front of my mom's crib. This skank starts yellin' 'bout how she don't give a fuck. How she gon' make sure we all burn up in here. So I went outside and told her to leave 'cause I got a baby inside. She gon' have the nerve to say fuck me and my baby. Now you know she had pulled her card with that one. So I done went ham on her." Rochelle continued to get krunk on her end of the phone.

"Y'all is crazy." I started to laugh. "Did she leave?"

"What you think? Hell, yeah, she got up outta here. Li'l Lo picked her up and threw her back in her car. Finally she drove off crying and screaming." Rochelle started laughing. "Girl, these bitches are crazy when they got a baby by these niggas," Rochelle confirmed.

"Was your mom there?" I asked.

"Nah. She had just left. That's when we heard the car alarm going crazy. By the time we got up, she was out there yellin' for Li'l Lo to come out and how she was gon' burn us up."

"That's a crazy situation right there. I guess today starting off bad for everybody."

"What happened to you?" Rochelle asked me.

"Girl, Marisa done went ham on me this morning. Up in this bitch acting crazy. Talkin' shit about me and Hood. All type of stuff. I'ma tell you about it when I see ya. I think I'ma get dressed, call Hood, and get up outta the crib for a minute, 'cause I can't get no rest here today."

"A'ight. Let me know what you're up to later. Maybe you can come through so we can talk. Charlene and Pig came through after shit popped off. So we sittin' here blazin'. I didn't want to call you because I knew you was tryin' to sleep, but I had to tell you what's going on because I knew you would be mad if I didn't."

"Yeah, let me know if that lunatic comes back because you know I will come over and slice her up. No doubt," I reminded her.

"I already know. Later." Rochelle hung up.

I can't believe Li'l Lo's baby momma came through with the drama. She should know better. You never bring your drama to some chick's house. Good thing Rochelle didn't call me because I would've gone over and got in her face for real. The situation would not be right for that chick when I was done. Rochelle and I are both known in the Brewster for kickin' asses. Over the last couple of years my life had changed so the only thing on my mind was surviving, not checking bitches, but they don't need to get it twisted 'cause I still would. Looks like today just shitting on both of us. Without giving it a second thought, I reached over and grabbed my cell phone again and pressed HOOD.

Chapter 27

I took me a quick shower and got dressed. I had called Hood to pick me up so I could get out of the house for a while and relax. So when he asked where I wanted to go, I immediately said his house. I texted Monica on her cell and told her to tell Li'l Bo to make sure she got home from school safe and that I would be back later. When Hood pulled up, I was outside waiting. I couldn't wait to get away for a while. On our way I didn't pay much attention to anything. I just lay my head back and listened to the music. For a minute I thought about my dad, but then I quickly erased that thought. I didn't want to think about nothing that would stress me out. So instead, I reached out to hold Hood's free hand while he balled down the interstate at full speed. For the first time in a long time I felt safe.

Finally we pulled into the Auburn Mills suburb addition. There were some nice, really beautiful homes. There were no cars parked on the side of the street, no prostitutes hanging out trying to flag the car down, and not a liquor store in sight. Instead, all I saw were perfectly landscaped green lawns with two- and three-car garages. Hood slowed down, then pulled into this yard with a circular driveway around the front. There was a three-car garage, which he parked behind instead of opening up.

"We here," he said after he turned off the ignition and took the key out. I just sat there. "Are you gon' get out?" he asked with a grin. I guess he noticed my reluctance.

I reached for the door handle and slowly got out. Hood walked around on my side and took me by the hand. Once inside, we stepped into this huge foyer and you could see this circular staircase that led upstairs. I paused and looked around in awe, not letting it show on my face. From where I stood, this house looked huge.

"Do you want to take a look around? Or would you like to have a seat?" he asked me.

"I'll sit for now. I'm a little tired." I rubbed the back of my neck with my free hand.

"Let's go in here." Hood led me off to the left into the living-room area with this huge Italian leather couch. The room was decorated beautifully. It had a woman's touch but everything in it was Italian this or that. On the wall hung a huge oil painting of a light-skinned woman who looked almost as if she was white. She was strikingly beautiful; she almost looked to be perfect. I would say her features were that of a mixed Angelina Jolie. But even with her light skin tone I could tell she was Hood's mother because they looked just alike except Hood had the skin of hot cocoa. The oil painting seemed to bring a breath of fresh air to the room. My staring at the painting was obvious.

"You hungry or want something to drink?" Hood sat down on his Italian leather couch beside me. The couch was so amazing; it seemed to swallow me whole. I immediately felt my sleep coming back on, but I decided to fight it.

"I'll take bottled water if you have any."

"A'ight, I'll be right back." Hood got up and disappeared.

My eyes started to get heavy by the time Hood came back with my water. "You wanna take a nap, baby girl." He passed me a Deja Blue water.

"No. I'm straight." I opened the water bottle and took a big swig, suddenly realizing how thirsty I really was.

"So you like the painting of my mother?"

"She's beautiful." I didn't hesitate to compliment.

"Thanks. That's the first thing I hung up when I moved into this house. I let my mother decorate this entire room since she would be hanging in here every day." Hood smiled.

"I could tell it was decorated by a woman. It's beautiful," I complimented. "Whenever you miss her, I'm sure you come in this room."

"Yep. Or I can call her with all this new technology." Hood let out a slight laugh. "For as long as I can remember it's been me and mom against the world." He had a smile on his face but sounded a little sad. He quickly changed the subject.

"So what's up with the classes? Everything straight?" He sounded concerned.

"Yeah, I'm loving it, but I've been feeling a little tired. Can't get no rest at home with my mom trippin'."

"Well, anytime you want to get away, you can always come here."

"Thanks."

"You sure you don't wanna take a nap?"

I shook my head no, the whole time looking at Hood and wanting to touch him or have him touch me. I needed him to touch me and not just hold my hand. I set my water next to me on the couch, then I turned my body completely facing Hood and reached out and kissed him full on the lips. At that very moment I felt my middle thump and start to melt. I was ready.

I took both hands and grabbed Hood by the face. Then I rose up on both knees and straddled him on the couch. As soon as I got on top of him I felt his hardness beating between my legs. Hood reached his head up and put his tongue deep inside my mouth. I had never had sex before, but my body seemed to naturally know what to do. As Hood worked his tongue inside and outside my mouth, my body started to rock back and forth, causing Hood to grip my ass tight and let out a soft moan that really started to turn me on. We slowly stopped for a moment. Hood looked at me and without saying a word, he lifted me up and carried me all the way up those circular stairs without taking his eyes away from me once.

When we reached his room, Hood laid me

down in this big, four-poster king-sized California luxurious bed. He undressed me piece by piece until I was buck naked. He looked me over from top to bottom with approving eyes. I sat up in the bed and reached up and pulled his shirt off, and I liked what I saw. Hood looked like nothing less than a Snickers bar that I couldn't wait to get a taste of. I reached down and started to unbuckle his pants, and when his pants dropped, the sight of his hard member made my heart thump from fear and excitement. Before I could think anything else, Hood gently laid me back on the bed and tasted every inch of me. When he seemed not to be able to take anymore, he came close to my middle and very gently began to ease inside of me. I let out a scream from the pain but letting Hood know it was the best pain I ever felt and wanted him to continue, and continue he did until we were fully connected. I was no longer a virgin, and without discussing it, Hood had taken his time with me. Without a doubt I was in love.

Chapter 28

I stayed at Hood's all day and got some much-needed rest. By the time Hood and I made it back to the Brewster it was dark outside, but everything seemed to be quiet. No drama going on. Hood got out and walked me to my apartment. The dope boys that were hanging out came over and gave a Hood a pound as we walked over to my building. As I unlocked the door I could hear Li'l Bo yelling and cursing. So I knew there was a problem.

"What happened?" I asked when I entered the apartment.

"Ma done stole my game, Mya. I'm sick of this shit!" he screamed while grabbing his hat off the couch.

"Yo, where you going?" I asked him.

"Out of this dump before I explode." He headed toward the door.

"No, you ain't going out there. It's getting late." I stepped in front of him.

"Mya, I don't need this right now. Now move," Li'l Bo ordered me.

"Mya, she broke the locks off our doors. She even stole our clothes," Monica intervened.

"What?" I slightly turned to look at Monica.

"Hell, yeah. She done took everything that she could sell for a rock," Li'l Bo said in a muffled tone.

"How long she been gone?" I asked.

"How we supposed to know? When we got here she was gone." Li'l Bo threw up his hands.

"What time did you get here?" I asked.

" 'Bout twenty minutes ago," Li'l Bo guessed.

"Twenty minutes? Where y'all been all day?" I really started to get pissed at him and Monica. I had given Monica instructions to have Li'l Bo bring her home right after school.

"We went to the mall," Monica said with her head down.

"Yo, who said y'all could go hang out? Monica, I specifically texted you and said for Li'l Bo to bring you home."

"Yeah, I know. But he wasn't coming home, though." She quickly glanced in Li'l Bo's direction, hoping for a way out.

"Why we gotta come straight home? Yo' ass ain't here. Where *you* been all day? Looks like you been hanging out to me," Li'l Bo yelled.

"Look, boy, you don't tell me what to do. I'm the oldest," I yelled back, but my voice got choked up. I went over and took a seat on the couch with everybody watching me. "I can't keep doing this shit." I started to cry, unable to control my emotions.

Li'l Bo thought I was crying because he yelled at me. "Look, Mya, I'm sorry." He sounded sincere.

Hood walked over to me to comfort me.

"It's okay Li'l Bo. You right. I should've known she was going do something crazy. I left and went out to Hood's crib today because she was trippin'. I woke up to her slamming the cabinets, and she was talkin' craziness about us having food and new clothes. She was mad about those locks on the doors too. I didn't want to hear her mouth no more so I just left, but you right, Li'l Bo. I'm sick of this too. We can't keep staying here."

"How about y'all move in with me? I got that big house with nobody but me in it," Hood suggested.

"I'm game," Li'l Bo quickly said.

"Thanks, but no thanks, Hood. I know you mean well, but we can't do that."

"Why not?" he asked.

"Yeah. Why not?" Li'l Bo sounded like Hood's echo.

"Because I said so." I threw Li'l Bo a "shut-the-fuck-up" look. "I appreciate the offer, but this is my brother and sister, so I have to take care of them. Tomorrow I'll get out and start looking for an apartment for us. You two can go with me if you want." I looked at Li'l Bo and Monica.

"Cool, as long as I can get my own room." Monica got off the couch. " 'Cause I ain't sharing one with no game-crazed freak."

"Yeah, whatever." Li'l Bo dismissed Monica with a wave of his hand.

"You two stop it. This ain't the time for that," I addressed them.

"Well, I'm going to bed. Hood, you sure you want to be in this family?" Monica asked with a smile on her face as she headed to our room.

"No doubt," Hood replied.

"Humph," Li'l Bo mumbled before heading to his room.

Finally we were alone again.

"Babe, if you won't come stay with me, let me pay for the crib. I'll do the down payment and hit your bills every month. That's the least I could do," Hood said, giving me a serious look.

"Hood, I appreciate your offers, but like I you told at first, no thanks. I can take care of us. I have some money put away from my dad. My moms don't know anything about it. We'll be straight for a while, plus I'm working now, and soon, I'll have my hair license. We're going to be all right. Don't worry, I got this," I assured him.

"A'ight, baby girl." Hood reached over and kissed me. I instantly got horny.

"Look, don't start nothin' we can't finish," I warned him.

"A'ight," he said as he caressed my right cheek. "Well, I need to make some stops and make a drop. Bricks can't wait. You know how it is. So I'ma hit ya later." He headed toward the door.

"Okay."

"Oh, what time do you want me to take you looking for this new crib? I could come through whatever time you need me to."

"Uh, we might catch the bus, but I'll call you if we need a ride."

"Mya, you ain't got to ride no damn bus." Hood gave that serious look again.

"Hood, we'll be okay. We've been doing this for a long time. Trust me." I gave him my normal, independent speech.

"A'ight." He gave up. "But you need anything, and I mean anything, you hit me on my cell."

He finally headed out the door after one last kiss. I know he wants to help, but he'll have to get used to not helping me. Like my dad said, ain't shit a nigga can do for me that I can't do for myself. Oh, except for one thing. I smiled as I thought about the day Hood and I had spent together. I turned and headed to my room to grab something to put on for bed. I had taken a shower at Hood's house so all I had to do was put on pajamas and jump in bed. I had a long day ahead of me tomorrow, looking for apartments.

Chapter 29

Looking for an apartment turned out to be more like a job than an adventure. We quickly learned it wasn't as easy as it sounded. Monica, Li'l Bo, and I had been out looking for three days. So far, we'd run up on every rat-infested apartment that Detroit had to offer. Our original plan was to try to stay as close to Mom as possible without staying in the Brewster so that we could check on her from time to time, but so far the apartments we had seen were worse than the Brewster. I had finally come to the conclusion that the only way to find something decent was to go out of this area. So today, that's exactly what I set out to do. It was only Monica and me, though. Li'l Bo said he was tired of looking so he stayed home. Monica and I boarded an early bus headed for the Detroit downtown area, and although it was early, the bus was already overcrowded. So we got off at the first downtown stop and started walking.

"Dang, Mya, you think we gon' find something that we can afford down here?" Monica said as she attempted to look up at the tall building we were standing in front of. I had attempted to look up also, but the building was just too high in the air.

"I hope so." I had an unsure mug on my face. "This building looks like a palace or something," I said and started back walking.

"Maybe we should just go back to the Brewster area. We can for sure afford something there. Or maybe you should just take Hood up on his offer. Let him pay the bills." Monica sounded defeated.

I stopped in my tracks. "Look, Monica, we don't need Hood to pay our way. I got this. Have we had Hood to get us through this far?" I sort of yelled in her face and started walking faster.

"No." Monica tried to take big steps to catch up with me.

"Right! So we don't need him now," I said, feeling bad for how I had just yelled at her. I stopped walking and turned to face her. We almost bumped directly into each other because of my sudden turn. "We are going to be okay. I have that job making pretty decent money. Pepper pays me really well to wash heads. Plus, we still got that money put aside so that'll take care of us for a while, if we spend it carefully, and soon I'll have my hair license. So things are looking up. I just need for you and Li'l Bo to believe in me."

"And I do. You really stepped up when Dad left. I believe in you." Monica reached out and hugged me.

At that moment I looked up and really noticed the building we were standing in front of and instantly I knew this is the one. This is what I had been looking for.

"This is it. Let's go inside." I grabbed Monica's hand, and we headed in.

Once inside the building, we looked around for a moment and were impressed. A representative told us they had apartments available and took us up to the fourth floor. When she opened the door to the apartment, I knew we had to get this one. I just hoped my pockets could afford to pay the rent. The apartment had three bedrooms with two full bathrooms. The master bedroom had a full bathroom. The living room area was huge with a built-in bar with bar stools. The kitchen was complete with granite countertops and all stainless steel appliances. I fell in love immediately, and to my surprise the rent would be only twelve hundred dollars a month with a two-year lease. The representative took us downstairs to do the paperwork. I had brought along references and proof of my job, but most important, I had brought along the money, which seemed to be all they cared about. I had to pay the first and last month's rent up front, which was no problem since I brought along five thousand dollars with me. The representative gave me the keys, and I was officially a tenant at River Place Luxury Apartments, downtown Detroit.

Since we were already downtown, we went to the furniture store and picked out beds, dressers, mattresses, and all those big items that we would need. We then headed over to Pier One, where we picked up some wall art and other designs that we were having delivered to the apartment. After that, we decided we wanted to go by Target to pick up some things. So instead of catching another crowded bus, we decided to call Hood, who picked us up right away. We shopped until about eight p.m. that night. Once we were finished, we decided to take the few things that we had to the apartment because everything else was being delivered the next day.

Back at the apartment, I unlocked the door with complete enthusiasm. Hood stepped in and looked around, nodding his head with approval. "You did good. I knew you had taste," he said with a huge grin on his face.

"You really like it?" I smiled.

"Yeah, plus it's safe. So I won't have to be worried about you, but I'll still get you a Glock. You never know."

"Hood, I don't need a Glock. You see all the security in this building?" I replied, knowing that I didn't need his gun because I was already packing.

"A'ight, but everyone around here needs to know I will blast a nigga and never ask a fucking question, a'ight?"

"A'ight," I mocked him and smiled.

"Let me grab all the stuff out of the car." Hood headed back outside to bring in all the bags.

"I'ma help, because I'm ready to go eat," Monica volunteered.

After everything was safely secured at the

apartment, we headed out to grab something to eat. Then we drove back to the Brewster. I had had a long day and was beat, so after hugging Hood good night, I went inside, jumped in the shower, and hit the bed. Monica told Li'l Bo all about the apartment, and I would tell Momma in the morning that we were moving out. I had decided not to make a big deal about her stealing our clothes, but I knew she wouldn't take us moving so well. She might even try to say I couldn't take Monica and Li'l Bo. I wasn't going to worry about that tonight. I would face it in the morning.

When I woke up the next morning, she still hadn't come home. So I told Li'l Bo and Monica to get dressed because we had to meet the people delivering the furniture today. Hood was going to pick us up by ten. First, I had to call Rochelle and tell her the big news. I called her cell but got no answer. As soon as I hung up the phone, it started to vibrate.

"Hello," I said into the phone.

"What's up?" Rochelle said, still sounding asleep.

"Are you still in bed?"

"Yep."

"Well, you need to get up, 'cause I know Tiny ain't still asleep."

"Girl, she's in there with Wynita." Rochelle yawned.

"Oh. Anyhow, I called to tell you I rented an apartment yesterday." I sounded excited.

"What? Oh snap. That's what's up." I heard Rochelle trying to sit up in her bed. "Where at?"

"River Place, downtown."

"Oh snap. Mya, those apartments are nice. When you moving in?"

"Today. I get all my furniture delivered today. That's why I'm up so early. Hood's about to pick me up and take me over there."

"A'ight, well, I'ma come through later today. You need me to help put together anything?"

"Heck, yeah," I quickly replied.

"Bet it up. Once I get up, I'll hit your cell."

"Later." I ended the call.

By the time I got off the phone with Rochelle and got dressed, Hood was knocking on the door. Li'l Bo answered and let him in.

"Yo, what's up?" I heard him greet Hood.

"Ain't nothin'," Hood replied.

"Hood, why don't you hook your brother-in-law up with them bricks? I'm ready to slice. Know wha'd I mean?" Li'l Bo tried to speak low.

"Hook you up with what?" I busted him. "Li'l Bo, don't make me get wit' you."

"Girl, what you talkin' 'bout," Li'l Bo said, giving me a huge grin.

"Yeah, whatever." I gave him a threatening look. "Monica, let's go," I yelled before we headed out the door.

When we made it to the first floor in our building and the elevator door opened, my heart skipped a beat. There in the middle of the hallway stood Luscious and Squeeze. My feet froze for like ten seconds. I couldn't move, and my stomach started to twist and turn. Paranoid, I thought I saw both of them mugging me. From somewhere deep within I found the courage to put one foot in front of the other. Hood, who was holding my hand, must have felt me tense up because he looked at me as if to see if I was okay. I gave him a fake reassuring smile.

Then my heart completely stopped when Squeeze started walking toward us. A second later, it was beating so loud and hard. I looked at Hood to see if he could hear it beating. If he heard it he didn't acknowledge, so I kept my focus on Squeeze. My grip on Hood's hand got stronger, and my armpits were sweating. I was sure I felt sweat drip down my arm. As Squeeze got closer, he approached Li'l Bo.

"Yo, what's up, my man?" Squeeze reached out and did a handshake with Li'l Bo.

"Shit," Li'l Bo responded, giving Squeeze's hand pound for pound.

"A'ight," was Squeeze's only reply. Then he looked at Hood. "Hood?" he said and nodded his head.

"Squeeze." Hood nodded back. This was the way leaders of crews addressed each other if there was no beef.

After that, Squeeze turned and walked back over to Luscious, who had got on his cell phone giving somebody the serious business. Whoever was on the other end of the phone was in jeopardy of getting killed. I was just glad it wasn't me. We stepped outside the building, and I was finally able to breathe. Without making it noticeable to everyone around me, I took in a huge gulp of air. That was the first time since the robbery I had laid eyes on Luscious or Squeeze. The sight of both of them scared me to death, but now I had something else on my mind. Like why in the hell was Squeeze approaching my brother like they hanging out or something? I would address that soon, but now just wasn't the time.

Chapter 30

Boom, boom, boom!

"Who is it?" I yelled while trying to pull on my robe so I could get to the front door. Someone was banging on it like they had lost their mind. Maybe Hood had left something since he had just left minutes before, but why would he be knocking like that? I know it ain't Li'l Bo or Monica because they have keys.

Boom, boom, boom!

"Hold up, I'm comin'." I start to get impatient. I swung the front door open and before I could say anything Rochelle stormed in right past me.

"He's out!" Rochelle paced the floor.

"Who?" I asked, confused.

"Mike."

"Oh shit. What happened?"

"Mya, I woke up and got ready to go into the kitchen to get Li'l Lo some water and there Mike is sittin' on my living-room couch holding Tiny. He scared the shit out of me! I almost pissed on myself. So I ask him how he got in. Of course, he says Wynita. So I start yelling for Wynita. That's when Mike says she left about ten minutes ago. I said how long you been here, then he said about thirty minutes, but he didn't want to wake me up. That's when he sat Tiny down and got off the couch to hug me. I hugged him back because I didn't know what else to do. Then out of nowhere Li'l Lo comes out of the room."

"Naw, man," I said out loud, already knowing it went down.

" 'Girl,' Mike said, 'Who da fuck is dis?' Li'l Lo said, 'Nigga, who is you?' That's when I cleared my throat. I looked at Li'l Lo and said, 'This Mike, Tiny's father; remember, I told you about him?' After that I told Mike that Li'l Lo was my man and he had to leave. Girl, this nigga hauled off and slapped me so hard spit flew outta my mouth. That's when Li'l Lo stole on him." Rochelle stopped talking for a minute and rubbed her red, swollen face.

"Anyway, they busted up all Wynita's furniture. So now she's so mad she spittin' fire. Mya, can you believe she came back wondering what happened? I got so mad I went off. I'm like, 'Wynita, why would you let Mike's crazy ass in here and you know Li'l Lo was here?' "

"What'd she say?" I had to ask.

"Talkin' about how she didn't know he was in there. Talkin' about they gon' replace her stuff that's broken. I told her to take that up with them. Then I told her I'm moving out. Now she over there crying about I'm trying to take Tiny away from her." Rochelle wiped tears off her face with the back of her hands. I reached over and handed her a Kleenex.

"That situation is all messed up. Where's Li'l Lo at now?"

"Shit, I was mad. I told him to get the fuck out too, just like Mike. I can't believe Mike's ass hit me."

I walked over and gave Rochelle a huge hug. "Well, at least Li'l Lo fucked him up."

"You know he did. I mean, me and Mike wasn't even together when he went to jail. Nigga talkin' about all he done for me. I told his punk ass I earned that so I don't owe him nothing. Plus, Tiny his daughter. Everything he did was for her, not me. After this stunt he better hope I let him see her."

"Are you hungry? I could whip you up some pancakes or somethin'." I tried to change the subject.

"I could eat." Rochelle rubbed her face again.

"A'ight." I headed to the kitchen with Rochelle on my trail.

"Where's Monica and Li'l Bo?"

"Monica's hanging out with one of her new friends, and Li'l Bo's ass in the street somewhere."

"You know what? I thought I seen him over by the Brewster when I was leaving, but I wasn't sure. I was in such a hurry to get away from over there."

"Yeah, I'ma bust his ass if I find out he slangin'."

"I hope not. You know these streets don't care who it swallow. Where Hood at?"

"Checkin' his traps. He just left right before

you came up." I grabbed some pancake mix out of the cabinet.

"Are you enjoying your new crib?" Rochelle reached in the fridge and grabbed the carton of eggs.

"Girl, yeah." I put a big grin on my face. "I still miss my mom sometimes, though. I go over once a week to visit with her just to make sure she's a'ight. Can you believe she didn't even ask where I live? Not once. I told her anyway, though." I shrugged my shoulders.

"Maybe she realized she had to let y'all go. I mean, I know she still loves all of y'all, she's just messed up right now." Rochelle sounded sincere. "Now I got to get Wynita to let me and Tiny go. She act like we gon' move out of the country or something. I think she should be happy to get us out, but she wants to keep me livin' with her forever. Mya, girl, I can't even scream when my man hittin' me from the back. Li'l Lo already got a condo waitin'. He pays a mortgage every month for a place he ain't slept at since we have been kickin' it. Yo, Mya, I just need some alone-time with my man without my momma being in the next room."

"I feel you." I smiled. "Hood and I have had sex in every room in this apartment except Li'l Bo's and Monica's rooms. And when they're here and I want to scream, I just go to Hood's house."

"I see he done put a smile on your face. Feels good to be sexed on a regular, don't it?" Rochelle asked with a grin.

"I know, right?" I laughed. I headed over to the

bar and grabbed some wine, popped the bottle, and while making pancakes, Rochelle and I talked about old times and got wasted. For the moment, for Rochelle, this morning's past events were a blur. She could face that situation again tomorrow.

Chapter 31

It had been a week since that situation with Rochelle had gone down and everything was back to normal. I had worked all week and attended my classes. So today was a good day for me to stay at home, relax, clean up, and do the laundry. Just like a lot of weekends lately, Monica and Li'l Bo were not at home, so I had peace and quiet. It was just me and Hood holding down the fort. I was walking around the house gathering everybody's laundry together while Hood followed me, trying to convince me to let him buy me a car. So I guess you can say I didn't exactly have peace and quiet. I had said no at least fifty times, but he didn't seem like he was going to give up anytime soon.

"Mya, I'm ya man. Ain't nothing wrong with me buying you a car. I ain't gon' have my girl catching no city bus. I have four vehicles, and you refuse to drive any of them. Why is that? Then you say no to me buying you a whip. I just don't get it."

We had been going back and forth about this

all morning. Hood didn't understand why I wouldn't at least drive one of his cars. Hood was a true baller, no doubt. Sittin' in his three-car garage was a 2008 white Bentley Continental, fully loaded, with an orange interior, a gray BMW M3 Concept, plus he had two Cadillac Escalade trucks. Who needs that many cars? He only had a three-car garage, so one of the Escalades had to be parked in his circular driveway. I told him if he kept buying whips he gonna have to change his address. What the hell? He was loaded with money, but that didn't have anything to do with me as far as I was concerned. How could I get him to see that? This bitching about getting me a car was getting on my last nerve.

"Look, I get that you're independent and you don't need a man for anything. I get that, but I'm ya man, and I'm not gon' have you walkin'. Period. I don't want to have to kill one of these niggas up if they get you in the wrong." Hood had that serious look on his face that he had all the time. So I know he ain't playing.

"Hood, if my walking bothers you that much, I will look into getting a car, okay?" I said while heading into Li'l Bo's room to get his dirty clothes.

"A'ight, baby girl," he finally said calmly, but something told me that he wasn't giving in too easy because he had been adamant about this all day. Or maybe I had won; maybe he was tired of arguing about it. Since I said I would look into it, he was cool with that. Either way, I was glad to get his ass off my trail following me from room to room with this.

After grabbing all of Li'l Bo's clothes out of his dirty hamper and throwing them into my wash pile, I noticed something fall out of his pocket. I reached down to pick it up thinking maybe it was some paper. But as I picked up the package to examine it for a couple of seconds, I recognized what I knew without a doubt to be cocaine. I almost fell backward as my body swayed.

"Hood!" I yelled so loud I heard an echo in my apartment, even though my place is fully furnished front to back.

"What, baby?" he questioned as he entered the room looking worried. He immediately recognized what I was holding in my hand. "Where did you get that?"

"It fell out of Li'l Bo's pocket. Oh God, Hood. What if he's using drugs?" Tears flooded my face.

Hood walked over and took it out of my hand. "This shit is that white too," he said, examining the bag. "I don't think he's using this. If he was, you would know it, trust me." Hood gave me a reassuring look.

"So he slangin' that shit? That's why he hangin' out so much. I knew it, but I've been too busy lately to approach him about this, but today I will."

"Look, Mya, you got to handle this the right way, because if you don't, you will push him to the streets for good."

"What the does that mean, Hood?" I got mad. "Are you telling me to give him a pat on the back, maybe even a round of applause?"

"That's not what I said, Mya. You got to handle this the right way, or you will make it worse. Li'l Bo ain't that little no more. He's a man now. He's tryin' to get his respect from the streets. At this point, he feels like he got something to prove."

"Well, you know what? I got something to prove, too." I snatched the dope out of Hood's hand, reached on his right side, and grabbed his nine-millimeter Glock, then headed toward the front door.

"Where are you going?"

"Over to the Brewster to get Li'l Bo."

"Why you need that nine?"

" 'Cause the first motherfucker who tries to stop me from gettin' my little brother, it's lights out for them." Tears were flowing down my face so fast I had to wipe them to keep from wetting my shirt.

"No, Mya." Hood grabbed the gun out of my hand.

"Oh, I am going over there. Now you can take me, or I'll catch a cab. Either way, I'm out." Hood followed me out the door. When we pulled up to the Brewster, it was packed outside as usual. Everyone was out: crack fiends, dope pushers, hoes, you name it. We rolled up on Li'l Bo chilling, hanging out, and trapping with about five other niggas. I jumped out of the truck heated.

"Yo, what you doing here, Mya?"

I immediately headed toward Li'l Bo. He started walking toward me so I wouldn't loud-talk him. He could tell by looking at me I was pissed. When I got in of front of him, I pulled out the bag of dope.

"What is this?" I opened the bag and let it pour out on the ground.

"Yo, what the fuck you doing?" Li'l Bo yelled.

"What did I tell you, nigga?" Before I knew it, I slapped him so hard he stumbled backward, then I grabbed him by his neck. Hood rushed up and pulled me off him.

"You have ruined everything!" I cried. "Everything that I have tried so hard to prevent."

"Mya, I told you I got to be a man. I can't have my older sister taking care of me like I'm some kid. I'm out here making money." Li'l Bo went in both his pockets and pulled out wads of cash. I noticed he had guns in his waist. It broke my heart. All I had sacrificed for my family and my baby brother was a dope boy.

"I know you working for Squeeze. He don't give a fuck about you. You fifteen, Li'l Bo," I cried. "Fifteen!" I repeated as crowds of people stood by watching me. I didn't care. I loved my brother with all my heart, and I just wanted to keep him safe.

"Take her home, Hood. She don't need to be out here." Li'l Bo turned around and walked back to his trap spot. Just like that, I had lost my brother to Squeeze. I had no more control. I hated Marisa and Lester for not being here to help me, expecting me to be the adult. How dare they put all this responsibility on me?

Chapter 32

For the next two days, Li'l Bo didn't come home. I was sick. I lay in bed both days thinking he would never come back. He had made it clear that he didn't want me taking care of him. So I didn't know if he would find his own crib or just lay around the trap houses. I was just plain worried. Monica tried to get me to eat, but I wasn't hungry. Hood tried to console me so he stayed by my side. He didn't check his traps for two days. He put Pig in charge just so he could hold me down. I knew without a doubt that he had mad love for me.

Although I appreciated him being there for me, the only thing on my mind was Squeeze. That nigga just seemed to be the root of my family's problems. My life had been going so good since the robbery. I had Hood in my life, I was working and going to school, I had the new crib for my brother and sister, and everything just seemed to be going in a positive direction. Even though I still worried about my mom, not seeing her come in the house high all the time was kind of unusual. Although I didn't like her getting high, I liked knowing she was safe. I had been thinking about my dad a lot lately and planned to go see him. My plan was to take Monica and Li'l Bo out to visit with him, but with all that was going on I just hadn't had the time. With things looking up on a positive note, I hadn't thought much about continuing to carry out my plan on Squeeze's crew.

Now the hate I felt for that nigga was at an all-time high. Since he couldn't seem to stay away from my family and since he was determined to ruin my family, I knew there was only one thing left for me to do, and that was to ruin Squeeze's life. You know, keep fucking with his money. After all, that will always get him where he lives. My thoughts were getting heavy until I heard a knock on my bedroom door.

"Come in," I said in a husky voice.

Li'l Bo walked in looking like he'd been up the whole two days he had been gone. He had changed clothes, and just like any trap boy he was geared from head to toe. He had on the big blinged-out diamond watch and the chain to match.

"What's up, sis?" he said. "Look, I'm sorry, but I tried to tell you. I promise I won't end up like Dad. You don't have to worry." He paused, and I saw a tear roll down his face. "Are you gon' say something? Yell or something, because I know you still pissed and shit."

"Damn right, I'm mad," I said without screaming at him like I really wanted to.

"Look, don't be mad at Squeeze. He's an a'ight dude. He just about his paper. I'ma be large just like him, and I ain't going to no damn jail."

"Li'l Bo, Squeeze is a snake. He ain't gon' let you be no more than a nickel-and-dime trap boy."

"Naw, it won't be like that, you watch. Do you want me to move out?" he asked while putting both his hands in his pocket. I didn't say anything, so he turned to leave.

"Li'l Bo," I said before he opened the door. "Promise me that you'll come home every night. Never stay out all night. I can't bear thinkin' you dead."

"Ah, Mya, that's what you worried about? Ain't nothing gon' happen to me. And I promise to come home every night." He walked over and gave me a kiss on the forehead and turned to leave the room.

I got so mad when he left the room I knocked everything off my nightstand. I couldn't make Li'l Bo stop trapping, but I could make Squeeze feel my pain. Squeeze owed me.

<hr />

Tuesday night was money pickup night for the Boone Squad, and I knew that all the trap boys would be loaded with at least fifty to sixty thousand apiece. So I set myself in place for my next robbery. I had been in the Brewster all day watching one of Squeeze's punk-ass trap boys by the name of Drake. Drake was a fine-ass redbone, but when anything came out of his mouth, he was an asshole. He loved to call women *bitches*. Too bad he wouldn't get to call me a bitch, since he wouldn't know I was a female.

Luscious always picked up Drake's stash third to last. So I knew I had to hit him before Luscious showed up. Drake had a vacant apartment in the Brewster that he didn't allow anyone in. I knew I had to be very quiet with Drake because those walls in the Brewster were paper-thin. My plan was to watch Drake go to his apartment, and I would come up from behind the building since his apartment was conveniently on the first floor. When he got ready to open up his door, I would put the Ruger to his head and order him to open the door quietly, then give me his stash. This time I wouldn't hit him in the head like I did Luscious. Instead, I would put some sleep aid up to his nose to make sure he was out. That way, when Luscious showed up to pick up his stacks, all he would have to do was wake Drake's punk ass up.

Drake had been standing outside for twenty minutes talking to some skank ho that seemed like she would never leave. Finally he gave her a pat on her big nasty butt, and she walked away. Soon as she walked away some crack fiend walked up to him and copped. Then Drake looked around the Brewster one last time and headed to his building.

As soon as he stuck that key in the door I came up from behind him and put the Ruger to his head. I ordered him to open the door and not say shit, and without saying a word or resisting, he did it. Once inside I started to ask him where the money was, but to my surprise, there it was sitting on the couch in a black bag that wasn't even zipped up. My first thought was *This nigga's crazy. What if someone had broken in here while he was out trappin'?* Oh, well, this just made it easier for me.

"Walk over to that couch and zip up that bag," I said in my practiced male tone. "Keep your back to me and no sudden moves or I blast."

He calmly walked over to the bag and zipped it up, then he quickly tried to grab for his side, but before he could even touch his shirt I blasted. Drake instantly dropped to the floor.

"A'ight, a'ight, man. Shit. You don't have to kill me over this shit."

"I told you no sudden moves, motherfucker," I quietly yelled while trying to keep my voice low. Luckily for him the bullet had only grazed his ear, which was bleeding.

"Lie still! If you move again I will put a bullet in your head, and this time I won't miss," I stated as I stepped over to the bag and quickly put it around my neck.

Nervous as hell thinking someone had heard the shot, I pulled out the rag with the sleep aid on it. Then I very quickly put the Ruger to Drake's head and ordered him to put the rag over his face. He seemed reluctant until I lifted the safety on the gun. One good inhale and he was out. To make sure he was out, I pulled his ear where the bullet had grazed him. Once I was sure, I took off the mask, opened the door, and made sure no one was in sight. Then I made a dash to the back of the building where I had a regular shopping bag hidden. I quickly removed the money from the black bag and put it into the shopping bag. With no one in sight, I took a long walk around the Brewster to the bus stop, where I boarded a bus that passed right by Luscious as he was about to enter into the Brewster.

Chapter 33

"That's fucked up," Hood said for the second time as he got dressed. He had just got out of the shower and was looking at the eight o'clock morning news report on TV.

"It is," was my only reply. According to the news, Drake had been found shot at point-blank range, two to the back of the head. When I heard that, I knew he had been the victim of one of his own crew. Luscious had shot him because he didn't have his trap money just like Phil said he would do. Luscious couldn't go to Squeeze without Drake's money or Drake's blood on his hands so he had no choice. Anyway, that was their problem. I didn't want to spend my time worrying about the Boone Squad.

It had been four days since that situation had happened. I was tired of hearing about it already. Rochelle had called and said she was going out, so I decided to roll. Hood agreed it had been a while since we had been out.

"So you gon' be ready when I get back tonight?" he asked me.

"Yep, I already told you I will be dressed, baby."

"A'ight," he said, and bent down and gave me a kiss and, of course, he had to slap me on the ass. That was one of his favorite things to do. I smiled at him. "Love that," he said with a smile, referring to my big butt.

"You better." I sucked my teeth.

When Hood left, I rolled over and went back to sleep. I was sleeping in today until it was time to hit the club. The sleep would do me good. Normally, Hood and I would both sleep until about ten a.m., but he said he had something to do early today. So I would take advantage of this sleep for both of us. I wanted to be well rested when I hit the club tonight because I was going to party my ass off. It had been a minute, and I couldn't wait.

I woke up about three p.m. and noticed Monica was not home again. She had been hanging out a lot lately with her new friend. I was glad she had a friend, though, because for the most part she was a loner. I figured she needed someone her age to talk to so I didn't make a big deal about it. I decided to make dinner so she could have something good to eat when she got home. After cooking and watching TV, I decided to pull out something to wear to the club. After carefully going through my closet I decided on this all-black Apple Bottom one-shoulder Kaza dress with a pair of Apple Bottom Shannon strappy stilettos. Satisfied with my choice, I jumped in the shower and did my makeup.

Putting on the finishing touches of my makeup, I heard Monica come in.

"It's about time you came home," I said, pretending to be upset.

"Well, you were knocked out so I went and hung out," she said, as she lay down across my bed.

"Where have you been and who is this new friend I haven't met yet?"

"Her name's Kisha. We hung out at the mall. Window-shopping and stuff." Monica shrugged her shoulders.

"Why you didn't ask for money for the mall?" I was looking through my mirror at her.

"Oh, I didn't want to shop. I just wanted to hang out. Besides, I still got some of the money you gave me last week."

"Well, I'm going out tonight. Are you going to be all right until Li'l Bo gets here?"

"Yeah, Mya, I'm not a baby," she reminded me with a smile.

"I know."

"Smells like you've been cookin', which is good because I'm hungry."

"Go eat then," I said as I headed over to the bed to start putting on my clothes.

"That outfit gon' look good on you." Monica pointed at my outfit that I had lying across the bed.

"I know, right?" I bragged.

By the time I was done getting dressed, Hood knocked on the door. He rushed in the house yelling my name, and from the sound of it he was pissed. "Mya, I done had to fuck one of your neighbors up

out in the parking lot. Punk-ass nigga hit my damn
Bentley. This nigga had the nerve to get out talkin'
shit."

"What?" I said in shock.

"Come check this shit out. I know the cops're
on the way."

We both ran out the front door, with Monica
trailing. Soon as the elevator stopped I was the first
to jump off running, but Monica and Hood didn't
seem to be in a hurry anymore. When I stepped
off the elevator I expected to see a crowd of people standing around this brutally beaten up body;
instead, I didn't see shit but a clear lobby. Besides
the doorman who spoke to me with his usual
smile, there was no one else in sight.

An uneasy feeling came over me as I stepped
outside and came face-to-face with this all-white
Range Rover with white rims wrapped in the
biggest red bow I've ever seen. In total shock, I
turned around to face Hood, who had a big smile
on his face. Shock quickly turned to anger.

"What the hell is this, Hood?" I pointed to the
truck. Then I looked at Monica. "You knew about
this, didn't you?" I asked her.

"Yeah. Ain't it nice, Mya?" Monica had a grin
on her face that at the moment looked stupid to
me. She walked slowly around the truck admiring
every inch of it.

"Well, you can just take it back. I already told
you I will get my own car!" I started walking back
toward the building.

"Mya," Hood yelled, "baby." He caught up to
me and grabbed my arm. "Look, I bought this

truck for you because I wanted you to have it." He used his sincere voice. "I know you take care of everything, but let somebody take care of you sometime, baby."

Tears start pouring down my face as I thought about my mother and what my father had told me. I knew I was being stubborn, but I didn't know how to accept the truck without feeling like I was needy or like another hood rat from the Brewster fucking for money. My independence was even more than I could bear. I was trying my hardest to find some peace in it.

"We need to leave for the club. Everybody gon' be waitin' on us." I dabbed at the tears running down my face, hoping not to mess up my makeup.

"A'ight. We'll roll in the truck. I'll drive it until you feel comfortable."

"What about the Bentley?" I questioned.

"It can stay here." Hood signaled for the doorman. "Aye, park this." Hood threw the doorman the keys to his Bentley.

"Monica, go back up and lock up. Li'l Bo should be home soon. Are you gon' be cool?"

"Yes, go ahead," Monica said with a smile on her face.

Hood and I jumped in the truck and balled out. I did a once-over glance when I got inside the truck, and it was nice. After that I didn't pay attention to much of anything in it, I had so much shit on my mind. I couldn't wait to get to the club because I needed a drink.

By the time we pulled up to the club, everyone else was just pulling in. Hood jumped out of the truck just in time to greet Pig.

"What's up, my nigga?" Pig said as he gave Hood a pound. "That's some new heat, right?" Pig pointed at the truck using some new slang.

"No doubt. Just picked this shit up for my baby," Hood replied.

"Them white rims is hittin' hard," Pig complimented.

"No doubt," Hood agreed.

Charlene walked up to the truck with Felicia in tow as I got out of the truck. At the same time I saw Rochelle pulling up with Li'l Lo.

"Mya, this you?" Charlene pointed to the truck.

I gave her a nod for yes since I didn't feel like giving her an answer.

"Umm, you must be lettin' Hood hit that hard." Charlene let out a laugh that I noticed was a little fake.

"What's up, bitches?" Rochelle walked up with a huge grin.

"Nothin'. Some of us just gettin' Range Rovers and what-not," Charlene said, and again, I thought maybe she sounded a little envious.

"Yo, Mya, this yo' heat?" Rochelle asked as she walked over to the Range Rover.

"Yep. Hood picked it up," I replied snidely, since Felicia seemed to be staring me down while Charlene kept making bitchy comments. "Anyway, did we come here to talk about this truck or get krunk?"

"I came to get krunk," Rochelle said matter-of-factly.

"Then let's do it, bitches," I said with a smile

and headed toward the club entrance. Hood and his crew followed. When we stepped in the club, it was VIP treatment to the fullest. Hood never received anything less. We had a VIP room with a fully stocked bar and waiters at our beck and call. We tossed back drinks and danced to the DJ for hours before shit started to get ugly.

"Mya, I swear if that bitch keeps staring at Li'l Lo, I'ma beat her ass," Rochelle sneered.

"Who?" I asked, looking around.

"Felicia. Every time I look up, that thirsty bitch staring at Li'l Lo."

"I don't know why Charlene carries that bitch around on her hip all the time anyway, but you know I got yo' back," I said while watching Charlene shake her ass all over Pig like she's auditioning for hoes most wanted. I didn't know what was going on with her, but Charlene was changing.

After fucking Pig on the dance floor with her clothes on, Charlene headed over to Rochelle and me.

"So what's up with you bitches tonight? Y'all actin' all stank."

"Yo, Charlene, why you always dragging Felicia's ass around wit' you?" Rochelle questioned her.

"She's my homie. We cool, you know that." Charlene downed a shot the waitress handed her.

"Well, I don't like the ho, and on top of that, I think she tryin' to push up on my man. You better tell her to step off before I fuck her up." Rochelle was getting mad.

"Chill, Rochelle, Felicia got a man." Charlene tried to defend her.

"Well, she better act like it, 'cause she tryin' it

tonight." Rochelle got up and walked over to the bar in VIP where Li'l Lo was getting a drink.

"So what's good wit' you, Mya?" Charlene pried. "'Cause ya girl trippin'." Charlene smiled, referring to Rochelle.

"Nothin'. Tryin' to get myself together. You know, move in a positive direction."

"Well, it looks like you got it together. You are sleeping with one of the baddest niggas in the game who got mad paper and as a result, you are livin' in a fly-ass crib, driving a bad-ass whip. I would say you got it all the way together," Charlene said with a shitty look on her face. "And to think you didn't even want to date his fine ass. I guess your senses finally kicked in." Charlene give a me another fake-ass smile and downed another shot of Hpnotiq.

"You know, Charlene, contrary to what you may think, I didn't start going out with Hood because of his money. None of that moves me. I'm with him because I wanna be," I said, growing tired of her little comments.

"Yeah, that's what they all say." Charlene gave me a wink and walked away.

What just happened? is all that ran through my mind. Why had I been getting the feeling that Charlene wasn't really happy for me? Greed was taking over her, but I didn't have time to be worried about the next person. I had my problems to get through. I'm sure Charlene was just going through a phase anyway. I'm sure that eventually she will be genuinely happy for me.

"Yo, baby, what's on ya mind?" Hood came up

behind me when I stood up. He had been to the restroom and had missed the conversation I had with Charlene.

"Nothing," I said with a smile and wrapped my hands around his neck and pulled him in for a big kiss.

"*That's* what I'm talkin' about." He grabbed both my butt cheeks, and I instantly got turned on.

"That ain't nothing. You wait until we leave here," I said, giving him something to look forward to.

"Bet, but we about to roll up over there." He pointed to where Pig, Li'l Lo, and other members of the Height Squad had posted up.

"Oh, go 'head. I need to run to the restroom anyway. These drinks are running through me."

"A'ight." Hood gave me a kiss.

I left VIP and headed for the restroom feeling good about the night. Somehow I was finally feeling okay about the truck. While I had no idea how long it would actually take me to drive it, I was feeling okay about accepting it from Hood. After all, I loved him, and he wasn't just any dude to me.

When I made it to the restroom I was glad to see I was the only one in there. All the stall doors were open. Which was good. The last thing I wanted to hear was a bunch of hoes chatting about their so-called ballers and what they had sexed him real good to get. Luckily I could get in, do my business in peace and quiet, and be out. As I finished up, I opened the stall door and my heart dropped.

"Where you been hidin', Mya? I haven't seen you around the Brewster," Phil inquired.

"I've been around. Why are you in the women's bathroom?" I tried to keep my cool.

"Look, bitch, don't act surprised to see me. I know what you did. It wasn't nobody but you."

"What the hell are you talkin' about? Nigga, you must be trippin'," I said as I tried to step around him to get out of the bathroom stall.

Phil grabbed my arm and pushed me up on the stall wall and closed the door.

"You must think I'm stupid! I remember all that shit we talked about that night. I know I was wasted, but I remember. At first I wasn't sure, but the other night when Luscious and me was gettin' high, he told me that dude voice sounded like a female impersonating a nigga. That's when it hit me. All that shit you had asked me—that's how you pulled it off."

"Get your hands off me, Phil." I struggled to break his grip.

"You listen to me. Nobody knows shit—yet." Tiny spit drops flew out of his mouth and smacked me in my face as he threatened me. "I want one hundred and fifty thousand of that money, or I will make sure that Squeeze finds out," he said while putting his lips close to my face like he was trying to kiss me. "You smell good, and you a bad bitch. I've been watching you all night." He put his head in the crease of my neck again and inhaled deeply. Taking in my scent, he smiled, then finally released me from his grip and opened the bathroom stall door.

I hastily walked around him.

"Oh, I know you were responsible for Drake too." He stared at me as he walked past me, then stopped. "You have until next Friday."

I stood there for a moment speechless with a million thoughts running through my mind. What was I going to do? This nigga was on to me. What if Hood found out I'm a stick-up bitch? If Squeeze finds out, I'm dead. Okay. I got to get myself together and go back to VIP. I looked in the mirror, checked my makeup to make sure I looked worry-free, and then headed back to VIP.

I stepped back in the VIP room to find Rochelle beating the shit out of Felicia. I immediately rushed over, grabbed a Grey Goose bottle off one of the tables, and smashed Felicia across the head.

"Trick," I yelled. "That's what you get for being a ho." I continued to yell as Hood grabbed me from behind, pulling me out of VIP. It took half the Height Squad to get Rochelle off Felicia. All I could see from where Hood had pulled me was Felicia falling out of VIP looking fucked up. That cheap hair weave she wears had gone wild. Her face was swelling up, and she was bleeding from the scalp where I had busted her with the bottle. Then out of nowhere, here comes Charlene talking shit.

"Why did you have to hit her, Mya? Rochelle had that situation under control."

"Because I felt like it." I got directly in Charlene's face.

"I'm on a warpath tonight. Any bitch or bitches

get in my way gettin' fucked up," I spat at her without blinking.

"Y'all must be jealous of her or something, because that was uncalled for." Charlene bent down and started picking up Felicia's stilettos. They must have come off during her beating. "Pig, get Felicia. Let's go." Charlene started walking toward the door with Felicia's shoes gathered in her hands.

"How about you just stop bringing that ho around?" I yelled while Charlene stomped away.

The way I felt right then was fuck both of them. The mood I was in was killer mode. Both of them chicks better walk away.

"You ready to go, baby?" Hood asked me.

"Hell, yeah. Let's get outta here." I gave the room a quick scan looking for Rochelle, but apparently she had already left with Li'l Lo.

Hood drove ninety all the way down the interstate to his crib. He didn't ask any questions; he didn't even ask if I wanted to go home. I guess he knew I had frustrations I needed to release. As soon as we got inside his crib I headed straight toward the staircase with Hood on my ass. I wanted him so bad I couldn't wait another step. At the edge of the staircase, I kicked off my Apple Bottom stilettos, turned around, and threw my tongue down his throat. Hood pulled my dress off and revealed my titties, which were hard and ready. He hungrily put them in his mouth and sucked. He then turned me around and bent me over the steps and pushed his hard member deep inside my hot juices, which quickly started to run down my leg. Hood was banging me so hard until we both released at the same time. Breathing hard, we both collapsed on the stairs tired as hell but wanting more. After two more intense rounds on the stairs we headed to the bedroom, where we stayed until ten a.m. the next morning.

Chapter 34

"*I'ma kill you, bitch, for screwing with my operation. You think you can rob me and get away with it? Well, you about to find out what I do to stank hoes who try to screw with my paper. Open your mouth wide, bitch, and suck my dick,*" Squeeze said, and then punched me in my face and blood flew out of my mouth.

"*Agh, fuck you, snake!*" I yelled in so much pain while I tried to squirm from under him.

"*Where you think you going, bitch?*" Squeeze grabbed me by my legs and pulled me back under him. "*Open wide, open wide,*" Squeeze kept yelling at me and laughing at the same time as he pried my bloody mouth open with his gun. "*Now suck on this, bitch!*"

"*NO, NO, NO,*" I kept yelling, and then everything went black.

BAM, BAM, BAM.

I sat straight up in my bed drenched in my own sweat. My hands immediately flew to my face and mouth feeling for blood, but there wasn't any. I had been dreaming. Thank God it was only a dream, but that banging on my door was real. Who the hell could that be?

"Who is banging on the door like that?" I yelled out loud, still lying in bed. "Monica, hurry up and get the door," I yelled again and lay back down attempting to pull my nerves back together.

BAM, BAM, BAM.

"Shit," I said as I jumped up and grabbed my robe. I must be the only one around here who can answer the door. I looked at the clock and noticed it was 5:22 in the evening. I had been asleep since Hood brought me home about 11:30 this morning. I had stayed at his house after we left the club. We'd been up going at it like mad people since we left the club. So I decided to get some rest when I made it home this morning.

I stuck my head in Monica's room and noticed she was gone. I didn't even check Li'l Bo's room because he never came home anymore except to sleep. Once he got up, ate, and was dressed, he was out for the day. Then my dream hit me again. What if it's Squeeze or someone from the Boone Squad here to take me out? Phil said no one knew but him, but I couldn't trust that nigga. I headed back to my room and grabbed both my Rugers, then went back to answer the door. Without asking who it was, I put one of my Rugers to the door so I could shoot if I had to. Then I looked out the peephole to see my mom, out of all people, standing at my door.

"Just a minute," I said through the door while I

tucked my guns under my robe and unlatched the door.

"What you doing in here?" she said while looking around when I let her in.

"Nothin'. I had to get decent. Why you knocking like you the police?" I threw back.

"Just wanted to make sure y'all heard me."

"Well, what brings you by? It took you long enough to come check on your children," I said sarcastically.

"Look at how you living. Y'all don't need me to come check on y'all. Where Monica at? I saw Li'l Bo hanging out on the block. Matter of fact, I always see him on the block. I guess you can't raise him no better than I could after all." She smirked at me.

"What you come here for? Huh?" I got irritated. "Monica is not here, and I'm in the bed." I sounded rude on purpose.

"I need some money," she said and started walking around in the living-room area.

"Ha," I gave a fake laugh. "I knew it was something that had nothing to do with us. Why didn't you ask Li'l Bo? He got plenty money."

" 'Cause I asked you. I don't want shit Li'l Bo makes from working with Squeeze." She screwed up her face like she had a bitter taste in her mouth. "Now are you going to give it to me or not? I don't have anything to eat in that damn apartment, and I need some feminine products."

"You would have food if you didn't sell your food stamps," I reminded her.

"Don't preach to me." She was getting mad and raised her voice.

"Okay. I'll give it to you. Sit down and wait here if you want to." I ran upstairs and grabbed my pink and white Coach bag and pulled out five hundred dollars. I hurried back downstairs. "Here, take it. Don't smoke it." My eyes pleaded with her but I knew the truth.

"Thank you, baby," she said and jumped up and gave me a taut hug, and before I could say anything else, she was out the door, gone back out into the street to cop more dope. I didn't want to give it to her, but maybe she would buy her some food for real. Who really knew? I just didn't feel like denying her.

I grabbed some orange juice out of the fridge and headed back to my bed to get my thoughts together. I tried to lie back down and get some more sleep, but every time I closed my eyes, I saw Squeeze or someone from the Boone Squad standing over me and I was looking up at the barrel of their gun.

I sat up in my bed knowing there was no way I would live too much longer with Phil knowing my secret. Even if I paid him he would threaten me all the time to get more money, or he may even try to kill me himself. After all, I wasn't stupid. Phil couldn't really tell on me without telling on himself. If Squeeze found out about what Phil had told me, Phil would be just as dead as I would be.

After a little more contemplating I knew I had to talk to Phil to come up with a better understanding. There was no way I would pay him to only be controlled by him with more threats. I had to talk to him face-to-face, but I had to make our conversation on my terms, and in order to do that, I would have to sneak up on him. I had to get into his apartment without him knowing it, and I had just the idea. I picked up my cell phone.

"Hi, this is Phil Harris's sister, Arlene. Phil went out of town over the weekend and left me in charge, but I seemed to have misplaced my key. Can someone come and let me in?"

"Uh, sure. I'll send someone right over," the female voice said.

"Oh, I'm not there right now. I will be there about six thirty," I lied, knowing the office closes at six.

"I'm sorry, we close the office at six, but we can stick an extra key in the mailbox by the door, and you can return the extra key tomorrow."

"Oh, thank you so much. I really appreciate it," I said and quickly hung up the phone.

That was easier than I thought. I guess that's what you get for living in the hood. They don't question nothing. That dumb chick should be fired on the spot.

Without another thought, I jumped in the shower and threw on one of my short-sleeve Baby Phat sweat suits with a pair of icy white Forces. Before heading out the door I stopped and looked at the keys to my Range Rover, which were conveniently lying on the bar. It took me only a split second to snatch them off the bar and head out the door.

I made it to the apartments Phil lived in at dark. I knew it would be a while before Phil made it to the crib since he would be out trapping, but I wanted to get that key to his apartment out of the mailbox before he made it home so I could hide inside. Once I got inside his apartment I looked around, and to be honest, Phil's crib was a real shit-hole. This nigga had an old twenty-five-inch regular TV in his living room with some old funky-looking furniture that looked like it had been donated. Squeeze clearly wasn't paying him shit. His bedroom looked the same. The nigga even had a mattress on the floor. Damn, I felt sorry for this nigga. He was dumb for real.

Suddenly, I heard the front door open. What was he doing home so early? I hadn't even decided where I wanted to hide. My plan was to sneak up on him in order to get him to listen to me. "Shit," I said in a muffled voice. I hit my leg on his closet door trying to get inside. I closed the door halfway so I could peek out to make sure he was alone. I could hear him moving around in the kitchen, and it sounded like he was dropping stuff. Then he came in his room and kicked off his shoes, and then pounced down on that old battered mattress on his floor. I was trying to think of what I would say to him, but then I was interrupted by Phil's loud snoring. I couldn't believe this nigga went to sleep that fast.

I slowly opened the closet door and crept over to Phil, where he was lying faceup on the mattress snoring. "Wake up, Phil," I said in a calm voice. Phil opened his eyes slowly like he thought he was dreaming. When he realized who I was, he bolted straight up.

"Mya? How da fuck you get in here?" He put bass in his voice.

"I let myself in," I said calmly, but I was nervous as hell.

"Bitch, you better have my money."

"Look, I came here so we can talk about this," I calmly said, but I was getting even more nervous by the way Phil was looking at me.

"Ain't shit to talk about. You pay me or you dead. Simple as that. And I don't appreciate you breaking into my crib." Phil stood up.

I felt beads of sweat popping out on my forehead.

"Phil, be real. Your life's in more danger than mine. Squeeze gon' put a bullet in your head before mine if he finds out you gave up his whole operation."

"Nah. Squeeze ain't gon' be worried about me, because right now, he worried about yo' little brother. Little young nigga think he slick just like you. Nigga been greasing his own pockets on the side. Li'l nigga think he slick. Just like you."

"What the hell are you talkin' about?"

"He be stealing money, and Squeeze all over that, but no need to worry 'cause soon . . ." Phil took two of his fingers and pointed them at my head like a gun and fake-pulled the trigger.

I tensed up. "You listen to me, you snitch-ass loser, if anything happens to my brother I will kill Squeeze, you, or whoever is responsible," I said.

My chest was heaving up and down so fast I felt like I was out of breath.

"Who da fuck you tryin' to threaten? Bitch, get out! Have my money by Friday like I said," he screamed at me.

I turned around and started walking up the short hallway. All of a sudden Phil grabbed me by the neck and started dragging me back toward his room.

"Phil," I tried to scream, but he had his grip so tight around my neck I couldn't speak.

"I changed my mind. I want the money *and* some of you," he said as he continued to drag me until he got to his room, and then he threw me on his mattress.

When he let me go I had to struggle to catch my breath. He immediately started unbuckling the belt to his pants while I was trying to catch my breath. I sat up trying to take in gulps of air.

"Lie back down, bitch." He got on top of me and started tugging at my pants. I dug my fingers in his eyes. He tried to punch me in my face, but I moved just in time. He grabbed me by my neck again. I kicked him in his nuts, and he fell backward. I got up, but I was still trying to catch my breath. I ran toward the door to his room, but I tripped on his shoe and fell on my knees. He grabbed me again by the neck and flipped me over.

"Stop fighting. You think you too good for me?"

"I am, motherfucker," I said while reaching down toward my right ankle where I had my Ruger strapped. Phil was trying to rip my shirt off, but before he could, I had my Ruger out and I pulled the trigger. Phil fell sideways off of me. I had shot him right between the eyes. Blood was pouring out the back of his head, and his eyes were wide open.

I quickly got up and looked around to make sure I didn't drop anything. I went back to the closet and wiped the doorknob to make sure I didn't leave a fingerprint. Then I quickly went to the bathroom to look in the mirror. There was no blood on me because all of it seemed to pour out the back of Phil's head when he hit the floor.

I wiped the front doorknob off and headed straight out the door to my truck. Once inside my truck I sat still. I didn't see anyone in sight. I didn't know what to do next. I hadn't planned on killing him. I had brought my gun along because it just felt right.

"Shit. Shit," I said, hitting my steering wheel. Finally, I started the Range Rover up and took off toward the Brewster, which was right around the corner. I had to get somewhere with a bathroom quick. My stomach was turning flips. I burst into my mom's apartment and headed straight to the bathroom, where I threw up. Sweat was pouring down my face. My mind was racing, and the only thing I could do was cry.

Murder was on my hands. I had killed him. I had no choice. It was him or me, and I wasn't an option. After throwing up, I ended up on my mom's living-room couch. I woke up the next morning to my mom calling my name.

"What you doing here? Why ain't you at home?" she fired questions at me.

I sat up on the couch. "I, uhh, I came by to see you last night. You wasn't here, so I sat and waited. I must have dozed off," I said while rubbing the sleep out of my eyes. "Did you get you some food yesterday?" I asked to change the subject.

"I didn't have time. I'll do it today," she lied.

"Yeah," was my only reply. My phone started vibrating. I looked at the caller ID. It was Monica. I decided not to answer. "I got to get outta here. I'll come by this week and check on you," I said before heading out the door.

Chapter 35

Everything had been cool since I had killed Phil. The whole thing blew over in the press, and no one in the hood seemed to care that he was dead. Somebody must've tried to rob him was the only thing I had heard. School had just started back for Monica and Li'l Bo. Surprisingly, Li'l Bo went back to school without me arguing with him about it.

Things had been good with him, but I had found a hundred thousand dollars in cash in his room in a shoebox, which confirmed for me what Phil had said about him stealing from Squeeze. I confronted him in outrage, and he assured me that he wasn't stealing from Squeeze. He said that he had been doing extra work on the side to make that money. I believed him, but I still watched him like a hawk to make sure he was safe. I would ride by the spots he trapped at all day to make sure shit was cool. I knew he had been putting in a lot of extra time so I chalked that shit up that Phil had said as hating. After all, he was probably just jealous of Li'l Bo. His ass had worked for Squeeze all that time, and he lived in a rathole. What a loser.

My classes were going good, and I was getting close to graduating. Things were looking up. Monica had still been hanging out and since school started back, she had been coming home later and later, but today, I'm letting her know that it ain't cool. But first, I needed to call Hood to see if he was still coming by tonight. He had been acting strange around me lately.

Last week he had hinted around about my money. I think he wondered how I could afford this place. I told him before I still had money my dad had left me, and he seemed to talk about the Boone Squad a lot and about some of the past shit that went down. It was like he wanted me to say something. I don't know, maybe I was just being paranoid. I just wanted to speak with him to see what's up.

"What's up, baby?" I said on the phone.

"Shit," Hood replied.

"Are you still coming through later? Or do you want me to come to your crib?"

"Ah, I'ma come by there. I got some moves to make first. I'ma hit you later when I'm done, but I gotta go." Hood hung up before I could say anything.

"Damn," I said, looking at my phone a little surprised. I threw the phone down, pissed, and then I heard Monica come through the door. It was like six p.m. She had been out of school for almost four hours. This shit was getting old.

"Yo, Monica? What the deal? Why you just gettin' home?"

"I went to the mall," she replied as she headed in the kitchen.

"Look, I know you got friends and everything, but you need to start coming home after school, all right? You can't be just gettin' out of school and coming home when you ready." I tried to stay calm, even though I was getting pissed.

"I just went to the mall, Mya." Monica looked at me like I was tripping.

"Aye, I don't care where you went. You heard me, right?"

"A'ight." Monica rolled her eyes, then grabbed a soda out of the fridge and went to her room pissed.

I didn't care. The last thing I need is her trying to do what she wants to do. I had already lost Li'l Bo to hustling. I wasn't gon' let her run wild too. Monica knows I hate to fuss at her, but if she kept this shit up, I was going to have to kick her ass. Rochelle's ringtone suddenly sang out on my phone, so I grabbed it.

"What's up?" I said as soon as I pressed TALK.

"Just got through gettin' krunk with Charlene. Listening to her complain about Pig. She talkin' about he ain't on her level and whatnot. I'm like, ho, he got you livin' like a queen. So what the hell are you talkin'?" Rochelle chattered.

"Girl, she crazy. Don't listen to her. Is she finally over you kicking her friend's ass?" I was laughing.

"She betta be. What choice did she have?" Rochelle said in her usual I-couldn't-care-less tone. "She asks why you don't call her up no more."

"Girl, please, I ain't thinkin' 'bout Charlene. She knows my number," I spat.

"That's what I was thinking. Fuck both of them," Rochelle cosigned. "Anyway, what's up wit' you? Nobody sees you since you started them classes."

"Rochelle, you crazy. It's only been about two weeks since I saw you." I laughed. "Anyway, you went out of town with Li'l Lo."

"I had fun too. While he was picking up them bricks I was lying on the beach," Rochelle bragged. "So where Hood's fine ass at?"

"Checkin' his traps. He's comin' over later."

"That's what's up." Rochelle smiled.

We sat on the phone and talked for about two hours. Somewhere during that time I must've gone to sleep because when I woke up it was morning. My cell phone was still in my hand. Monica and Li'l Bo had just yelled to me that they were leaving for school. The first thing on my mind was Hood. He told me he would call, so I immediately checked my phone, but I had no missed calls from him.

He was really acting strange. This behavior just wasn't like him. What if he knew about the robberies and just wasn't telling me? I dialed his number, and it went straight to voice mail. Fuck all this! I decided to go over to his crib. I jumped in the shower and was sliding into some Seven jeans when someone started knocking on my door.

I looked through the peephole, and there was Hood. I opened the door, pissed.

"Where the hell you been at?" I jumped in his face.

"Making moves," he said in calm but irritated voice.

"No, skip all that. Are you messing off with some slut, Hood? 'Cause if you are, tell me now," I demanded.

"Yo, what are you talkin' about? I don't have time for that shit," Hood pleaded his case.

"You know what? Just get out." I pointed to the door.

Hood grabbed me and started kissing me. I tried to resist by releasing myself from his grip, but he kept on until I gave in to his kisses that I love so much. I love him so much. Hood laid me down right there in the middle of the floor. He pulled my wife beater shirt over my head and started kissing me all the way down to my belly, then he pulled off my jeans. Once the jeans and thong panties came off, Hood's face headed south straight between my legs, where he dipped his face and didn't come up for air until my juices were all over his mouth. At that point, he slid inside me, and I brought my hips up to meet him and ride him until he released all his frustration inside me.

Panting and out of breath, I lay in Hood's arms where I feel so safe. We lay for almost an hour, and I had started to doze off.

"I had to kill two niggas last night," Hood confessed.

"Huh?" I said, coming out of my nap.

"You heard me right. Pig had to make some pickups for me a couple of weeks back. Somehow he got into a fight with Charlene and he ran a little behind so the deal didn't go through. Shit got crazy after that. Dude thought we was tryin' to set him up.

"I had to wait all this time to hear from the dude what they wanted to do after we had convinced them it was just a mistake. Me and Pig was supposed to meet with them last night. This time dude sent these young niggas who thought they would make a name for themselves by robbing us. So I smoked both of them. I dead niggas all the time, and normally, I don't think twice about it, but they were young, like Li'l Bo's age, Mya. I don't pride myself on killin' kids regardless of the situation. I may be a killer, but I ain't no monster."

"Baby, it was you or them, so you did what you had to do," I said, understanding when your back is against the wall.

"I know, but, baby, I just want you to know I done had a lot of shit on my mind the last couple of weeks waitin' on this deal. It was huge; a lot of money was ridin' on it. Then this popped off last night. I still ended up gettin' the bricks, though. When dude found out what happened, he personally came out hisself to meet with us. I'm just now gettin' this shit wrapped up this morning. That's why I didn't come or call last night. I'm sorry."

"I'm sorry, too. For not trusting you, but I'm

going to make it up to you," I said while climbing on top of Hood. I bounced down hard and rode him so good he released two times, back to back.

"I love you," are the sweetest words I heard coming from his mouth.

Chapter 36

Friday night we were all at the club kickin' it, having mad fun. Hood and his crew were popping bottles all night celebrating their success with the deal that had gone through, which had brought in some major dough. The whole crew was eating, and everybody was happy.

Even Charlene was happy, so I know Pig must have laced her pockets something fat. To Rochelle's and my surprise, she didn't have Felicia with her tonight. Instead, Nina had come out with her. The way she always has Felicia with her, I was surprised that Nina and Charlene were still best friends, and the fact that we had not seen Nina for a while made it good to see her.

All of the Boone Squad was in the club doing their thing, and I actually felt good. I had no bad nerves at all. I felt like things were coming together, even though I still wanted to fuck Squeeze up every time I saw him, and I had not ruled that

out. It would be in due time. Right now, I just
wanted the party to never stop.

"Mya, girl, you about to blind me with yo' wrist.
That ice is blingin'," Charlene complimented my
diamond-accented bracelet that Hood had surprised me with right before we came out.

"Girl, Hood just got me this. It's like ice on my
wrist," I bragged.

"All of you chicks are doing big thangs. Ballers
and shit," Nina yelled over the loud music.

"Don't worry, Nina. We gon' have to find you
one too," Rochelle said as she puffed on the blunt
Charlene had just passed her.

"Don't waste your time, Rochelle. I've been tryin'
to hook her up, but she got the Mya syndrome."
Charlene laughed. "Rochelle, you remember how
she was trippin' when Hood tried to hook up with
her?"

"She was acting crazy, but she came around."
Rochelle passed the blunt to Nina.

"I told you I'm cool. I don't need a hookup. I
like being alone. Less damn drama." Nina hit the
blunt, then passed it to me.

"Nah, I'm cool. I don't smoke," I reminded
her.

"Well, keep the rotation going." Charlene
reached across me for the blunt, and we all started
laughing.

We had a good night—no arguing, no fighting, everybody was cool. If things could be like this
all the time I would be happy as hell, but we all
know nothing ever stays the same. I had planned
on going to Hood's crib for the night, but we de-

cided to head back to my crib since it was closer, and because we were both equally wasted. For some reason, though, I had this weird feeling.

When we finally made it to my crib, it was almost four in the morning. I checked on Monica, and she was knocked out snoring like she had run a marathon. I walked a door down to Li'l Bo's room to find him not in bed. At first I thought maybe he was in the bathroom, but the door was wide open and the light was off. I headed straight back to Monica's room.

"Monica, wake up." I shook her. "Did Li'l Bo come home?"

"Huh?" Monica said, barely opening up her eyes, which irritated me.

"Did Li'l Bo come home? 'Cause he's not here."

"Oh, nope. He didn't come home, so I went to bed. I thought he would be here by now." Monica sat up on her elbows.

I headed back to the living room and grabbed my cell off the bar. Then I dialed Li'l Bo's number. It rang until the voice mail picked up.

"Yo, where the hell are you? Get your ass home," I screamed in the phone before hanging up.

"You think he's a'ight?" Monica came out of her room rubbing sleep from her eyes.

"I guess." I threw both my hands up. "But I'ma kick his butt, though, when he gets here. I'm going to bed." I headed toward my room.

"Li'l Bo didn't come home yet," I said to Hood when I got to my room, where he was lying across the bed already half asleep.

"Don't worry, baby. The trap be like that; some nights you just can't get away."

"Well, he could at least answer his phone." I bounced down on the bed while typing a text to Li'l Bo telling him to call me.

"Come here." Hood reached out for me, and I lay down in his arms. As much as I wanted not to worry, the pit of my stomach was sending me different signals. Something wasn't right. Li'l Bo had promised me he would come home every night, and so far he had. I tried to keep my eyes open, but they kept getting heavy and before I knew it, it was daylight.

I sat straight up in the bed. Hood was still asleep, and we had both slept in our clothes. I looked at my cell phone. No reply text from Li'l Bo and no missed calls. I got out of the bed and headed down the hall to his room. His bed was still empty. My heart silently skipped a beat.

"Monica," I yelled, feeling sick to my stomach.

Monica came out of her room fully dressed in a hurry. "What?" she asked with a worried look.

"He still didn't come home. Li'l Bo is still not here." I immediately dialed his number again.

"Straight to voice mail." I hung up the phone. "We're going to look for him." I headed back to my room to grab my shoes.

"Hood, wake up. Li'l Bo still ain't here. I'm going to look for him. I have a bad feeling," I said with my voice getting choked up.

"A'ight. I'ma go wit' you. I'ma call my crew and get them lookin'."

"Yeah, I'll call Rochelle and Charlene," I said while dialing my cell phone.

We hopped in Hood's white Escalade and headed straight to the Brewster. When we got there, it was like a normal day in the hood. People were hanging out already. We rode by all Li'l Bo's trap spots without sight of him. I rode up on Rochelle and Charlene scanning the blocks looking for Li'l Bo. Hood's crew was looking for him, and so far, nobody had seen him.

I was running out of ideas. I started dialing on my cell phone again. "Yo, Squeeze, have you seen Li'l Bo?" I asked in a hurried tone.

"Who da fuck is this?" Squeeze caught an attitude.

"Mya, his sister." I got mad. "Have you seen him?"

"Aye, what's up, li'l momma?"

"Squeeze, this ain't no social call. Have you seen Li'l Bo or not?"

"Nah, I ain't seen my man. Why? What's the problem?"

"There ain't no problem besides he didn't come home. If you see him, have him call me."

"No doubt. You still—"

I hung up before he could finish. I hated his snake ass.

Hood and Monica were just staring at me. "Says he hasn't seen him, but I don't believe that nigga," I spat. "Where is he at, Hood?" Tears started to roll down my face.

"Look, let's go back to the crib. Maybe he's there now," Hood suggested, not answering my question.

I dialed Li'l Bo's phone all the way back to my crib, and it kept going to voice mail. My hands and legs started to tremble. Something was wrong and, just like I thought when we got back home, there was no sign of Li'l Bo.

At that point Monica and I really started freaking out, but I chilled so I could be strong for her. *KNOCK, KNOCK, KNOCK.*

We all looked at one another because what if it was the cops with bad news? Hood walked over to open the door. It was Rochelle, Charlene, and niggas from the Height Squad.

"Everybody we talked to, even them niggas he trap with, say they ain't seen him," Rochelle said with tears rolling down her face.

"But he'll come home. He might just be out with some chick. He is at that age," Charlene threw in and shrugged her shoulders.

"I hope so," I said, shaking my head back and forth.

Hood was talking with his crew, then he headed back over to me.

"I'ma go back out, talk to his trap partners myself. They got respect for me."

"A'ight." I gave him a hug.

To try to get my mind off Li'l Bo, Charlene and Rochelle started talking about the club the night before to get me laughing. Charlene made some sandwiches so we ate that and drank some wine. Monica went to her room for a nap. The wine gave us all a buzz because before we knew it, we all had dozed off. I woke up to banging on the door.

I looked out the peephole. It was Hood. After all this time we had been dating he still wouldn't use his key. I used my key to his crib all the time when I went over to visit him, but he never used his key over here. When I opened the door Hood had a strange look on his face.

"They found him," he said in a muffled voice.

I was confused. "They? Who found him? What do you mean found him? Where is he? Did you tell him to bring his ass home? Did you tell him I'm pissed?" Tears started rolling down my face.

Tears started progressing down Hood's face too.

"NO, HOOD!" I yelled. "NO, NO!" I started pounding on his chest.

Monica ran out of her room crying. "OH, GOD, NO! WHERE'S MY BROTHER AT, MYA? NO!" Monica fell to the floor crying. "LI'L BO, AWWW!" Monica continued to scream. I rushed over to her, and we held each other and cried.

Rochelle and Charlene were trying to comfort us while Hood was trying to get us off the floor. My worst fears had come to pass.

Chapter 37

Li'l Bo had been found behind one of the buildings he trapped in front of over in the Brewster-Douglass Projects. He had been shot five times, and no one heard anything. Because that's the way it goes in the hood. Closed mouths. All we knew was that all his money and dope was gone. They had even taken his shoes. According to homicide, it was a robbery gone bad, but the truth was he was just another young black dope boy that they didn't give a fuck about.

Today was the day of the service. I had made all the plans by myself because my momma was nowhere in sight. I hadn't seen her, but I knew she knew about it. Avoiding real-life issues was one of her natural talents. Monica and I had been up to prison to tell my dad, but he already knew when we got there. They had to put him on lockdown because he had lost it. The warden wouldn't even allow him to come to the funeral. My dad had threatened to kill all of them, the guards and war-

den included. The pain was even deeper for me
and Monica. No comfort from our mother or father, but we got dressed and prepared to go see
our only brother for the last time.

Hood had barely left my side since everything
happened. Squeeze had offered to pay for everything, but I refused to let that nigga pay for anything that had to do with my brother. As far as I
was concerned, it was his fault for letting Li'l Bo
work for him.

When we made it to the service, there was our
mother dressed up, looking the part of a mother
mourning her only son. Her face looked terrible;
her eyes looked like they were swollen shut from
all the crying she had been doing, but I couldn't
make myself go to her. Deep down inside I was
angry with her, and to my surprise, Monica didn't
leave my side either. She stayed close to me.

After the services, we had rented a hall for the
people to eat, but Monica and I chose to go home
instead. Hood came home with us, and Rochelle
and Li'l Lo came over. We hung out and got
fucked up.

Two weeks had gone by since the funeral.
Monica and I tried to get back on schedule, even
though we both needed a boost. We were sitting
around doing laundry when our mom all of a sudden showed up. Monica let her in.

"Hey, Mom." Monica gave her a big hug.

I didn't say anything. I just continued to fold
clothes.

"Hey, Mya," she spoke.

"Hey," I said, tight-lipped.

"How are y'all getting along?"

I didn't answer so Monica started talking. "We're doing okay. I went back to school trying to keep busy, and Mya went back to work. So we're doing all right," she lied.

"That's, that's good," Mom replied as she cleared her throat with a gurgling sound. "I been missin' y'all a lot."

None of us said anything for a moment. It was quiet. I tried to remain cool because the pure sight of her made me so damn angry.

"I've been thinkin' about getting clean."

After that I couldn't take any more of her babble bullshit.

"You been thinkin' about getting clean?" I mocked her. "You been thinkin' about getting clean?" I repeated. "Well, God bless America! Your fifteen-year-old son is dead, lying in his grave, and you thinkin' . . . about gettin' clean. You are *so* pathetic." I got off the couch and lunged at my mother fist first. Monica grabbed me and held me back.

"All you have done is ruin our lives. Li'l Bo wouldn't be dead if you had been a real mother to us. That's right, he's dead because of you." I pointed at her with a flood of hot tears pouring down my face.

"Because you would rather suck on a glass dick than be there for your kids, all because a man got locked up. Please, get over it. Men go away all the time," I screamed at the top of my lungs. "You know what? I hate you. I hate you. I *hate* you," I screamed from my shattered soul. "Now I want you to get out of my house and never come back. Stay away from me and Monica. We no longer have a mother," I said, huffing in short hurried breaths with my fist still balled.

My mother stood looking defeated, tears progressing down her face. She turned and walked slowly toward the door. "I love you, Mya." She turned around to face us again with her hand on the doorknob. "No matter how much you hate me, I love you and Monica. I'ma do what's right because it ain't too late." She turned and walked out the door.

"YEAH, WHATEVER!" I screamed at the closed door.

Chapter 38

*"**B**itch, I told you not to play wit' me."* Squeeze had his *sweaty hands over my mouth while I twisted and turned trying to break free. I needed air. I was suffocating. My hands were tied behind my back, and my feet were strapped to a chair. I was pleading with my eyes for him to let me come up for air, but he just made his grip tighter over my mouth.*

"I'ma kill you, motherfucka, if you don't let my sister go," I could hear Li'l Bo yelling, but his face was *nowhere in sight. As Squeeze's grip got tighter my breathing came less, and Li'l Bo's voice started to fade. I was dying.*

"Li'l Bo!" I screamed and sat straight up in bed.

"Mya, it's only a dream." Hood tried to comfort me.

I looked around the room and noticed I was at home in bed. Hood was right there with me. I had been dreaming again. I had been having these dreams for about a week, and each time I woke up with a racing heart, drenched in my own sweat.

"Whew," I said, panting, "I had another dream that I saw Li'l Bo."

"It's all right. That's normal." Hood wiped my forehead with his hand.

"Baby, can you get me some water?" I asked him. "My throat is dry."

"Whatever you need." Hood got out of the bed and headed straight for the kitchen. He came back with Dasani water. I drank long and hard since I was so thirsty. I tried to relax for a while, then lay back down to sleep. No sooner than Hood's head hit the pillow he was off to sleep again. While my mind felt exhausted, I couldn't go back to sleep so easily. For some reason, I felt like Li'l Bo was trying to tell me something, and the more I thought about that, I wondered about Squeeze. He had been so willing to help out when Li'l Bo died, but I'd never forgotten what Phil's snitch ass had said about Squeeze.

Phil had told me that Squeeze thought Li'l Bo was stealing from him. Li'l Bo had me convinced that everything was legit, and that he was making that money for putting in extra work, so I stopped tripping. Now I kept having all these dreams about Squeeze trying to kill me. What if that nigga had Li'l Bo killed? Or what if he knew what happened to Li'l Bo?

I needed to find out what his grimy ass was up to.

<hr />

The next day when I finally got rid of Hood, I rolled over to the Brewster to see what was up in the projects. Maybe I could get a peek at Squeeze, you know, see what his ass was getting into. Normally his nasty ass would be hanging out trying to pull with some young tramp, but today, I rolled up on him and he was checking with his young crews making sure they didn't forget he would pop a cap in their ass.

I had been watching him for about two hours, and it started getting dark, then he got a call on his cell so he walked off from the crowd. He was all smiles, showing off that nasty-ass gold in his mouth, so I figured he was either on the phone with a bitch or talking about money. Either way, when he jumped in his money-green Bentley, I was right on his trail. I had to see what this nigga was up to. If he had anything to do with my brother getting killed, it was lights out for him. No questions asked.

I had been following Squeeze for about an hour all the way on the other side of Detroit when finally he pulled into the Marriott Hotel. What was he doing here? This nigga had a mansion out in the hills with the white folks, or so I had heard. Why would he need to meet a bitch at a hotel? Unless he was on some business, but usually coke deals didn't go down at the Marriott, not with niggas like Squeeze. Either way, I had to know what was up so I was going to hang around.

Riding around the parking lot, Squeeze finally pulled inside a spot next to a car that looked just like Charlene's candy-apple-red Benz. That was confirmed when I saw the plates, QUEEN B. Oh snap! Why would Squeeze be parking next to Charlene's car at the Marriott? This had to be a coincidence.

Squeeze jumped up out of the Bentley and disappeared into the hotel.

I know Charlene's ass couldn't be sleeping around with Squeeze because if she was, Pig was going to kill that bitch. Then there was going to be a war between crews. But I could just be jumping to conclusions because I hadn't seen them together.

I didn't have to wait long for my answer. I saw Squeeze pimping out of the hotel, and he headed straight to Charlene's Benz. When he reached the Benz, he grabbed Felicia by both her ass cheeks and tongued her down. Felicia popped the alarm on Charlene's Benz, jumped in, and balled out. Not before I saw Squeeze go into his pocket and hand her a wad of stacks.

I had to duck down 'cause Felicia blew right past me. Soon, my heart slowed back to normal. I thought Charlene had fucked up, and Felicia was a ho just like I thought. I knew Charlene knew what that bitch was up to, but if Pig finds out Felicia was using the Benz he bought Charlene to go meet Squeeze in, he was going to fuck Charlene's ass up anyway.

Squeeze finally jumped back in his Bentley. I thought about following his ass some more, but after that shake-up, I took my ass to Hood's crib 'cause he was waiting on me.

Chapter 39

It had been two days since I had followed Squeeze, and to be honest, I couldn't get that picture with him and Felicia out of my mind. At this point, I didn't know what to think. I wanted to talk to Rochelle about it, but she had been MIA for a minute. I didn't want to mention it to Hood because I know he wouldn't like the idea of me following Squeeze and putting myself in harm's way. So for now, this information was just stuck in my head. I couldn't help but think Felicia was a ho just like we thought she was. That bitch would sleep with anybody for some money. Either way, I didn't see any suspicious acts from Squeeze regarding Li'l Bo, but I would be watching his ass.

I had to get this situation off my mind. It was time to get out of this bed and kick today off instead of lying here thinking about this bullshit. I was supposed to have class today, but the shop was closed for some electrical repairs. Rochelle and I decided to grab lunch and do some shopping. We were finally gonna hook up today, but I thought I'd leave the bit about Felicia out of the conversation. I didn't want to piss her off talking about Felicia. Because right now, she still got heat for her.

"Baby, you up?" I started rubbing Hood's back.

"Yep," Hood said in a stifled tone.

"You want some breakfast? I could whip some up real fast."

"Nah, I'm cool." Hood turned over and gave me a kiss on the cheek. "I got to meet with Pig this morning; we got a run to make. I'ma grab something on the way. Matter fact, I need to jump in the shower so I can head out. What you got planned today?" he asked, getting out of the bed, headed for the shower.

"Just lunch and some sho—" I got cut off by Hood's phone when it started to vibrate.

Hood reached down and picked up the phone off the nightstand. "What's good?" Hood spoke into the phone. "Yo, what's yo' point, nigga? A'ight, I'm on my way." Hood hung up the phone and reached for the clothes he had on yesterday.

"I thought you were going to get in the shower?"

"Yeah, I know. Look, baby, I gotta go. I'ma holla at you later." Hood got dressed so fast my head was spinning.

"Is everything okay?" I asked, a little worried. It wasn't like Hood to put back on the same clothes he had worn the day before and leave without taking a shower.

"Oh, hell, yeah." He smiled. "Just gotta leave now. Got some shit to handle ASAP, but I'll call you." He gave me a quick kiss and was gone.

I wondered for a moment what that was all about, but I chalked it up it to Height Squad business. I grabbed my robe and headed down the hallway to make sure Monica was up for school.

The closer I got to the bathroom in the hallway, I thought I heard gagging.

"Monica?" I knocked on the door. "You okay?"

"Yeah," she hastily replied.

"Okay." I started to walk away again, and this time I heard it loud and clear. Monica was in the bathroom throwing up. I tried to open the bathroom door, but she had locked it.

"Monica, unlock this door," I demanded.

"A'ight. I'm comin' out," Monica said in voice that sounded less than okay. When she opened up the door, her face looked terrible. She looked like she had been throwing up all night. Her face was pale, and her eyes were big and bulging. She clearly needed a doctor.

"What's wrong?" I asked her. "What did you eat last night?" I continued to inquire. Monica dropped her head like she didn't want to talk to me. "Monica, what's going on? Why didn't you wake me up and tell me you were sick?"

Still no words from Monica. The more I looked at her, the more she seemed different. Something had changed.

"Get dressed. You're going to the doctor," I said.

"I don't need to go to no doctor, Mya. I'm fine." Monica tried to regain her normal voice, but she was outvoted by her stomach. She turned and made a quick dash for the toilet, where she hurled again.

By the time we made it to the doctor's office, Monica was exhausted from puking. Once we made it to the examining room, the doctor ran some blood tests on her and within an hour he came back with the results. Monica was pregnant.

"Pregnant! What does that mean?" I shouted at the doctor.

"It means that in nine months she is going to have a baby," he answered in a sarcastic but polite tone.

"Moni . . ." My chest started to rise and fall quickly. I thought I was going to suffocate. I couldn't breathe. The doctor rushed over to me and grabbed my arm.

"Just breathe. Take deep, slow breaths. You're having a panic attack."

Finally my breathing returned to normal.

"Mya, I'm sorry." Tears were pouring down Monica's cheeks.

"How? Who?" I tried to ask but a full question would not come.

"Look, you two go home and discuss this. Monica, I need to see you at least once a month, but because of your age, I would like to see you more often. Stop at the desk and make your next appointment."

On the way home the words still did not come. I was so upset I thought it was best that I didn't say anything.

When I pulled up, I noticed Hood had already returned. I thought he would be gone most of the day. I immediately wondered if he had finally used his key. Maybe him being there was a good idea to keep me from killing Monica.

When I opened the door to the apartment, I noticed Hood sitting on the couch with his head buried in his hands.

"Hood," I said, instantly knowing something was wrong. I walked over closer with Monica on my heels. "Hood, baby," I said again as I got down on my knees in front of him. "What's wrong?" I pulled both of his hands from his face. His face was wet from tears. "What happened, baby?"

"They done shot my nigga."

"Who? Pig?" My heart dropped. "Is he all right?" I asked. Hood didn't say anything. He just gave me a look that told me everything I needed to know. "Why? What happened?"

"I don't know. I got a call from one of my trap boys this morning saying Pig didn't meet him at four this morning and wouldn't answer his cell. So I went over to Pig's crib 'cause that nigga always answers his cell. That's where I found him, still in his car with a bullet to the head, two to the chest."

"What?" I said, still in shock. "Baby, I am so sorry." I hugged him tight. "I know Charlene's fucked up right now. Maybe I should call her." I stood up.

"Charlene, man, that bitch was nowhere to be found. I tried to call her and got no answer."

"What?" I said again, still shocked. "You think she's all right?" I began to get worried about her.

"Yeah, she's all right, but she gotta answer to me, and if she had anything to do with what happened to Pig, she's DEAD!" Hood said with certainty.

"She wouldn't have anything to do wit' that," I tried to defend Charlene. "Hood, I been knowing Charlene since I was in grade school. She may be conceited, but I don't think—"

"You don't think?" Hood gave me a look that was full of anger and hurt. "Look, Mya, somebody gotta answer for this shit. The Brewster is about to be a war zone until somebody tells me what happened to Pig. Whoever I think's guilty is a dead motherfucker walkin'." Hood stood up pounding his chest while he was talking, but more tears started pouring down his face.

Immediately, Hood bounced back down on the couch, and I followed suit in his arms trying to comfort and console my man. Monica just stood there in disbelief.

"I am sorry about your friend, Hood," she said before strolling off to her room. She had her own problems weighing on her shoulders.

There was just too much going on. Monica and I were still trying to get over the death of our own brother, and now she was pregnant. On top of all that, Pig was killed. Everything was just getting crazy instead of better. With all this heavy stuff on my mind, before I knew it, Hood had fallen asleep and I did too, but when I opened my eyes after a nice long nap, he was gone. I tried calling him but got no answer. The only thing I could do was lie back down on the couch and pray that he came back to me. Alive.

Chapter 40

Two days had gone by and I still had not heard shit from Hood. I stopped calling him yesterday. I had come to the conclusion that when he was ready to talk he would call me. I didn't even bother going to his crib, even though I had two keys and all the codes to his alarm systems. I knew he wasn't home. I had left him messages letting him know that I loved him.

I didn't leave the house for anything. In fact, the only time I had been out of bed was to shower and cook for Monica. Since she was pregnant, I made sure she had breakfast before school, and I cooked dinner for her. I had called Pepper and told her I wouldn't be coming into work or class this week. I just had too much on my mind.

I decided to call Rochelle to see if she had seen Hood. We had only talked briefly the day Hood had disappeared on me. According to her, Li'l Lo was tripping on killing niggas ASAP. I knew her hands were tied too.

"What's up?" I said into the phone when Rochelle answered.

"Nothing. Just layin' up watching TV. Li'l Lo gone, and Tiny over at Wynita's house."

"So how you like playin' wifey since y'all moved up in Li'l Lo's crib?"

"It's cool. Ain't got Wynita yellin' at me all day, but I miss that sometimes." Rochelle laughed.

"I know, right?" I laughed at the thought of Wynita giving Rochelle the business.

"So what's up wit' Hood? He still MIA along with my man?" Rochelle asked.

"Hell, yeah. Li'l Lo been home?"

"Nope. You know Hood got all them niggas combin' the block. Until they get some info he ain't gon' let them outta his sight," Rochelle said matter-of-factly.

"That shit's crazy," I mouthed with irritation.

"Well, anyway, I'm sick of sittin' up in here. I'm 'bout to roll over to yo' crib. Tiny gon' be at Wynita's all week. Ain't no tellin' when Li'l Lo comin' home. I'm lonely."

"A'ight, then, bet. I'll see you in a bit." I ended the call and headed to the shower to throw on some decent clothes because I looked a mess.

Rochelle was knocking on my door in no time.

"What's up?" I hugged Rochelle when she came inside the door. I didn't realize how much I missed being around her until she walked in my house. We hadn't been spending much time together since our lives had changed.

"Girl, you look like you got shit on yo' mind," Rochelle said with a hint of concern.

"Rochelle, what don't I have on my mind? I

think I just miss my dad so much," I said, as tears started running down my face. Rochelle reached back over and hugged me again.

"Talk to me, Mya. What's up? I know I haven't been there for you like I should, but I'm always a phone call away," Rochelle said as tears started rolling down her cheeks.

"I know. I'm cool. Damn, girl," I said, sniffling while wiping my tears. "I didn't mean to make you cry." I started laughing, and Rochelle started laughing too.

"Come on over here and sit down. I need to tell you something." Rochelle and I both bounced down on one of my living-room sofas.

"Go head. Spit it out," Rochelle rushed me.

"Monica's pregnant."

"She's *what?*" Rochelle said in almost a whisper.

"Yep. I found out the same day that Pig was found dead. I had taken her to the doctor that morning because she had been sick."

"By who?" Rochelle asked.

"Don't know." I hunched my shoulders. "We haven't talked about it much, and when I asked her she wouldn't tell me. I didn't want to pressure her because the whole thing makes me want to choke her to death."

"Damn," Rochelle said, shaking her head back and forth. "Have you told your mom?"

"Not yet, but I will. Better yet, I'm going to make Monica tell her," I said in a disappointed tone. "I still don't have nothing to say to my mom. I just can't believe that I have been around here tryin' to make life better for us, and she messes up like this. Rochelle, I didn't even know she was interested in boys yet. I mean, damn . . . am I that blind? I was supposed to be takin' care of both Monica and Li'l Bo, but maybe I just messed up both of their lives." My voice got choked up.

"Mya, don't say that because you know it ain't true. Stuff happens. You can't blame yourself. All you can do now is love Monica and help her get through this and make sure that she continues with her education."

"How can I do that when I don't even know what to say to her? I can't find the words, because I'm so full of anger."

"Don't worry, you will," Rochelle assured me.

"Enough about me." I repositioned myself on the couch. "Have you heard anything from Charlene yet?" I started wiping my face.

"Hell, no. I don't know what's up with that chick. I've been callin' her, and she won't answer my calls. I called her mom's crib yesterday, and they say she ain't there."

"That's weird. Maybe she's dealing with Pig's family tryin' to get him buried or something."

"Or maybe she's somewhere distraught. I don't know. All I know is I ain't heard from her. She better come correct 'cause Li'l Lo talkin' about blasting her ass if she don't talk. He thinks she knows what happened. At least who shot him, but I don't know." Rochelle looked defeated.

"Hood's pissed at her too," I validated. "And I don't know if this means anything but I saw Felicia meeting up with Squeeze at the Marriott. The strange part is she was driving Charlene's car."

"What? Why you withholding information like

that from me?" Rochelle was hyped, on the edge of her seat.

"Look, I didn't know if you were ready to be talkin' about Felicia yet. Since you still got heat for her and shit. I'm sure this doesn't have shit to do wit' anythin'. It just proves that Charlene's losin' her motherfucking mind."

"I know. That bitch silly, lettin' that ho drive her whip. But fuck that, Charlene ain't crazy enough to do no stupid shit like puttin' Pig in harm's way."

"I agree witcha on that."

"I tried to tell Li'l Lo Charlene's tryin' to clear her head up right now because as far as I know she loved Pig. She may be greedy, but she was feelin' him."

"That's what I told Hood."

"If anything, she's scared that whoever murked Pig lookin' for her too." Rochelle sounded convinced.

"Maybe," I said, before we were interrupted by a knock on the door.

I looked out the peephole to see Hood standing in the hallway. "Baby!" I hugged Hood when I opened the door. He hugged me and held on tight. In fact, he was pulling me so close our pelvises were linking.

"You a'ight?" he asked.

"Yeah, at least now that I see you." I grinned.

"What's up, Hood?" Rochelle said, getting up off the couch.

"What's up, Rochelle?" Hood replied back.

"Where Li'l Lo at?" she asked.

"He should be at the crib by now. That's where

he was headed when I left him about half an hour ago."

"His ass bet—" Rochelle was cut off by her ringing phone.

"Hello. A'ight, baby, I'm on my way," Rochelle said with a huge grin on her face as she ended the call.

"I would stay and chat, but I gotta go." Rochelle headed straight for the door without turning around.

"I'll call you later," I yelled after her.

Hood headed over to the couch. I followed him, hot on his heels. I was following so close I almost stepped on the back of his red and black Jordans.

"So what's been up?" I said as soon as we sat down facing each other.

"Been out puttin' gats to niggas' heads, trying to find out what the streets is sayin'. Got all my people workin'. Last couple of days I been over at Pig's momma's crib, helping her with shit to bury him. We got all that arranged now. Basically, I just been tryin' to be there for her, you know? I'm like her son."

"That's nice of you, baby. You know, being there for her and all," I said sincerely, knowing exactly what she was going through. I was and still am sick from Li'l Bo's sudden death. Every day I wonder if I would ever truly get over it.

"He would do the same for me," Hood assured me. We sat in silence for a couple of minutes.

"Did I ever tell you how I got my name?" Hood said with a chuckle, but hurt was written all over his face.

"No."

"Ever since I was a little man, I been running my block. My momma was a dope fiend. I mean, ever since I was four that's how I remember her. This dope pusher who went by the name of Monster was her pusher and pimp. So every Saturday night, here comes Monster banging on our door looking for moms." Hood stopped talkin' for a minute with a killer look in his eyes. "Every Saturday night here comes Monster. That nigga would beat my momma all the way out of the house to the block and make her work the corner, and she would fight him every step of the way because even though she was a fiend, she hated selling her body. By the time I was seven, I had grown a hate so bad for him until it cut my breath off to look at him. One day I decided I had had enough. I was gon' dead that nigga, and it wasn't gon' be no secret. I wanted everybody to know I took his life. Me, a little nigga. So the next Saturday when he came up the block, I was there waitin' on him before he reached my building. The block was hot, and everybody was out. I stepped to him and without saying so much as spit, I pulled the trigger and hit him right in the heart. Monster dropped to his knees lookin' me dead in the eye, and that's when I put one between his eyes. That was the end of that nigga. When cops showed up, no one had heard or seen shit, and I had earned my respect. From that day forward, niggas off the block called me Hood." Hood finished with a distant look in his eyes.

"So is that why you say Arizona is good for your moms?" I asked.

"Yeah, she got clean after that situation, though. Not long after that I started working the block stacking dough. I bought that house and moved us out of the projects. Right after that, she decided she wanted to move to Arizona to be close to her sister. She loves it out there. I think it's good for her. I bought her a store because she loves clothes and design."

"Wow, she owns a store? That's a big transition," I said, thinking about my messed-up life. "Monica's pregnant," I blurted out.

"Ah, damn," was Hood's shocked reply.

"Yep. You know, Hood . . . it seems like my family has not been functional since my dad got locked up. I have a mom and a dad, yet still I feel all alone in this world. Most times I feel like they're both dead. You are so lucky to have your mom back."

"Mya, you don't have to feel alone. You have me, and even though things are fucked up for me right now, I'm still here for you and Monica. She's like my li'l sister. I was an only child, so I know what lonely feels like. When I met Pig, we instantly became brothers . . . blood brothers. Now I got to learn to live without him. Right now, I don't see how that's possible because inside, I just want to go and murk any and everyone I think may be responsible." Hood's jaw was so tight I could almost hear his teeth clicking. "Maybe Monica having this baby is a gift from God to your family," he said, his voice full of grief.

"I guess I never thought of it that way. I wish my mom was around to help us. You know, tell us what to do." I shrugged my shoulders. Hood had made a point.

"Speaking of your mom, I saw her yesterday when I was in the Brewster. She was carryin' bags of groceries."

"My mother carryin' groceries? Hood, my mother don't buy food. Crack is her only meal, and it's been that way since my dad got locked up," I said sarcastically as I got up off the couch.

"I think you should go visit her."

I changed the subject. "I think we should get something to eat."

Go visit my mother? I didn't know what was on Hood's mind. I was still pissed at her. I still blamed her for what happened to Li'l Bo because she hadn't put us first in her life. She was selfish. But I was curious about her carrying groceries. I wonder what was really in her fucking shopping bags. I just hoped it wasn't crack she had stolen from somebody. I couldn't take somebody else close to me getting killed.

Chapter 41

I had been tossing and turning all night long. Different scenes kept running through my mind. I kept dreaming Rochelle was running through the Brewster naked, yelling for Tiny. I felt weird in my dream. I woke up twice and got some water. I didn't know why I was having a bad dream about Rochelle, but I figured it was because I ate so much before going to bed. After talking with Hood yesterday, Monica had come home and he took us out to eat. We ate so much I thought I would bust, and after we got home, I called Rochelle like I told her I would. So maybe that's why I was dreaming about her since I talked to her right before I dozed off to sleep on a full stomach. I was just falling back to sleep, but now my phone started ringing. I instantly reached over and grabbed it since it was Rochelle's ringtone, but it was only four o'clock in the morning.

"Ahh, ahh! Help me, Mya! Please, help! Ahh!"

"Rochelle . . . Rochelle!" I yelled back into the

phone. Hood jumped up and grabbed the phone out of my hand.

"Rochelle, put Li'l Lo on the phone!" Hood yelled into the phone. "Shit! It went dead! Let's go!" Hood jumped up out of bed and we shot out the door with Monica in tow asking what happened.

Hood drove over a hundred all the way to Li'l Lo's crib. When we pulled up, we saw lights flashing from about ten cop cars and two ambulances. We jumped out of the truck and headed toward the front of the crowd trying to get through.

"Step back. You have to step back." Some black cop tried to stop us, but Hood pushed him out of the way. Then the cop came back with more force.

"Man, get the hell outta my way!" Hood pushed the cop on the ground, then five other policemen rushed him.

"We have to get up there!" I yelled with tears streaming down my face. "That's our family."

"Man, you have to stay back. There's been a murder up there," a light-skinned cop spoke in a more soothing tone.

"No, no, no!!" I fell to the ground and started yelling for Rochelle. That's when I saw them bring a stretcher out covered up. I tried to run to it, but the light-skinned cop blocked me. Hood was on the ground, several men trying to contain him.

"Mya!" I heard Rochelle yell my name as she ran toward me.

"Oh my God! Are you okay?" I cried and hugged her at the same time. Quickly I stepped back a little to give her a once-over glance. She was covered in blood, but she appeared to be fine. So whose blood was she covered in? I didn't have to wait long for my answer.

"It's Li'l Lo! He's dead!" Rochelle started screaming again. By now, the cops had let Hood go and he came over.

"Rochelle, what happened?" Hood tried to sound calm as he looked at all the blood Rochelle was covered in.

"I do . . . I don't know. We were lying in bed asleep. Next thing I know, two armed guys in masks were standing over us. Before Li'l Lo could move, they shot him like six times, maybe even more. They just kept firing at him. Then they ran out." Rochelle started crying again and shaking uncontrollably.

"*That's it?*" Hood looked like he was off in a distant land. "They just shot him and left? You know what? Fuck this. I'm out!" Hood yelled, and with that, he jumped in the truck and balled out. I stayed with Rochelle. She had to tell the cops what happened. Then Ms. Wynita pulled up. I started to get nervous. Shit was completely out of control; anybody could be next.

Chapter 42

It had been two weeks since we buried Pig and Li'l Lo, and nothing was back to normal. Charlene had finally resurfaced at Pig's funeral, talking about she didn't know what happened. I believed her because she was busted up, looking like she had been crying for months. At that point she just didn't know what she was going to do. She claims someone had been following her. That's why she hid out.

Hood hadn't talked about the murders since the funeral. A couple of people had been killed in the Brewster. Word in the streets was that Hood had killed them for not telling what they knew. Hood didn't talk to me about what he did with his beloved nine-millimeter, so I didn't bring it up.

Rochelle had been staying back in the Brewster with Ms. Wynita. She had been holing up in the apartment just about every day. I had gone by yesterday to hang out with her and do her hair, just to make her feel good. While I was over there

I had the feeling I should go visit my mom, but I decided to wait until today so I could take Monica along with me, because she needed to let Mom know that she was going to have a baby.

Standing outside of her apartment brought back memories of all the hurt and disappointment. I almost grabbed Monica by the hand and ran for the exit because what if we knocked on the door and she was not home? It would bring back too many old, hurtful memories for sure of our mother never being home. I didn't want to get Monica's hopes up because more than likely Mom was out copping some dope. Before I could act on what I was contemplating, Monica knocked on the door and, to my surprise, it immediately swung open.

"Hey," Momma said with a huge smile on her face. Monica and I both paused for a minute. We had to because this well put-together lady was not the Marisa we knew. At least not for a long time. This was the Marisa that we knew when Lester was around. One thing I knew for sure. There was only one way she could look like this and that was if she was clean. Hood knew. That's why he told me to go visit her. Why didn't he just tell me?

Tears started to pour down Monica's face. She reached out and hugged Momma so tight that Momma stumbled back a bit.

"Momma . . . you look so good. Wow," Monica said, shocked. She stepped back and did another all-over glance. "You really . . . look good."

"Thanks, baby. Are you going to come in, Mya?" she asked me before I allowed my feet to step one in front of the other. Inside the apartment everything looked clean and cared for. Compared to when we left this apartment, it had been receiving some true love. Some of our baby pictures were hanging on the wall that I hadn't seen in years.

"Place looks nice," I said in a calm voice.

"You like it? I have been trying to make this place feel like home again. I think I missed that feeling." She looked at Monica, then me, and gave us a grin.

"Hmm," was my only reply.

"So what brings you two by? I been hoping to see you. I just didn't know when would be a good time for me to stop by your place," she said, and then got quiet for about thirty seconds. "You guys hungry? I just made a meat loaf, and it's way too much for me to eat alone."

"Uh, no. We just came by for a minute. Monica needs to talk to you about something." Feeling a little nervous, I squeezed both of my hands in the tight pockets of my Dereon skinny jeans.

"Yeah, about that . . ." Monica was also nervous.

"Monica?" she inquired after Monica didn't say anything else.

"I, uhh . . . well, I just wanted to tell you that I'm going to be having a baby. A—" Monica was abruptly cut off.

"Ohhh . . . Monica, I'm sooo sorry, baby, I haven't been there for you. This is my fault."

"It's okay. It's not your fault. I did this." Monica started to cry. Momma came over and hugged her.

"You can count on me now. You can both count on me. I'm going to be there for you, I promise. I'm clean, and that's the way I'm going to stay. I ain't gon' lose no more of my kids to crack. I love you too much for that." She started crying, then I started crying. All the overwhelming crying sent all of us into one big family hug. For the first time in a long time, we were a family again. And I knew I needed my momma as much as she needed me.

Chapter 43

Hood had disappeared. I had not heard shit from him. I went by the crib a couple of times, but there was no sign that he had even been staying there. He had a Mexican lady that would come in and clean up twice a week. I spoke with her, and she hadn't even seen him, so I didn't know where he was. I thought maybe he had gone to visit his mom in Arizona, but deep down, I knew he was trying to find out who exactly had Pig and Li'l Lo killed. Hood was taking Pig's death really hard. They were like brothers, and he had to avenge his murder and their coconspirator, if there was one. I just wished he would at least call so I would know how things were going. I needed to know that he was okay.

I had been trying to focus on my graduation that was coming up. I had finally finished all my classes and completed all the hours I needed for my beautician's license. Things were still crazy, but I was moving on. Monica and Momma called themselves in the kitchen making quesadillas while I sat on this damn couch and racked my brain over the well-being of my man. I knew that if anything happened to him then I would be next to go on a killing spree. I had to find out where Hood was.

KNOCK, KNOCK, KNOCK.

Maybe that's him. I jumped off the couch and ran to the door.

"Dang, Mya, slow down." Monica smiled. She had been on cloud nine since we had Momma back in our lives.

I opened the door to find Rochelle standing in the hallway.

"I need to talk to you." Rochelle rushed past me.

"Hey, Rochelle," Momma said.

"Hey, Mrs. Marisa," Rochelle spoke back. I always thought it was weird how everyone in the hood called each other's parents by their first name with Mrs. in the front. "What's up, Monica?" Rochelle said in a rush.

"What's going on?" I asked, while walking on Rochelle's heels, knowing she had something important to tell. She looked at Monica and Momma, then back to me, like she needed to get an okay in order to proceed.

"It's okay. What's up?" I assured her.

"Have you talked to Hood today?"

"Rochelle, I still haven't talked to Hood, just like we discussed yesterday. What's going on? If you know something, spit it out." I got agitated.

"The streets are talkin' mad shit."

"What are they saying? Spit it out!"

"Luscious from the Boone Squad is dead."

Monica bent over and held her mouth like she had to throw up.

"Monica, you okay?" Mom asked, concerned. Monica slowly nodded her head.

I looked back at Rochelle. "What does this have to do with Hood?" I could feel a headache coming on.

"Word on the streets is, Hood popped him late last night because apparently he killed Pig and sent somebody to kill Hood, but they killed Li'l Lo by mistake."

"What? WHAT?" I yelled.

"Anyway, Hood killed Luscious late last night."

"No, no." Monica's muffled sounds finally turned to full-blown crying. This time I rushed over to Monica, who had dropped to the floor. Clearly she was upset or in pain.

"Monica, why are you crying? Are you in pain?" I asked, worried.

"Why did he have to kill him?" Monica cried.

"Who? What are you talking about?" I was confused.

"Luscious. Why did Hood have to kill him? I'm going to need him. He is my baby's daddy, Mya."

"Monica!" I hauled off and slapped the shit out of her. Momma and Rochelle both grabbed me.

"Why would you do that, Monica? Huh?! Ain't that crew taken enough from us? Maybe even our own brother?" I cried my eyes out.

"He wouldn't do that!" Monica tried to defend Luscious.

"Yeah, and how do you know that?" I asked as I yanked myself free from Rochelle's and my momma's grasps. "Let me go," I said, as they released their grip on me. I headed to my room in total shock. *This craziness would never end* was my only thought.

Chapter 44

After Monica dropped that bomb on me, I went to my room and got dressed. I left the house in a hurry. I needed to go by 4EverStylz and just relax. I thought maybe Pepper could use me to wash some heads, but when I got there, she wasn't even in. So I just sat in Pepper's area trying to get my thoughts together. I guess I dozed off, because hours later Pepper woke me up.

"Wake up, sleepyhead," Pepper said in a light tone.

"Oh, hey. I must have dozed off," I said as I stretched.

"What brings you in today? I thought you were hanging out with your family."

"Yeah, that was my plan, but I just had too much going on there."

"What's up? Talk to me. You look like you got the weight of the world on your shoulders." Pepper had a concerned look on her face.

"It's nothing I can't handle. I'm fine." I tried to smooth it over.

"Mya, ever since I met you, you have been this independent, 'I can do it all by myself' young lady. I admire you for that, but you need to know that it is okay to sometimes let someone in." Pepper sounded sincere.

"You know, ever since my father went to prison everything just seemed to go downhill. Here, lately, shit looks up, and then right back down. I'm just not sure about the signals life is giving me. My brother being killed has been the hardest for me to deal with, me not knowing who killed him, but still trying to deal with that. Then my sister getting pregnant. It has been so much I just think I'm giving up, Pepper. I can't do this any more." Tears spilled down my face.

"Mya, you are strong, and I know that whatever comes your way you will be okay, but at this point, you need to let your past go, because you can't change anything in it. Trust me, I know. I was raped at the age of nine by a grown-ass man. If that wasn't enough, he raped and shot my mother right in front of me. For years I struggled with that, almost committing suicide because I felt just like you. I just couldn't go on. Then God put someone in my life that told me exactly what I just told you. Once I accepted that, I discovered I was better for my pain. My journey went on until I came into your life, and it will continue." Pepper had tears pouring down her face. I got up and gave her a huge hug because I needed to hear that.

"Thank you so much, Pepper. I needed that. On a more positive note, what am I going to do after graduation? Are you going to continue to let me wash heads until I get a spot at a salon?" I babbled on.

"I don't know how to tell you this, so I will just say it." Pepper paused for a brief moment. "I'm closing the salon and moving back to Florida."

"What? Why?" I questioned.

"I just have to. My family that still lives there needs me. My father has been really sick, and my younger sister needs help. I just have to go back." Pepper looked so sad.

"If it's for your family, I understand. They come first." I would hate to see her leave. Pepper had been a positive force in my life. She had helped me open myself up to my dreams.

"But don't worry. You are still going to graduate in a couple of weeks and get your hair license. I am so proud of you."

"Thanks, Pepper. Well, I need to get going. I'm going to go home and check on my family. When I left today, I was really upset so I need to go home and apologize."

"All right, I'm going to hang around here. I got some things I need to take care of," she said.

I left the shop feeling happy and sad. I was going to miss Pepper because she had made a major change in my life. Without her, I would not be on my way to receive my school certificate or my hair license. On my way to the car I thought about what Pepper said about moving on. That's why, when I made it home, I was going to apologize to Monica. For some odd reason, though, I started to feel a little nervous, but I was not sure why. Then my phone started singing Hood's ringtone. I quickly answered it.

"Hel—" Something heavy came down on me, and everything went black.

Chapter 45

*S*wish!

Someone threw a bucket of cold water in my face. All I could think was they must have been trying to kill me because the water was deathly ice cold.

"Wake up, bitch!" I heard a female voice that I recognized yelling at me.

"Aggh," I moaned, trying to come out of a drowsy state with a pain in the back of my head that was pounding. Before I could open my eyes, more water came at me.

Swish!

"Bitch, I said wake up!" the familiar voice yelled at me again.

My eyes started to flutter open, and I saw two shadows, but it took a minute for the figures to become clear.

"Charlene?" I said, confused.

"Yeah, it's me. Wake yo' ass up," she sneered at me.

"Charlene, what are you doing?" I said, trying to move. Then I realized that I had been tied to a chair with my hands tied behind my back. My head was pounding so bad I felt like I was about to die.

"Charlene, what's going on? Why am I tied to this chair?" I tried to wiggle my hands around.

"You hear that, baby? She wants to know why she's tied to that chair." Charlene started laughing.

I looked up and saw who she was referring to as "baby" and to my surprise: "Squeeze? What are you doing here?" I looked from Squeeze to Charlene with confusion written across my face. Why would I be in a room tied to a chair with these two people? With Squeeze, maybe, but Charlene? Why?

"Bitch, you don't talk to him." Charlene rushed over and slapped me in the face.

"That's right, baby, keep her in check," Squeeze cheered Charlene on while smoking on a blunt.

"Mya, Mya, with your fine ass. You think you smart just like yo dead brother."

"Fuck you, motherfucker! Don't ever bring up my brother!" I yelled and struggled to get out of the chair.

"That little nigga thought he could steal from me and get away wit' it."

"My brother ain't steal from you."

"Yeah, he stole from me, and that's why I had to kill him. I liked the little nigga, but he was a thief," Squeeze sneered at me.

"So *you* did it. I knew you were a snake. Just like you beat my momma, talkin' 'bout she stole from you. Don't nobody have to steal from you. You're a fake gangster with no heart. I promise, I'ma kill you when I get outta this chair," I warned him in deadly voice.

"Bitch, you ain't gettin' outta that chair, so save your threats," Charlene jumped in.

"And you supposed to be my friend." I looked at Charlene with disgust. "How you gon' be helping this nigga? Pig has only been dead a couple of weeks, and you already sleeping with another crew. He should have known you was just thirsty like all the other hoes in the Brewster. But FYI, bitch, your so-called friend Felicia, that skank already been sleeping with him." I nodded in Squeeze's direction. "Yeah, I saw them at a hotel together." I released a big grin.

Charlene let out this vicious laugh that echoed in the room, and that's when I realized the bitch was pure evil.

"First off, Pig was weak! That nigga let me run him. On top of that, his money was too short, and as for me and you being friends, bitch, please. You are just like Rochelle; both of you bitches are haters. That's right. Both of you are jealous of me and Felicia. And as far as Felicia, I know she been messin' with Squeeze because sometimes my man likes to do threesomes. We pay Felicia to be down with that. So when you saw her at that hotel, probably the Marriott a couple weeks ago, I was inside. I just stayed all night so I wouldn't have to go home to Pig's sorry ass."

"So you been sleeping with Squeeze behind Pig's back. That's why you had Pig killed. Bitch, you are sick." I spat those words at her.

"I didn't have shit to do with him being killed, nor did my man, but to be honest, it was a convenience."

"You know what? When I get out of this chair, I'ma kill your trifling ass," I said as a chill went down my spine and I saw a worried look on Charlene's face.

"Bitch, you don't need to be worried about killing me. You need to be worried about what Squeeze gon' do to you."

"Fuck Squeeze!" I yelled, and then spit directly in Squeeze's face.

"Fuck me? Fuck me? No, fuck you!" Squeeze bent over and punched me in my face.

I saw stars for at least two minutes as blood flew out of my mouth.

"Now what I want to know from you is, where is my money?" Squeeze got directly in my face with his foul-smelling breath.

I almost peed myself. He knew. I went speechless for a brief moment, but only a moment. I would keep my cool.

"I don't know what you talkin' about," I said, looking him dead in his beady eyes.

Squeeze grabbed me by the neck and started choking me, and everything started going black.

"Squeeze, let her go! If you kill her, she can't tell you where the money is." Charlene grabbed at his hands, and he released his grip.

"Look, I know you got my money because Phil told that you did the robberies, bitch, before his sorry ass got killed. Now all I want you to do is tell me where my money at." Squeeze tried to use a calm voice, but I knew the nigga was in killing mode.

"I already told you, I don't know what you talkin' about, and even if I did, I wouldn't tell you," I said through my gritted teeth.

"You know what, you little fucking bitch? I'm going to blow your brains out, and I'ma enjoy it. Then I'm going to go fuck that little sister of yours and kill her and that crackhead-ass momma of yours. First, I'm going to let you suck on this because I have been waitin' on this for a long time," he said as he started to unbuckle his pants. I could see the uneasy jealous look on Charlene's face.

"Why do want her to do that? What is that about?"

"Shut the hell up!" Squeeze turned and yelled at her. He finally got his pants unbuckled.

Charlene ran over in a fit of jealousy. "Squeeze, if you do that I'm through wit' you." She tried to grab his arm.

Squeeze turned and slapped Charlene in the face. She flew across the room and fell on her knees.

"I told you to get back!" he yelled, then turned his attention back to me. "Now open up wide and suck this gently." Squeeze came close to my mouth with his dick in his hand, and then we heard a strange noise.

"What da fuck was that?" Squeeze turned and looked at Charlene with his gun drawn to where he heard the noise come from. Out of the dark stepped Hood.

Hood and Squeeze drew their guns on each

other at the same time. My heart was racing, hoping Squeeze didn't shoot first.

"Nigga, step back from my girl!" Hood yelled.

"Well, well, if it ain't Hood. Nigga, what you doing here? I thought you busy out there killing niggas from my crew. Now you come to get me?"

"Damn right. You had Luscious kill Pig just so you can have this thirsty bitch?" Hood nodded his head in Charlene's direction.

"Nigga, don't be call—" Charlene was cut off by Hood.

"Bitch, shut the fuck up. You next," Hood warned. "Let my girl go. It's me you want to kill, not Mya. She don't have shit to do with why y'all going after my crew."

"Nigga, is that what you think? I'm going after your crew? I didn't have nothin' to do with what happened to Pig or Li'l Lo. That was something Luscious was on. Nigga had heat for you and Pig because that little nigga y'all killed about a month back was his half brother. I told that nigga to let that ride because his brother pulled a foul move when he tried to rob y'all, but nah, that nigga overruled me. I was gon' deal wit' his ass later for going against what I said, but first I had other business to focus on, like your girl here and my money."

"Why you kidnap my girl?"

" 'Cause she is the one who's responsible for robbing my crew. Yeah, those robberies you heard about, she did it. You should give a round of applause to your gangster bitch. Robbing dope boys for the stacks and pullin' that shit off. I have to admit it myself, she a bad bitch."

Hood's whole facial expression changed.

"I know you didn't know about it or have nothing to do with it because it started before you started messing with her. But you know it's a code to that shit, so she got to die."

Hood looked at me really hard and the only expression I could read was his love for me. He didn't give a fuck about what Squeeze was saying. He was telling me to get ready.

"Look, nigga, this my last time tellin' you untie my girl and let her go," Hood said, as he lifted his safety on his nine-millimeter Glock.

The whole time I had been working my hands free.

"Nigga, be real. You know I can't do that. Her life belongs to me now." Squeeze started to lift his safety.

"Tell him, ba—" Charlene started to say, but before she finished, I was out of my chair. I grabbed the knife off the table she was standing by and stabbed her in the upper chest, but she wasn't dead.

"Pleaass . . . My . . ." Charlene tried to get out.

"Bitch, it's too late," I said, before plunging that knife in her neck. Blood splattered everywhere.

In the middle of me jumping Charlene, Squeeze had lost his concentration for just a minute, and Hood had shot him in the shoulder. Squeeze fired his gun, but the bullet missed Hood. I raced over to Hood, who was about to end Squeeze's pitiful-ass life. I quickly grabbed the gun out of his hand before he could blast because I had made a promise to Squeeze that I planned to keep.

I walked slowly over to him. "Yeah, I robbed your crew, but the next time you want to beat up somebody's mother, you should think about that shit. As for Li'l Bo, this is from him—a special delivery to you, by me. Die!" I yelled.

"Fuck you, bitch. I'll see you in hell," Squeeze said in pain, holding his shoulder.

"You first, motherfucker." I released everything Hood had left in the chamber. I wanted to send Squeeze off in style. His blood splattered all over me. I took my finger and got a sample off my face and licked it. I had to have a taste of this sweet revenge.

Chapter 46

One year later

It had been a year since all that crazy mayhem had gone down, but life was moving on for the better. We had all found some peace in all the craziness that had transpired. My mother had been clean for more than a year. I was so proud of her. She had gotten a full-time job and was in school studying to become an LPN. We had all finally been down to the prison as a family to visit my dad after he was let out of lockdown. We were still dealing with Li'l Bo's death as a family, even though Dad remained locked up. We made regular trips down to see him. He was really keeping his head up, and he was excited about his new grandbaby.

Monica was doing well. She finally had the baby, and we as a family named the baby Imani. Imani was so precious. She looked just like Monica, and she was being spoiled rotten and loved. Monica had gone back to school and had plans on graduating. She wanted to get a job, but I told her no. I just wanted her to focus on going to school and taking care of Imani. Finances were not a problem for her. I think she secretly still wanted Luscious in her life for Imani's sake, but she was moving on in a positive direction, and she seemed not to be jaded by her shattered past.

Rochelle was doing great. She had found her own apartment and finally moved out on her own, just her and Tiny. She had a new job and was now going back to school to get her hair license. She was also dating this new guy who was out of the ordinary for her. He wasn't in the game, to my surprise. He was an English schoolteacher. She and Tiny had been spending a lot of time with him, so I was happy for her.

I had finally met Hood's mother, and she came down to our wedding and I loved her. We got along great. That's right. Hood and I got married a couple months ago, and we were doing good. I had moved in with Hood, and Monica, Imani, and Momma stayed in the apartment. I paid all the bills so they didn't have to worry about that. Everything was going great. I had been trying to convince Hood to get out of the game. He had plenty of money, and Pig was no longer around. I thought maybe he could do something different, but he still hadn't agreed, so we were still talking about that one.

I had graduated and received my license, and I couldn't have been happier. Last week I had my grand opening for my new salon that Hood had purchased for me. Hood had surprised me and purchased Pepper's old salon 4EverStylz. I re-

named it "Stylz by Design." That's where I was
headed now. I had to be there when Rochelle arrived, and she was always one of the first to get
there. I had hired her to wash heads like Pepper
had started me off without a license. Turns out my
girl had a few stylz up her sleeve too, so she plans
on being one of my stylists as soon as she finishes
school.

Normally when I made it to the salon, Rochelle
would be just pulling in right before me. This morning she must've been running late because I didn't
see her anywhere. I pulled my silver Mercedes-
Benz CLS550 that Hood purchased for me as a
wedding gift into my assigned parking space.

Once inside, I looked around my shop, still admiring the unbelievable fact that it's mine. All of it
and everything in it belonged to me. My husband
had purchased this salon just for me. It had been a
long and rough road for me, but I had done it.
Looking around the shop, tears rolled down my
face for the loss of Li'l Bo, my only brother who I
loved so much. I know he would be happy for me.
Tears also rolled down my face for the excitement
of the new direction that my family was going. I had
reasons to keep my head up, but right now, I
needed to stop being so emotional and start putting
up my inventory. I had some hair products that I ordered for the salon that came in yesterday so while
no one was in the shop this would be a good time
to put them away.

When I made it to the back I heard someone
come in, so Rochelle must have finally arrived.

"I'm back here, Rochelle," I yelled. She was

getting close because I could feel her presence. I turned around to playfully scold her for being late.

"What da fu . . ." I said as the products in my hands hit the floor.

When I turned around, I found myself staring down the barrel of a gun, and the person holding the gun was supposedly dead. I guess the dead do sometimes come back to life.

"I thought you were dead," I said with a slight tremble in my voice.

"Well, bitch, you thought wrong," Luscious said with an evil grin. "You robbed me, then Drake, and you killed Phil. Then yo' man kills my brother. What you thought? You and your man could just fuck over me, then get rid of me? Bitch, I could never let that happen."

"Fuck Phil. He's the one who gave up y'all operation. If you had any balls you would have killed him yourself because in the end, I was just gettin' it," I spat.

"Whatever, bitch. Tell yo' man the next time, before he walks away, to make sure the body cold. Oh, my bad, bitch, you ain't gon' ever see him again. That's right. After I kill you, I'ma go murk that motherfucker. Then I'm going home to Monica and my baby so we can be a family," he said with a smirk on his face.

"Fuck you, Luscious! I should've killed you when I had the chance, motherfucker!" I yelled as I ran toward him.

POP, POP, POP!

DON'T MISS

Saundra's tale of revenge, Detroit-style, in
HER SWEETEST REVENGE 2

Noire's newest story, "The Crushed Ice Clique" in
BAD BEHAVIOR

Chapter 1

Pop. Pop. Pop.

"Agh!" I screamed as the hot bullet that left Luscious's gun pierced my left shoulder. Grabbing my shoulder, I instantly felt the hot blood start dripping down my sleeve. But the thud of Luscious's body hitting the ground had my attention. Then Luscious disappeared and on the ground in his spot Monica lay covered in blood. "MONICA, MONICA!!" I yelled over and over.

"Mya!" I heard someone yelling my name, but my body was frozen in one spot. Panic set in as I tried to force myself toward Monica. "Mya," I heard my name again. I felt myself blacking out.

"Mya." I finally opened my eyes and realized it was Hood shaking me, calling my name. "Babe, it's only a dream again. You at home and safe. So is Monica." I looked around the room as I realized I was home in my bed. "Shit, I hate these dreams." I sat up then slightly, pushed my Donna Karan stitched quilt off me, and climbed out of the bed.

Realizing I had interrupted Hood's sleep again, I apologized. "And I'm really sorry for waking you up with this shit again." I went into our master bathroom to wipe all the perspiration off my forehead that had built up while I was panicking in my dreaming.

"It's a'ight, you know I got you. Besides I'm 'bout to get up anyway. Gotta handle business." As usual, I could always count on Hood to be supportive. No matter what. But I was sick of having these dreams. It had been well over a year since Luscious had tried to sneak up on me at Stylz by Design to take me out. He thought he had me too, but his plan had failed when Monica came out of nowhere and shot him in the back of the head, killing him instantly. I was lucky, because had it not been for my sister Monica, I would be dead. Luscious did end up shooting me in the shoulder, but I recovered so fast it was like a pat on the back. To be honest, the dreams were worse than getting shot.

The only regret I had about the whole incident was Monica getting caught up in the middle. I hated that she now had murder on her hands. Even worse, it was her daughter Imani's father that she had killed. It was only a coincidence that she had even showed up at the shop that morning. On her way to school she remembered she needed money. She later said that she had attempted to call my cell but got no answer so she came because she knew that was where I would be. As she pulled in, she happened to see Luscious, who she thought was dead, slip into my shop. Monica said she knew he was up to something and without a second thought she grabbed the .22 pistol that Hood had given her for protection out of the glove compartment of her all-white 2012 Dodge Charger. Just as she entered the back of the shop, she saw me running toward Luscious as he fired shots at me. So even though I regret her having to kill Imani's dad, I thank God that she did.

As I came out of the bathroom, Hood headed into our triple-sized walk-in closet. "Well, since I'm up, would you like me to make you some breakfast? A little eggs, bacon, maybe some hash browns," I offered. There was no way I was going back to sleep. I refused to close my eyes only to get a glimpse of Luscious. Hell no. I would stay woke.

I had told Rochelle I was coming in late today since I stayed over the night before, but what the heck, I might as well drag my ass in. I could get an early start on inventory since I didn't have any appointments scheduled. Even though I owned the shop, I still had a few special clients. And for my services they paid top dollar.

"Nah, babe, I'm good. I'ma meet up with my people early this morning so I'll just grab some on the way." Hood walked into the bathroom as I plopped back down on the bed and quietly contemplated my next move. I decided a latte would do me good so I made the kitchen a part of my mission for the morning. Not soon after Hood left the house I jumped in the shower. An hour later I had searched through my closet and fished out a pair of white Vince tennis shorts with a black Helmut Lang tank. I completed the outfit with Alexander

Wang ankle-strap sandals. I had to admit my new style was classic. I had put the Brewster Projects dressing behind me. At least a little bit—I still would represent from time to time. With not as much as one glance in the mirror, I concluded I was ready to head out.

Chapter 1

Honore Morales and her cousin Cucci Momma Jones were two beautiful but thirsty tricksters from the hustle hard blocks of Hollis, Queens. Get-money bitches who were all about that life, Cucci and Honore had grown up together in the wicked and wily projects where they learned the art of scheming and skullduggery from some of the best street legends in the game.

While Cucci Momma was a ghetto princess extraordinaire who rocked the latest fashions, slung the silkiest Brazilian, and sported the type of smooth cocoa-colored body that was displayed on the cover of *Big Booty* magazine, her BFF Honore was softer in tone and easier on the eyes, although no less tricky or deadly about her business. Honore had a classic type of beauty about her, and she was known to stop traffic and weaken the coldest of ballers and mesmerize them with her hazel eyes, honey-colored skin, rudely bodacious ass, shapely legs, and long, wavy hair.

On the real, Honore's package was put together way too perfectly for her to be so damn broke, and right now her brain was deep in scheme mode as she played with a sticky ball of gum in her mouth and gazed at the ceiling with a bored look on her mug. The sounds of smacking and slurping rose in the air as an OG named Chimp Charlie crammed his face deeper between her soft thighs and slurped up her sweet juice like his long, pink tongue was a twisty-turny crazy straw.

Charlie gasped in delight as he came up for air then dove right back in headfirst again, but Honore's mind was on a million other things as she got her pussy ate from one end to the other. The musty motel room they were in was chilly and the television was blaring on channel seven. Honore sucked her teeth, wishing this shit was over with already and pissed as hell that she was even lying there with her legs cocked open in the first damn place.

"This shit feel good, don't it, baby?" Chimp Charlie bragged as he lifted his peasy gray head up from outta her wet box. "I know you like what ol' Charlie be puttin' on you 'cause this pussy is wet as fuck."

"Nigga shut up," Honore ordered as she looked down and rolled her eyes at the ancient baller in disgust. "More eating and less talking. I ain't got all day to be messing with you. I gotta go to work tonight. Time is money, yo."

Honore pushed his face back into position and Charlie went back at it.

Stupid-ass nigga! she thought as his tongue swirled around her clit and he spread her thick ass-cheeks wide so he could toss her salad and add extra dressing.

As old and ugly as Chimp Charlie was, and as much as he made her skin crawl, Honore knew she was lucky to have a simp like him to yank back and forth on a string. It wasn't every day that you could find a limp-dick old-head who was willing to drop big dollars just to eat your coochie out like it was buttery grits and eggs. And even though her pussy was dead to Charlie's mouth mauling right now, Honore gapped her legs open even wider and let him have at it because business was bad in the hood and she needed to put some cash in her pockets real quick.

Honore prided herself on her ability to turn a dollar, but the street hustle she had going with her cousin Cucci was getting harder and harder to maintain these days. Out of desperation the two of them had started managing a small stable of strippers and renting them out as dancers and escorts, but lately them bitches were getting thirstier and thirstier by the hour. Every time Honore turned around one of them thots had their hand out demanding more and more of the cut. For some reason them bitches had it in their heads that they were doing all the work and Cucci and Honore were collecting all the profit. They didn't understand that advertising sex parties on P.O.F and other Internet sites wasn't as easy as it sounded. All those types of places were on the government radar these days, and undercover vice-types were lurking around mad corners left and right looking to make a bust. Them ungrateful pole freaks didn't realize how risky it was for Cucci and Honore to search for the right tricks who had heavy pockets, set up the parties, pick out just the right spot, and provide the proper security so the girls didn't get licked and picked every time they opened their legs.

But with her and Cucci holding tight to the purse strings, some of the girls had already started branching off on their own, and Honore was getting more and more frustrated and desperate for cash every day. On the real, a bitch like her had expensive tastes. Plus, she owed niggas money for this and that, and now her aunt was hollering about making her pay rent too. If things kept going like this then her ends wasn't never gonna fuckin' meet, and since right now she needed get her nails done, her brows waxed, and some fresh new gear to drape on her phat sexy ass, giving up the trim to Chimp Charlie was her best fall-back hustle of the day.

Honore rolled her hazel eyes and glared up at the ceiling as Charlie's false teeth clicked together and raked over her clit. Everything had been going real smoovy and groovy for them up until just a few months ago when outta nowhere they got shit on by the game. Her and Cucci had been working as prime money mules for a hood legend named Sly McFly, and under his street guidance and cut-throat protection they had been bringing home the bacon, the spare ribs, and the pork chops too.

Sly happened to be Honore's godfather *and* Cucci's step-daddy, so he stayed looking out for both of them. He was a real OG from back in the day who had already earned his stripes living the thug life, and now in his older age he was all about stacking chips and living the high life.

Sly moved product, collected payments, and ran businesses all over Hollis, Queens, and with his type of trade constantly flourishing he kept all his workers laced nice and lovely. Not only did he keep Cucci and Honore looking like two bright shiny dimes, he footed the bills and taught them the business of the streets while they partied their asses off and lived like project princesses.

But all that good shit was a wash now. Sly's old ass had got caught up in a trick bag a few months earlier, and now the pigs had him locked up out on the Rock with no bail. His high-priced lawyers had promised that he was gonna beat the case when it went to court, but in the meantime, while they waited for that to happen, Honore and Cucci were left out there on their own to fend for themselves and keep their pockets up the best way they knew how.

Honore gazed down between her legs and frowned at the sight of the peasy gray head that was rotating around in big slow circles and lapping at her clit. Chimp Charlie was Sly McFly's personal driver and one of his very best friends. He was also a fat stankin' slob-ass nigga with a lotta money who didn't mind tricking it off. Cucci Momma had been fucking with Chimp Charlie ever since she was a teenager, and recently Honore had secretly slid right in on her cousin's game so she could get some of that bank too.

On the low-low and dipping way behind Cucci's back, Honore had started letting Charlie get a lil sniff and a taste here and there in exchange for a few dollars, and like a hopeless dope fiend, he had gotten addicted to her prime body. Honore felt kinda shitty for cutting in on Cucci's dough, and she couldn't stand Chimp Charlie's wrinkled, ashy ass not even a little bit, but she kept up her "lease and lick" game because the fat OG paid it like he weighed it. Besides, whenever her other little side hustles slowed down Honore could always fall back on chimp-ass, trick-ass Charlie, and just like a trained puppy, he would come running.

Honore lay back on the raggedy lint-balled bed-spread and stared at the ceiling again. She tried to relax as Charlie lapped at her pussy with his extra-long, abnormal tongue. That shit slithered like a garden snake, and he stiffened it and probed up inside her tunnel deep enough to touch her damn cervix.

The effect of Charlie's head game was starting to kick in, and despite her reluctance Honore began to hump against his face. Her clit throbbed like crazy as Charlie swirled his tongue around and around until it grew long and stiff. Dipping his tongue deeply inside her pussy hole, he gathered a glob of warm sticky cream and rubbed it all over her clit. Honore started humping harder, mad that her body was responding even though her mind didn't want it to. Charlie slid his big rough hands under her thick booty cheeks and lifted her up slightly. He looked like he was eating a gourmet meal, and Honore was practically helpless as she gapped her legs open wider and surrendered to him. Her fingers were all in that peasy hair of his as she fucked the shit outta his face. He sucked and swirled and massaged her soft ass until her whole body was on fire. Warm juices ran outta Honore's pussy slit like a river, and all that liquid sugar trickled down and dripped right into her ass crack. Charlie went after that juice like it was liquid gold. He probed his tongue around her asshole and licked that juice right on up.

Soon a feeling of irritation mixed with pleasure overtook Honore and she couldn't hold her nut back no more. She reached up her body and squeezed her firm, melon-sized breasts and fingered her stiff nipples until tiny sparks shot off in her clit. Moaning loudly, she humped real hard a few times until her clit started quivering and jerking, and then she whimpered with pleasure and released a hot shot of sweet cum all over Charlie's big lips and scraggly mustache.

"Okay, okay, now get up," Honore barked as soon as she caught her breath. She had busted her a big one and now she wanted that nigga offa her. She pushed his sticky face from between her legs and frowned. "Good job nigga, it was better than the last time."

"I bet it was," Charlie said as he wiped her wetness from around his mouth and chuckled. "This shit been getting better and better, ain't that right? I'ma have yo ass turned all the way out soon, girl."

"Nigga please," Honore scoffed as she got up and walked naked toward the bathroom. She could feel Charlie's eyes glued to her bold round ass the entire way. "I'm a paper-chaser, dummy. How the fuck you gonna turn me out? Plus, your tongue is short and kinda rough. I've had better."

"Shut ya broke ass up." Charlie laughed as he laid back on the bed and wagged his snake tongue out at her. "You know my shit is damn near as long as my dick."

Speaking of dick, Charlie reached down between his legs and grabbed his. After all that pussy he had eaten his shit was still limp and soft. Unfortunately, he had just fucked another young chick right before Honore called him, and that's why he wasn't able to get his shit up for her. One erection a week was about all he could muster up at his age, although his mind still wanted pussy every day.

Charlie could have easily fronted Honore off when she called begging for money like he was broke or he wasn't interested in seeing her, but he liked the girl. He didn't mind coming up off the few dollars he had in his stash, but he had wanted to eat Honore's pretty pussy a lil bit first, that's all.

"You ain't chasing shit!" Charlie called out to her in a delayed reaction. "You still running around here with them lil bum-ass looking-for-a-come-up niggas who barely got pocket change, baby! What you need to do is bag you a baller, Honore! I know you waiting on Sly to get out, but I'm telling you I can put you on to some real ends with the type of shot you got."

"Miss me with that shit, Charlie," Honore yelled back at him. "Sly McFly ain't raise me to be out there on the streets selling my ass, nigga! I get other silly bitches to do that shit for me. I only hit you off with some pussy every now and then because it's quick and easy. Besides, I'm beautiful and I got a good brain. My time is coming, ya heard? A smart bitch like me is only gonna stay down for so long. Trust and believe, Sly or no Sly, I'ma be on my feet in a minute, son."

"That's what all the hoes say." Charlie grinned as he flipped through the channels on the small television. "I been running game for years out here, and one thing I know is this city is too big not to be getting some real paper, especially with a face and a body like yours. You, Cucci Momma, and all them lil chickenhead broads y'all be trickin off in that escort service just ain't the move, baby girl. Y'all need to put some real heavy action down and get out there and grind."

"Don't you worry yourself about our bizz, fat boy," Honore said as she cut on the water and wet a rag so she could clean herself up. "Me and Cucci know how to handle our handle."

Honore was steady popping shit, but Charlie was absolutely right though. The escort business wasn't what it needed to be. Bitches in their line of work were fickle these days. They were all about getting that cash any way they could, but they didn't really wanna work hard for it. If they wasn't showing up at the parties late, then they were showing up high, or sometimes not even showing up at all. Them lazy bitches were straight up trifling, too. After Cucci and Honore busted their brains to get everything all set up, the strippers would walk in looking tired and worn out and putting on some lil weak-type performances and half-ass dancing so bad their customers' dicks wouldn't even get hard. Yeah, Charlie was 100 percent correct. This escort game was almost played. It was time to for her and Cucci to put their heads together and rack the fuck up.

And the motivation was right there too.

Honore was a natural-born stunna and she

wanted everything. She wanted to live the high life and claim her spot in the glamorous world of drugs and money. She loved stepping out fly and rocking the latest purses and shoes. She knew she had a sweet face and a killer body, and she knew she was smart enough to touch some real cake too. All she had to do was find a solid hustle and then work the right angle to pull it off. And once Honore got her foot in the right door she would kick that bad boy all the way open!

The ambition was deeply embedded inside her and she would do whatever it took to get what she wanted. No matter who she had to let eat her pussy from time to time, or who she had to double-cross and scheme on, Honore Morales was determined to find her a new hustle and get her life!